A SHROUD
FOR ROWENA

VIRGINIA RATH

A SHROUD FOR ROWENA

VIRGINIA RATH

COACHWHIP PUBLICATIONS
Greenville, Ohio

A Shroud for Rowena, by Virginia Rath
© 2019 Coachwhip Publications

Published 1947
No claims made on public domain material.
Cover image: Horse © Chris Gorgio

CoachwhipBooks.com

ISBN 1-61646-486-0
ISBN-13 978-1-61646-486-8

A SHROUD FOR ROWENA

To
Mary Collins

PROLOGUE

It was February of 1939 when Rowena Talcott walked away from "the old Talcott place" on Broadway and out of her small, well-ordered world.

Rowena had left the house only once before during the day, going out into driving wind and rain with letters her father wanted mailed; returning with damp ankles and a wrecked umbrella. Remembering that, her aunt, Sophia Talcott, called to her when she heard her come out of her bedroom around eight o'clock that evening:

"You'd better take my umbrella since yours turned inside-out. It may rain again and it's nine blocks to the Lymans' house."

There was what Sophia, decidedly not a fanciful woman, felt was "an odd pause." Then Rowena came into her aunt's bedroom, saying in her gentle voice:

"Perhaps I'd better take it though I don't like to ask to borrow it—"

"Nonsense. My umbrella isn't so valuable as all that. You'll find it in the corner over there."

As Rowena crossed the room, Sophia noted that she was wearing a new blue spring print, new blue gabardine pumps, a new dark-blue straw hat. She had her raincoat over one arm and carried an old purse, an unusually large and very shabby affair of black suede.

Being determinedly noninterventionist, Sophia did not say: Why risk having a new outfit rained on when you're going only to Bess Lyman's? She said instead: "You look very nice," even while she reflected that, despite frequent periods of semi-starvation, Rowena had gained a few more pounds recently.

"Do you like the dress?" Rowena turned to face her aunt. "I got this in a shop people are beginning to talk about—Gisele's. Their prices are high but the proprietor does the designing. His name is Dundas, which is odd—"

"Not at all. All couturiers aren't French and the best are usually men." Sophia adjusted her noseglasses. "Hmm. Very smart. You'll wear it forever and it's very distinctive, especially that draped yoke. Don't forget the umbrella, child."

Rowena picked up the umbrella. The frame had been re-covered half a dozen times since Sophia's father had given the umbrella to her thirty-two years ago, on her sixteenth birthday, but the ivory handle was imperishable—a beautifully carved horse's head with flowing mane, lovely in itself and quite unsuitable as a handle for a woman's umbrella.

"My dear father," Sophia observed, unsentimentally, "had an amazing amount of naturally bad taste. Run along—and close the door."

Rowena said, "Good night, auntie," and closed the door. The thick hall carpet swallowed her footsteps as Sophia picked up her book.

Downstairs in his small, book-stuffed study, St. George—Sophia's brother, Rowena's father—was reading the morning newspapers. This was a chore that he reserved for after-dinner hours when he had time to work himself into a really enjoyable rage.

For St. George Talcott (see *Who's Who*) was cursed with intelligence and the belief that history repeats itself. He found it infuriating that the average person, for whom he had a vast contempt, did not consider the name of Munich a stench in the nostrils.

He was wrestling belligerently with the sheets of a refractory daily paper and muttering to himself when he heard what he afterward very loosely described as "a slight thud" in the hall. He surged to his feet and burst from the study, a stocky man of fifty-five with an unbelievable beard, still black, still springing buoyantly from a center parting. He combed it with his fingers as he faced his older daughter in the hall that February night in 1939.

"Great heavenly honk, girl! Can't a man have a quiet hour of study after dinner without—"

"I only dropped my purse, Papa," Rowena said composedly. Rowena, like all of St. George's family, accepted him as an interesting natural phenomenon, although, since he was an old-fashioned literary lion, most people found him more terrifying than the African variety.

"Never knew a purse to make so much noise. I suppose you've all your earthly possessions in it, since it's the size of a young suitcase. Gadding again?"

"Bess Lyman wants me to make a fourth at bridge with her sister and Mr. Lyman."

St. George snorted. "Bess Lyman—hah! Scurrying about from one worthy cause to another—"

"Including Chinese war relief, Papa. And you are always talking about—"

"I am a voice crying in the wilderness. Well, I predict—"

"Whatever it is, don't forget to predict it in your diary, Papa," Rowena said sweetly.

Papa was not offended. Every night, when he had digested the day's news, St. George wrote up his diary. He not only expected that it would be published after his death but had arranged that it should be. He said:

"I will stand or fall in the eyes of posterity by my predictions. Already Herr Hitler is insisting that Danzig is engraved on his heart. There will be war—soon. And one day the Japanese will slug us when we aren't looking. Right now we consider it a matter of some importance that in ten days we'll open a world's fair on Treasure Island—a sideshow for complacent idiots who—"

He stopped, sniffing. "You're wearing that god-damned perfume—what d'you call it? Faugh! Sickeningly sweet stuff."

"Jasmine. And I use very little, Papa. I like it."

"'But O, the smell of that jasmine flower!'" St. George quoted absently. "You're all decked out in new clothes, young lady, rain or no rain."

"I'm tired of my winter things. I wanted something special this spring. I thought this dress was slenderizing when I saw it on someone else who's too plump. I don't think it's fair," Rowena said, "that I should keep gaining weight besides being the only stupid one of a clever family!"

St. George blinked. He said, in his gentlest tones, which could be heard only on the ground floor instead of throughout the house, "You aren't stupid, Rowena. The rest of us are dangerously facile and we're show-offs. I don't think you're too plump, either. But you're thirty and it's time you were marrying. You have two beaux you can't keep dangling forever. It's time you made up your mind, don't you think?"

"Yes," Rowena said slowly, "high time. And I—I have come to a decision, Papa. No, I won't talk about it tonight. It's getting late and . . . . Good night, Papa."

"Good night." St. George watched his daughter go toward the front door, her new hat brave above her drab raincoat. "Do you have your key?"

Rowena turned and smiled at him. She said, "Yes, Papa," and added—it was the last time she spoke to him—"'Curfew shall not ring tonight.'"

St. George went back to his study and forgot Rowena. He took out his current diary and in writing, wonderful to behold and fearful to decipher, recorded various vitriolic comments regarding the statesmen of the day. Then he took up *The Decline and Fall* and went to his bedroom.

He read late, slept late, and was shaken awake by Sophia, who told him bleakly, "Rowena's bed hasn't been slept in and Bess Lyman says that she hadn't asked her to play bridge last night. The Lymans had an engagement elsewhere. And a burglar broke into the house last night."

"Burglar?" St. George chose this more comprehensible of two disturbing facts. "Here? How d'you know?"

"I woke and heard some noise in Rowena's room. It was two o'clock and I was surprised that she was so late getting home, but it wasn't my affair so I went back to sleep. This morning cook found a kitchen window open—one that's low to the ground. And in the dining room the silverware had been taken from the sideboard drawer and was on the table. Also, Rowena's bureau drawers are disarranged and her jewel box emptied on the bureau. She had no jewelry worth taking. She wore her pearls last night and nothing is missing."

"Even if there was a burglar and he was frightened away before he could bundle up the silver, that still could have been Rowena in her own room at two o'clock this morning," St. George said.

"What was she doing between eight o'clock and two A.M., then? Why did she come back at all? If she came back to get something, she could have found it without turning her bureau drawers inside-out. You know how fantastically neat Rowena was in all her arrangements."

"Must you be so damned logical, Sophia?"

"I haven't called the police, yet, about the burglary or to notify them Rowena is missing. Do you want me to?"

"Fancy we'd better," St. George said heavily. "I don't like to risk embarrassing the poor girl in case she comes back but she shouldn't worry us, dammit! I suppose she carried identification cards and so on in her purse?"

"Yes. And tabs with her name woven into them on her underthings."

"That rather lets out the emergency hospitals, doesn't it? I'll call the police but—great heavenly honk—it's preposterous! Rowena can't just walk out of our lives. She'll come back—"

"Or," Sophia said, her harshly colored face suddenly sickly white, "the police will—find her . . . ."

Rowena did not come back and the police did not find her. Inevitably, since her description and her portraits were splashed over newspapers from Pacific to Atlantic, Rowena was "seen"—in New England, in Canada, in Mexico, in San Francisco.

Between February and May, St. George traveled to Seattle, to Des Moines, to San Antonio to scrutinize women who might be Rowena. When he returned from Texas, where he had confronted a lady who was suffering from amnesia but resembled Rowena only superficially, he bellowed for the hundredth time, "The police are a set of bungling half-wits," and took himself to a private detective.

He chose one at random—a Henry Hunt, of whom the San Francisco police said bitterly, "We probably never will catch the bastard with his pants down. He's too damn smart."

For the next three months Mr. Hunt pursued his devious ways, apparently unaware that the police were interested in his activities. Then, one day in July he faced St. George in his study and told him:

"I've done my best though I came on the case when it was cold. There doesn't seem to be any reason why your daughter should have disappeared voluntarily. Usually in these cases we ask . . . Do you mind if I'm quite frank, sir?"

"What am I paying you for?" St. George grunted.

"For nothing, I'm afraid. When an unmarried woman your daughter's age disappears, we usually suspect a disappointment in love. But it seems she could have married either of two men." Mr. Hunt was merely reproachful, "I must say that you never bothered to explain any of your household to me so I—"

"Why should I do your detecting for you, Mr. Hunt? Besides, I thought you'd better form your own opinions, if any. If you want mine, for what they're worth . . . About eight years ago I decided to engage a resident secretary—male. I was weary of genteel females who swooned when I uttered a good old Anglo-Saxon word and fled my study in tears when I ever so slightly, and always with some provocation, raised my voice."

Mr. Hunt, listening to St. George's well-rounded, carrying accents, grinned slightly.

"I was fortunate enough to find Joel Gloster. His mother was Russian; it was convenient for me that he knew Russian. His parents left him a small income which he had eked out by ghost-writing and translating. Of course he is only a talented dabbler in the arts and never will be anything more.

"I am sometimes foolish enough to lend the light of my countenance to these very little theaters that present mostly Russian and French plays. Joel was connected with one of these groups. That's how I happened to meet him as you no doubt know.

"He types well, knows some shorthand and admires me," St. George said calmly. "So he fitted easily into our family circle. In time—about six months ago—he asked Rowena to marry him. I gave him my blessing. It wouldn't have been a brilliant match for her but I thought she should marry and am selfish enough to have liked thinking that she and Joel would stay on here if they did marry. Neither of us tried to force her to a quick decision—"

"Miss Rowena's other young man seems to be a different sort than Gloster," Hunt suggested.

"Yes. There's nothing precious or literary about Bob Lovell. His father was my old friend; he died when Bob was sixteen and Bob came to live with us as my ward. Always seemed to be happy with us though he's a hearty, healthy specimen with hair on his chest.

"He's had his own establishment since he graduated from college—by the skin of his teeth—and went into insurance. But he still has the run of the house. He's Rowena's age but I was surprised when, shortly after Joel had made his declaration in form, Bob said he had learned to appreciate Rowena and wanted to marry her. Rivalry might have entered into it. Bob and Joel never liked each other."

"Lovell insists that your daughter had promised to give him an answer in a few days and he was so sure she'd say 'yes' that he had his mother's ring reset for her. He did have the ring reset. But Gloster says he's sure Rowena was going to marry him, so where are you? At least you can't see her as an unwilling spinster. So, did anyone want to kill her? Apparently not. You have another daughter and a son, but your son is self-supporting, and you're hale and hearty and haven't made a will in Rowena's favor or any will at all. And if she's dead," Hunt said, "where is her body?

"The police went over this neighborhood with a fine-tooth comb. They interviewed every taxi driver, streetcar conductor, everyone at the railroad and bus stations, investigated every auto accident or near-accident. And you were never asked to ransom her. I've done everything the police did, all over again, maybe better than they did, but here I am, saying it's just one of those things and there's no use you throwing good money after bad."

St. George did not roar at Mr. Hunt. He twisted his fingers into his beard and said: "I suppose you are right. My sister, my other children, who haven't complained about this damnable, degrading publicity, should be considered. So—what do I owe you?"

Hunt named a sum that would have caused those who knew his price schedule to raise skeptical eyebrows and ask "When did you go cut-rate?" St. George, who had no notion that Mr. Hunt's expense accounts usually soared to dizzy heights, raised his eyebrows, too. He grumbled, "Related to Jesse James, are you?" wrote a check, gave it to Hunt and saw him to the door.

After that Rowena became a useful topic of conversation to those who had known her or knew someone who knew someone who had known her. And often those whose egos bore the imprint of St. George's large, deflating foot would end the discussion with a pitying, "Poor St. George has never been the same man since . . . ."

St. George never played the role of bereaved father. But sometimes he sat as long as an hour without doing anything at all; and he took to listening to the radio, which he had always dismissed as "a child of Satan, conceived by and for those who won't or can't read."

And as time went on—1939, 1940, 1941—the grave, sonorous voices that came over the radio were an echo of the predictions set down in St. George's gargantuan diary. Above all else he had enjoyed being proven in the eyes of his rivals that which he always knew he was—right. Yet one day he said suddenly to Sophia, "I'm tired."

He went on when he saw the difficult tears in her eyes: "I'm not whining, old lady. It's ironic that I was confronted with one problem my stupendous intellect couldn't solve. And that I'll die without having solved the problem of Rowena's disappearance—"

But he lived through 1941, to say "I told you so," and to see his one son off to Camp Ord in June of 1942 with the comment, "A scholar by nature and education; a Ph.D. at twenty-two at great expense. And now cannon fodder. That's civilization. And since one reverts to the vernacular on these occasions—give them hell, Chris!"

The next day he made his will. His lawyer testified later that when he tried to reason with him, St. George could be heard throughout the De Young building.

"Draw that will up exactly as I've outlined it, you fat fool, and see that it gets some publicity! Call this will fanciful," St. George went on more temperately, "but I've no illusions about Rowena. If she *can* come back, this will bring her back. And don't argue! I saw a doctor yesterday. He gave me six months. I give myself six weeks."

Actually it was less than six weeks before Sophia found him dead at his desk, his dog-eared copy of the *Meditations of Marcus Aurelius* open on his knees at a page that bore the words: "Think not disdainfully of death, but look on it with favour; for even death is one of the things that Nature wills." It was then, the newspapers were quick to recall, more than three years since Rowena had disappeared.

Long before that, before he had had time to cash St. George's check, Inspector Sullivan of the Homicide detail had invited Henry Hunt to "come down to my office for a little talk."

When, dapper and jaunty, Hunt entered Sullivan's office, he found waiting to meet him: McElroy, of Traffic; Rush, of Missing Persons; and

Nicholas Prevost, not then an inspector, attached to the Burglary detail. Hunt grinned derisively.

"Gentlemen, I am honored. You're going to ask me if I know where Rowena Talcott is, dead or alive. You know I went over the same ground as you did—"

"But you're such a smart little crook," McElroy said pleasantly. "They don't like us to bribe people, but there's nothing to keep you from doing it."

"Thank you, Mac," Hunt said affably, "but you'll have to write this off as one of my few failures."

"Someday, Harry, you're going to find yourself minus your license," Sullivan predicted.

"If I ever do, it won't be your doing, Jim, on account of I'm moving to Los Angeles."

"Oh, are you? I heard you wanted to and that you've got a pal there who'd take you into partnership, only he wants you to put some capital, cash down, into the business and—"

"How you do go on, Jim. But mother told me there would be days like this if I insisted on being a detective. Still, it's better than taking in washing. I don't like L.A. but the fog here is bad for my bronchial tubes." Hunt coughed hollowly. "Good-bye, gentlemen. I'll see you in jail; me looking at you from outside the bars."

He walked toward the door before Nicholas Prevost said in his silky-soft voice: "As one expert to another, was that a bona fide burglary at the Talcott home the night Rowena disappeared? A professional job?"

Hunt turned and stared at Prevost; at his admirably tailored suit, the admirable shoulders therein, and the dark, faintly Slavic face above them. Hunt's small eyes were bright and wary. He said, in his quick, high-pitched voice, "Since you ask so politely—no, I don't think it was a professional job. I leave it to you to find out why someone tried to make it look like one. Good-bye, boys."

He went out and closed the door behind him. Rush swore, expertly and monotonously.

Prevost said slowly, "So Harry's wanted to buy into that L.A. agency for some time? And even though we know how much money he's had to put out this spring and how much he needs now, after three months on the Talcott case, he can suddenly buy into that L.A. agency and move down there, bag and baggage. Is that coincidence? I wonder. . . ."

PART ONE

I

The train from Los Angeles was late but there were almost enough taxis at Third and Townsend; enough at least for servicemen who were glad to share a ride. The driver of one Yellow, having deposited two young and downy second lieutenants at the Plaza Hotel, looked back toward his third passenger.

This was the quiet, very thin, blond PFC who wore the Purple Heart, Good Conduct Medal and European Theater ribbons and used a cane when he walked. Without being asked, he repeated the address he had given.

"Oh sure: that's on Broadway near Octavia. Where'd you see action, soldier?"

"Salerno, Anzio, Cassino, Rome. . . ."

"You done your share. Hope you don't mind me askin'? I was in for two years but they said I was too old. Maybe, but army life was restful, compared with hacking in San Francisco in war-time. I never got farther than Texas—"

"I was in Texas, too," the soldier said politely.

"Ain't that the damndest state? Get in it and you can't get out, even if you ride all day long. . . ."

The driver's opinions of Texas lasted out Van Ness and well into Broadway before he slowed down, trying to make out house numbers on a not too well-lighted street.

His fare said, "It's that large old gray house," and the cabbie began, "Why that's the old Tal—" and stopped.

"Yes," the other agreed with the stoical courtesy of one inured to such remarks, "it's the old Talcott House. Don't get out. I can manage my bag."

He put his bag on the sidewalk, handed the driver two dollar bills and acknowledged his, "Good luck, soldier," with an oddly shy, very appealing grin.

Driving away, the cabbie thought: "That'd be the brother of the girl who disappeared. Rowena, her name was. Seems like a nice guy."

He looked back. "He's still standin' there, just staring. Well, why not?"

The house had a bad case of architectural acne. It was turreted, gabled, cupolaed, balconied, bay-windowed. All this and wooden lace, too, thought Christopher Marlowe Talcott. He murmured,

"Seek as you might, you'll never find its like else-where; but though not at all humble, it's home," and drew an appreciative breath of the foggy air that, on a warmish September night, smelled of fish and oil and sewers, gas mains, flowers and sea salt.

He was glad, Chris decided, that he had wired only: "May arrive home tonight. Not certain, so stand by but don't try to meet train."

It was better to stand here alone, to have time to realize and savor the fact that he was alive. Listed as missing for two months, he was home and he still had two legs even if one was mainly a memorial to the surgeons' ingenuity and perseverance.

Being submerged by a tidal wave of family at the station would have been unnerving. He would not let himself admit that he had wanted to be met at the station by one person; that he had waited ten minutes before he took a cab, looking for Anice. One rather expected that a fiancée might risk his not arriving tonight, might be willing to wait for a train that was late, might . . .

He told himself determinedly that there was some very good reason why Anice hadn't met him. He had only to walk up the front steps and in a few minutes she would be in his arms. Then why, said a nagging small voice, do you put off that moment? Because, Chris answered, the family will be there, too, and becoming acquainted with the family again will take some doing.

It's not odd that I should feel that, he thought. So many feel the same, even when it's a mother and father or wife they're going home to. They all say: "It's going to be tough, because the people at home haven't any idea what it was like and never will have."

Oh, Chris added quickly, at least Aunt Sophia knew there was a war going on, to coin a phrase. No sister of Father's would be less than very well-informed. It won't be difficult to pick up where I left off with Aunt Sophia. She was always an onlooker, always impersonal, and she's no fool. . . .

Neither is Daphne but—thinking of Daphne and her infrequent letters, Chris shrugged wearily. It was best to take his sister as she was; disregard her when she was difficult and not trouble yourself to try to excuse her.

As to Daphne's husband, Mark Vibert, Chris had never felt that he and his brother-in-law were more than moderately well-acquainted., But at least Mark was intelligent and tactful and had been in the Army for some time, though he hadn't gotten overseas before he was given a medical discharge. Mark was apt to have a vague notion of what questions one would rather not be asked.

And Bob Lovell's blithe assumption that there never was anything to be tactful about was sometimes helpful. Chris rather hoped that Bob was already in the house, but it was possible that he wouldn't be able to make it tonight. He was in the Navy, "still a lieutenant," he had complained in his last letter to Chris, "and still in the city at the same old desk."

At least he and Mark had been shaken out of their smooth-worn little grooves by the war. But Joel Gloster had remained in his ivory tower. . . .

Well, but after all, Chris asked himself, would I be so scornful of Joel if I hadn't been so rudely yanked from my own little ivory tower? I was a complacent little professor for most of my adult life; I delivered popular lectures on Mrs. Radcliffe, Miss Edgeworth, Miss Burney, Jane Austen and the Brontes. I pointed with pride to my slim volume in appreciation of Jane Austen. But it was readable and discerning; the critics said so, Chris thought quickly, and then grinned deprecatingly.

And, he reflected, I am twenty-nine, while Joel is nearly forty. Joel had never pretended that he was anxious to put on any sort of uniform, and a punctured eardrum had very handily taken care of any possibility that he might be forced to do so.

And Joel apparently had never considered working in some essential wartime industry. St.

George had named Joel his literary executor and
Joel had, so far as Chris knew, put in the last three
years revising a collection of essays and editing St.
George's monumental diaries. Naturally, he had
gone on living in St. George's home. No doubt
the women had been glad to have him there while
Mark was in the Army and there were only Sophia,
Daphne and Anice to rattle about in the huge,
three-storied house.

For Anice had promised . . . Abruptly, Chris's
long jaw squared. He looked at the cane hanging
over one bony wrist, threw it out into the street,
lifted his bag and limped up the front steps. From
one pocket he drew out the key that had been his
particular rabbit's foot for more than three years.

He unlocked the door and stepped into a long
narrow hall that imprisoned an odor of old wood,
old carpets, dust and cedar-scented furniture pol-
ish. There were two square parlors at the front of
the house whose doors faced each other across the
hall. One of these was a little ajar.

Chris tiptoed over to it and for a few minutes
stood there looking at the people gathered in the
room. . . .

II

Sophia Talcott was knitting, seated in an ancient rocking-chair. Sophia wore a prewar sweater

and an imported tweed skirt, a cameo pin larger than a silver dollar, woolen stockings and scuffed brogues.

At eighteen Sophia had "put up her hair" and up it had stayed. She cared no more that her hairdress happened to be fashionable now than she had when it, and the hats that crowned it, had been disparagingly likened to Queen Mary's.

Recalling those hats, Chris grinned reminiscently before he thought: but Aunt Sophia looks an old woman now. Perhaps she does have more than just a conscientious, tepid auntly affection for me. If she does, she's put in some bad months— two when I was reported missing, besides all the time until July when it was touch-and-go whether or not I'd keep my leg. If that mattered to her a great deal, no wonder that she looks so much older.

His sister Daphne did not. As usual, she was curled into a very large chair, her tiny slippers tucked under her house coat. In time gone by, Chris had wished he might throttle whoever had first declared that Daphne looked like one of her own kittens.

Daphne, like Sophia, Chris and St. George, "wrote." That is, as naturally as she breathed, she drew charming pictures of cats—full-grown, half-grown, and kittens preferred. As an artist she did not approach Claire Newberry though Daphne seemed happily unaware of that. The texts of her books, Chris had always pronounced "maudlin." However, she had a large following, tirelessly addressed all sorts of clubs, and never missed any gatherings that could be termed "literary."

And now Chris grinned a brotherly grin and reflected that Daphne did look like a fluffy kitten or grown-up child with her soft yellow hair and round blue eyes and soft, boneless little body. A Siamese was sprawled over her shoulder with its head under her chin, "talking" to her. Daphne had been so often photographed with her living models that she liked always to have a cat about to complete her picture of herself.

She went on stroking the Siamese but her voice was as sharp as its babyish quality permitted when she said, "You will do as you like, Aunt Sophia. You always do. But I don't think it would be kind, and neither does Mark."

"My dear Daphne," said the man who stood behind her chair, "would you mind now and then asking me what is my opinion on some given subject, before you announce to the world what *you* want said opinion to be?"

Chris, still unnoticed at the door, lifted his eyebrows, thinking that this was the first time he had ever heard Mark speak rudely to Daphne.

He thought he knew why Daphne had married Mark. She had been seeing him constantly
for some time before Rowena walked out of their
lives. Mark was attractive, had inherited a bookstore as well known to San Franciscans as Paul
Elder's or Newbegin's. His income was adequate,
and he and Daphne knew the same people.

When Rowena had been gone for a year, Daphne married him, and they took over the third floor
of the old house. For by then people were beginning to remark that Daphne was twenty-eight and
still unmarried, and her vanity was sensitive and
voracious; yet she wanted only to be cherished
and admired by a husband.

And to Chris's continuing surprise, Mark had
seemed to want to cherish Daphne; and, if he did
not always pretend to admire her, he appeared to
find her amusing when she was outrageous. He
was not amused now and his voice was frigid as he
went on:

"Chris is intelligent, though he was well-bred
to the point of being slightly ineffectual, as all of
us were or are, except for St. George—"

Chris never knew if protesting murmurs followed this speech. For at last he let himself think
what this homecoming would have been if his
father had been here; how St. George would have

made an exultant banner of his great beard and bellowed for the liquid equivalent of the fatted calf and sung a particularly ribald version of "Mademoiselle from Armentières."

St. George's son swallowed hard and closed his eyes. When he opened them, Mark was saying, "But after the last three years, I doubt that Chris is so persistently well-bred, and he may have acquired some perspective on his nearest and dearest."

Mark smiled unpleasantly. A muscle jumped in his thin cheek and Chris noticed the two perpetual, fretful parallel lines between his dark brows.

"One can do that even if he goes no farther and fares no worse than an Army camp in these United States. And Chris is in love."

Chris's stomach muscles tightened slowly. He let himself admit that Anice was not in the living room. He no longer tried to believe that she had chosen to remain upstairs until the others greeted him.

For Anice was as much "family" as Bob Lovell or Joel Gloster and though Bob was not here, Joel was. He sleeked back his thinning hair, saying in his pleasant but over-cultivated voice, "You are right, Mark, but so is Daphne. Chris has been through experiences that fortunately none of us can even begin to visualize—"

"You do not need to emphasize the fact that I was turned out of the Army because of chronic indigestion," Mark said.

"Darling, you mustn't be sensitive. We understand."

"What do you understand, Daphne?" Mark asked.

"That its men of breeding and education who find communal life so trying that they become tense and can't eat the horrible Army food and so they—"

"But we were talking about Chris, Daphne," Joel said firmly. "And would anyone recommend that we greet him with a—well, with what? A ghost story? Give him time to become adjusted again, I say."

"Would you," Sophia said quietly, "advise waiting until his thirtieth birthday?"

It had seemed for so many months so very doubtful that he would live to be thirty, that a full minute passed before Chris decided that Sophia must have St. George's will in mind. And then he had to make an effort to recall, in detail, the provisions of the will.

St. George had directed that his estate should not be settled until Chris's thirtieth birthday, in late February of 1946. On that date, seven years

and some days would have passed since Rowena's
disappearance. If, before that date, Rowena appeared, she was to receive one-half the estate when
it was settled. The other half was to be divided
between Daphne and Chris, except for five thousand dollars each to Joel, Sophia and Bob Lovell.
Sophia's legacy was only a token of gratitude since
she had, many years ago, inherited half of her
father's large estate.

The will had ended with the provision, that if
on Chris's thirtieth birthday Rowena must be presumed legally dead, her inheritance would revert,
share and share alike, to Daphne and Chris.

And now Joel was saying quickly, "My dear Sophia, Chris will not be thirty for several months.
And long before that—"

"Long before that, two minutes after he gets
here, Chris will want to know why Anice isn't
here," Mark said. "And what will you tell him,
wise guy?"

"Yes, what will you tell me?" Chris asked, step-
ping into the room.

They crowded around him. Sophia took him to
her firm, flat bosom; Daphne stood on tiptoe to
kiss him; Mark shook his hand violently; and Joel
said too heartily, "You're looking very fit, my dear
fellow."

Chris found himself in a chair with a glass of the Talcott ceremonial sherry in his hand, answering their questions. Yes, he felt very well. No, he did not have to use a cane now. Yes, the San Francisco fog looked better than blue Italian skies to him.

"What a pity you didn't call on Santayana when you were in Rome," Daphne remarked. "Father knew him—"

"He corresponded with him acrimoniously," Chris said, adding dryly, "And I should think it might occur, even to you, that I had certain military duties to perform, in and about Rome. I don't think they would have relieved me from them so that I could carry Father's posthumous regards to Santayana. Where is Anice?"

"Were you standing at the door for some time? I was afraid of that," Sophia sighed. "Anice moved in July. She is living with a friend in an apartment on some street off Union. I tried to persuade her to stay until you came home—"

"We all did," Joel said. "We—is that the doorbell? It should be Bob. He said he would drop by to see if you had arrived."

Bob Lovell breezed in, brisk and hearty in Navy blue, slapping Chris on the back with: "Hail, the conquering hero comes! Landlord, fill the flowing

bowl and let joy be unconfined. You look a hundred per cent, old man. Boy, did I envy you, in
the thick of things while I'm still chained to that
ol' desk chair—" He looked about and whistled.
"Oh? Joy is too much confined, maybe? Anice?"

"Anice," Sophia agreed.

"I told her you'd expect to find her here, Chris.
She wouldn't write you when she moved. She just
shook her head and looked frightened."

"Perhaps she was frightened," Daphne drawled.
"Frightened that we might open Chris's eyes to
what she really is."

III

"Daphne," Sophia said warningly.

"Oh, auntie! Chris is going to—" Daphne
turned to her brother and stopped abruptly. "You
do want the truth, don't you?" she said placatingly,
"It's better to—Chris, don't scowl at me like that!"

Chris did not answer. He was shaken by a hot
resentment large enough to cast over everyone
there. It was an old resentment that he had deliberately folded away but now that he took it out and
looked at it, he found that it had worn very well.

He had met Anice King at the home of friends
in San Rafael early in 1942. He had asked her
to marry him the day after St. George's funeral,
knowing he would soon be leaving Fort Ord. That

is, he had asked her to wait for him. For a long time he had been determined that they would not marry until the war was over. Anice had never wanted to wait; and, after a year in the Army, Chris absorbed the "live while you can" philosophy of most of his fellows, and forgot his scruples. He and Anice were to have been married during his last leave, in May of 1943.

Daphne openly opposed the engagement and marriage. She said that Anice was "pretty, in a common way. But she has no family, no education, no breeding."

Sophia had told her astringently not to be stupid. Anice's father had been a respected and unusually well-loved doctor. It was a pity he hadn't made money; that he couldn't send Anice to college; and that she felt she was needed at home, since her mother was dead.

But, as Anice had helped her father in his office, besides keeping his house, she had no difficulty in getting a position in a doctor's office in San Francisco when her father died soon after she met Chris. And, Sophia pointed out, she had grave doubts as to Daphne's ability to earn her own living in any but one way; and that way was not by drawing pictures of cats.

But though she squelched Daphne briefly, Sophia did not pretend any enthusiasm for the impending marriage. She said: "It's your life, Chris. I don't approve of hasty wartime marriages. And if you do return safely, I wonder how congenial you and Anice will be."

"Father said—"

"He said: 'She's a well-favored wench, my boy,' and nudged you in the ribs. I believe St. George, who only met Anice once, considered her in the light of a pleasant diversion which he thought you entitled to. It's not her lack of formal education that I object to, Chris. But all your interests in life have been academic and cultural; matters that are a closed book to Anice. Perhaps she will be good for you; perhaps you will change. When the war is over you'll be less the professor and Anice better fitted to be a professor's wife."

In slightly different words, without encouragement, Joel had echoed Sophia, "Better plan to give her a correspondence course in English lit'rature, old chap." Mark had not volunteered an opinion. He had only told Daphne, "Lay off, my pet. The boy is in love, even as you and I."

Bob had been customarily forthright. "She's a luscious morsel but take it from me, she's got an eye to the main chance. . . . Oh, all right, if you feel that way about it. Your ol' Uncle Bob gives you his blessing—"

But they were not married, with or without anyone's blessing. Anice came down with an especially
virulent type of flu and was in a hospital when
Chris reluctantly had to leave San Francisco.

Sophia had promised to look after Anice; had
said she would, and did, bring her from the hospital to this house and installed her in one of the
vacant bedrooms.

When she could answer his letters, Anice had
promised to ".... stay with Aunt Sophia. I had to
let my apartment go and now it's harder every day
to find anywhere at all to live. The doctor says
I mustn't work for three or four months. I hate
to be obligated to anyone, and as soon as I can
get back to work I'll pay room and board, if they
don't mind my staying here till you get back. . . ."

Chris forced himself to speak in what he hoped
was a reasonable tone of voice.

"Anice promised me to stay here, where I'd
know there was someone to look after her if she
was ill again. She went back to her job as soon as
she could. She paid you a fair sum for room and
board. You are not precisely cramped for space in
this family ark. So why—"

He ground out the words with sudden, uncon-
trollable violence. "So why did you drive her away
from here! Speak your piece, Daphne, my pet!

What should I know about Anice that it's your sisterly duty to tell me?"

"Just that your little Anice came home stinko one night this June and fell on the stairs, and—"

"I doubt if that is true," Joel said mildly. "Neurotic the girl certainly is but—"

"Neurotic—Anice?" Chris said hotly. "I've never known anyone more sane and levelheaded!"

"She's certainly practical," Bob agreed. "She had a soft thing here so I don't think she'd have moved out if she hadn't been really scared."

"If she wasn't cock-eyed, how did she get that bruise on her cheek?" Daphne said softly.

"Bruise? What—"

"Chris! Listen to me, please." Sophia put down her knitting. "It is true that Anice came home late when we were all in bed and—"

"I assure you that I did not expect her to lead the life of a nun, simply because she is engaged to me."

"That is neither here nor there. Anice came in and she did fall on the stairs. I heard her. By the time I was up, she was in her room with the door locked. She was not intoxicated to the point where her enunciation was affected. She said she had tripped and fallen, coming upstairs in the dark. The next morning there was a bruise high on her cheek.

"I believe that she ran up the stairs. I think I heard her before she fell and fully awakened me. I know that she was gasping and half-sobbing when she spoke to me afterward. And that is all I know except that several weeks later she told me that she was going to leave us, and did."

"I see." Chris stood up. "Is there a car available? No, don't tell me to wait until tomorrow!"

"I have my car and I know where Anice lives, old man," Bob said soothingly. "I helped her move because Daphne had the only car with gas in it that day—"

Daphne interrupted. "I had an important engagement and with the ridiculous shortage of gasoline and taxis before the war ended, I couldn't very well have—"

"Later on I'd just love to hear what a nasty old war it was, Daffy," Chris said bitingly. "I'm really relieved that you survived it when I remember the extreme hardships and deprivations you described in your letters."

He limped toward the hall; stopped suddenly. "Was Henry Hunt the private detective Father hired to try to find Rowena? . . . Well! Don't any of you remember?"

"The name was Hunt but why do you ask?" Sophia said slowly.

"There was a fellow in my platoon who had been a private detective in Los Angeles. Even in the Army there were guys who realized that I was *the* Rowena Talcott's brother. Quite a few of them read *True Detective* and similar publications. This fellow was professionally interested. He mentioned Henry Hunt and I asked him what he knew of Hunt.

"He said that 'they don't come any smarter or any crookeder than Harry.' I told him that Father had squawked to high Heaven when he paid Hunt's fee. But when I mentioned what the amount was, my friend whistled and said: 'Hell, for Harry that was peanuts. I can't figure it unless—well, Harry did sometimes give a sucker a break and while he charges all the law allows and then some, he does like to give value received.'

"That was all he would say, then. He had his guts blown out the next day. I think I would like to talk to Henry Hunt. Come on, Bob. . . ."

IV

Chris did not speak again until Bob turned from Broadway toward Union to avoid the dead end street at Broadway and Jones. Then he asked:

"Didn't Mark come home just before Christmas? Long enough ago to have . . . have . . ."

"Readjusted himself? I don't know what's eating old Mark," Bob said. "Of course it hurts a guy's pride to be thrown out of the Army because of stomach ulcers. It's not a heroic complaint. But Mark's thirty-one. This is a young man's war. I'm thirty-seven and, for all my talk about wanting to see action, I know I'm not young enough to take it. I'd think Mark would be glad to be home but he doesn't act like it. He's on the ragged edge and Daffy's not helpful. We know our Daffy—worse luck."

"Joel hasn't changed."

"Christ, no! Still the trusted and faithful old family friend. I think I know why he called Anice neurotic. Sophia gave her Rowena's bedroom and—"

"Oh? Still, we never closed it and Father very sensibly had Rowena's belongings put away. However—"

"Don't blame Sophia. She gave Anice her choice, and Rowena's room is one of the best. But around April, Anice asked Joel if Sophia would be offended if she moved into another bedroom. Joel wanted to know why she wanted to make the change; but when he questioned her all she would say was that sometimes the room 'smelled funny.'"

"But, good Lord—"

"Joel mentioned the possibility of a dead rat in the walls but Anice said it wasn't an unpleasant smell—just 'funny'. She can be stubborn, you know. She moved into another room, but I have a hunch she made some other complaint that Joel thought wasn't 'quite the thing' and wouldn't repeat."

Bob swung the car across Columbus Avenue, past the square that lay like a green doormat before the gray, sky-reaching bulk of St. Peter's and St. Paul's, on up a hill and into an alley where flat-fronted houses faced one another across a narrow strip of pavement.

He stopped before a nondescript building with one fairly large window and an outside staircase. "This is it, pal. It's respectable. There's a light in the window so she's probably home. I'll get myself a few drinks and be back in an hour or so. Right up the stairs; first door to the left—"

Chris was tired. His patched-together leg ached and the dirty stairs were steep. He climbed them slowly and stopped to rest before he reached their top. He stood with his back against a wall, sniffing a sour, fruity odor that suggested that someone near-by had a few casks of homemade wine in a basement close at hand.

Then a door on the landing opened and Anice came out, her pale, heart-shaped face framed by dusky hair curling softly to her shoulders. She stared down into the uncertain light, not seeing him for a moment. "I thought I heard . . . Chris! Oh Chris, darling!"

Somehow Chris was up the last half-dozen steps and Anice was in his arms, fitting them as if she had been custom-tailored for them. When he had done kissing her he still stood and murmured maudlin remarks against her soft black hair.

Presently she drew him into a long room furnished with good taste; cheap chintz and wicker, with a drop-leaf table and a home-painted cupboard filled with dishes at one end; a solid-looking couch in another corner. The bright cover folded over a chair suggested that the couch would pretend to be a divan in the daytime but now it was unashamedly a bed.

"I sleep here," Anice said. "There's a bedroom but that's Marion's since it's her apartment. She isn't home now—"

She switched on the center lights and turned to look at Chris. "Oh, honey, you're so thin and white! You wrote you were feeling fine—"

"'Tolerable,' I said," Chris reminded her.

"Yes, but— Well, but you can walk and in spite of what you finally wrote, I was afraid . . . I knew you'd hate being lame, though all I cared about was to have you home. And you are home and—"

"Didn't you know I might be home tonight?"

"No. They didn't tell me—"

"I'll speak to someone about that," Chris said grimly.

"Oh, it doesn't matter. I wouldn't have wanted to see you for the first time in a mob. And you have come as soon as you could, and—" Anice's pointed chin jerked and she burst into tears. "I'm ashamed to do this, but it's b-been so long and s-so h-horrible!"

Chris sat down in a large chair and beckoned to her. "Come here! Yes, you can safely sit on my left knee. You are as tiny as Daphne and three times as pretty. You make her look washed-out and her true age. Is that why she doesn't like you?"

Anice burrowed into his shoulder and laughed hysterically.

"She doesn't like you, does she?" Chris persisted.

"No, and I don't like Daphne. Did any woman ever, really?"

"She's never had an intimate woman friend."

"I'll bet! Probably I'm jealous of her." Anice sat up, found a handkerchief in the pocket of her yellow house coat and dried her eyes. "She's an artist and well-known and has a husband I think's a swell guy. She patronized me and cut me out of conversations by talking about people and things I don't know about. You may not believe me—"

"I know Daffy. But when you first went there, I was on my way overseas and then Mark was drafted—"

"She kicked up an awful row because she felt *her* husband should be excepted but she didn't miss Mark like most women miss their husbands. She had their whole third floor apartment to herself instead of just her bedroom. I'll bet you have no idea how much she spends on herself. I couldn't help wishing I had clothes like hers and she tossed me a few old things I couldn't resist taking, but I should have known better—"

"That doesn't matter. Why did you move from Rowena's room?" Chris said. "Didn't you know—"

"I knew it was her room. That didn't bother me at first. But when you were reported missing, probably killed, last February, I lay awake nights . . . . I'd have to stop thinking about you to keep from going crazy and I'd find myself wondering about Rowena. And that first week in February the first odd thing happened.

"I'd wake up feeling like someone had been in the room. Then one morning when I began dressing I discovered someone had been in my bureau drawers—"

"But you once told me, dear, that your bureau drawers look as if they've been stirred up with a stick, so if nothing was missing—"

"Nothing was missing," Anice said coldly. "And my bureau drawers are always a mess. That's the point! Someone had straightened them and laid everything in neat piles. Everything was in order —bras and slips and handkerchiefs, just so."

Chris stiffened. He started to say, "But Rowena was fantastically neat. Her bureau drawers always were just so—geometrically exact." He didn't say it. He managed a facetious: "Do you walk in your sleep, darling? Tell me the worst now."

Anice put his arms aside and stood up. "You sound like Joel. I won't bother to tell you the rest."

"I believe you, dear. I find it—disturbing though it may have been a stupid practical joke."

"But where does the joke come in?"

"If it was a joke, you didn't have the necessary information to think what someone wanted you to think, because I never talked to you about Rowena," Chris said slowly. "But you were frightened—"

"At first I was curious and mad. I wanted to catch whoever was playing games so I didn't lock my door. About a week later, I sat up in bed one night, feeling someone had been around. But I was alone. Then I smelled this perfume. It was a funny, very sweet odor, not like any I know; not quite like rose—"

"Jasmine?" Chris said rigidly.

"I don't know. I never had any of that."

"Rowena used to wear it. She had some on the night she disappeared."

"Oh." Anice shivered. "If I'd known that— It may not have been jasmine. But the smell got on my nerves. It seemed to me it was always in the room. I stuck it out through February until April and then I asked for another room."

"And what frightened you that night in June when you dashed up the stairway and fell and hurt yourself?"

"Didn't Daphne tell you I was only billy-goat drunk?" Anice said bitterly. "And Joel had laughed at me about the perfume though I spoke of it just as a funny smell. And when I spoke about the bureau drawers, he acted like I was accusing someone of being a thief. So after that I kept my mouth shut. But—did—did Rowena keep her bureau drawers in apple-pie order, Chris?"

"Yes, she did, Anice."

"Then I wasn't the only person who didn't tell all they knew. Well, that night I came home late. I'd been out with a lonesome soldier. I did go out quite a bit, Chris, but I'd never go steady with anyone. I had a key to the front door and the house was dark and quiet. I tried not to make any noise. When I got opposite the living room door, it wasn't closed. I stopped because I thought I heard someone in there—"

Then, Anice said, she had tiptoed over to the living room door and looked into the room. For several moments she sensed sound rather than heard it; sound resulting from slow, deliberate, meaningless movement that was hardly more than a stirring of one blacker shadow in the midst of motionless shadow.

Gradually that moving shadow took on a certain form; a vague and terrifying resemblance to a human form. A faceless figure of no precise height, but one with arms that moved in what Anice later decided were gestures. Later, because suddenly someone began to sing, very softly, slowly and clearly. . . .

"I know the tune. The words sounded foreign," Anice said and she hummed a twice-repeated refrain that made Chris's mouth go dry and his palms wet.

As a household they'd had what many would have called odd diversions. They liked charades and word-games and they "recited," not seriously but trying to see who could be most absurd.

Each of them had his favorite poem when elocution was in order. Bob's was "Give Me Three Grains of Corn, Mother"; Chris's "Lasca"; Daphne's "The Mistletoe Bough"; Sophia did "Over the Hill to the Poorhouse" with gestures remembered from her girlhood; but Rowena had always, surprisingly, outdone them all. Sometimes she recited "Curfew Shall Not Ring Tonight" but her specialty had been Bulwer Lytton's "Aux Italiens."

And now, as Anice was silent, Chris was suddenly back in that late Victorian parlor that had reassuringly resisted years and change. It was any night when they had drifted from conversation to recitation and Rowena held the center of the stage.

She had, hamming it gloriously, reached the final stanza of "Aux Italiens," embellishing it with absurd gestures that always delighted her audience.

"But O, the smell of that Jasmine flower!"

(Left hand outstretched, cupped hand slowly raised to Rowena's neat little nose while she seemed to sniff ecstatically at an imaginary flower—)

"And O! that music! and O, the way
That voice rang out from the donjon tower—"

(Right hand out, then left; then both hands clasped over Rowena's breast as she sang softly and slowly:)

"*Non ti scordar di me*
Non ti scordar di me!"

V

Remembering this, Chris had closed his eyes without knowing it, until Anice said anxiously:

"Chris, you don't look well!" Then, as he stood up, shaking his head, "Did—did Rowena sing that song? I remember it's from *Il Trovatore*—"

"It is also part of a poem that Rowena used to recite—with gestures. No dear, someone was trying to frighten you, or us, through you."

"I was frightened. I lost my nerve when I heard that ghostly singing in that dark room. I turned and ran and fell on the stairs; got up and into my room and locked the door before Miss Sophia heard me."

"Joel didn't wake up?"

"No. It takes a lot to wake him when he's sleeping on his good ear, he says. But Chris, you don't believe in ghosts? And you do think Rowena is dead, don't you?"

"I don't know what to believe. I didn't intend to leave you so soon but I think I'd better talk to Aunt Sophia before she goes to sleep."

"I know." Anice gave him a gentle push toward the door. "A car just drove into the alley. It's probably Bob. Good night, Chris. Don't call me at the office; the doctor doesn't like it. I'll be home tomorrow by six o'clock."

Bob was mellow after three quick ones, inclined to be brotherly and solicitous.

Chris said curtly, "No, Anice and I didn't quarrel. I'm tired and didn't want to keep you waiting. What will you do when you leave the Navy? Go back into insurance?"

"If nothing better comes up. I haven't missed any chances to establish useful connections," Bob said candidly. "It's been rather expensive at times but you do meet useful people when you're in Supply. You can afford to take a long rest. I don't suppose you've spent half your monthly allowance from the estate."

"I must have a good bank balance. Aunt Sophia will know. She had my power of attorney and sent me money when I wanted it. I suppose that eventually I will go back to California if they still have a place for me in the English department."

Chris kept the conversation going along these lines until they reached the old house on Broadway. Then he got out of the car quickly, said, "Thanks, Bob. I'll be seeing you," and let himself into the house.

The living room was empty but there was a light in St. George's study. Joel, Chris supposed, was still editing St. George's diaries. While undoubtedly they needed stringent editing, Chris hoped that Joel would not end by sucking all the marrow from the bone.

Sophia called to him as he reached the top of the stairway. She was sitting up in bed with a book on her knees, wearing a shapeless purple woolen bed jacket.

"Our furnace is old and cantankerous and it was impossible to keep a handyman during the war," she remarked. "We have a cook and one maid, on and off. We pay them absurd wages and they're remarkably incompetent. It's hard to realize that we ever had cooks like Zinnia, and maids who polished furniture."

"I thought Zinnia would be an old family servitor but, just for a handful of silver, she left us. But she adored Rowena and didn't leave us until Rowena had—had gone. I saw Anice, Aunt Sophia."

Sophia sighed. "Yes? Why did Anice move out of Rowena's room and what frightened her the night that she fell on the stairway?"

Chris told her. Despite her strongly marked features, Sophia could be remarkably wooden-faced. She only wrapped her hug-me-tight more closely about her shoulders and said:

"Well? What do you think, Chris?"

"I have to admit that Anice's story could be pure fiction if someone gave her the necessary facts about Rowena. But I don't see why any of you should conspire with her. Or what she could gain by conspiring with one of you."

"No more do I. When we got your wire, Chris, I did try to reach Anice. She wasn't home yet and I very foolishly told Daphne to be sure to call her. Daphne 'forgot to.'" Sophia shrugged. "Well, even though you love her, you do have to admit that, so far as you know, you had only her word for it that her story was true.

"However, at least twice I noticed an odor of jasmine in Rowena's room and made Daphne admit that she did, too. Of course Anice could have sprinkled jasmine about the room to back up her story. But I believe her story because I have one of my own to tell and I can offer proof, of a sort, that I'm not lying; though it's proof I would rather not have."

"What do you mean, Aunt Sophia?"

"About three weeks before Anice left us, Bob asked all of us to go to the theater. Then I came down with a heavy cold and at the last minute decided to stay home. I let the servants go and had the house to myself. It was a cold, rainy night so I went to bed early, only to wake and find that I was hungry. I started down to the kitchen for a glass of milk; used the front stairway but didn't bother to turn on the hall lights.

"When I reached the lower hall I thought I heard someone in St. George's study. I opened the

door and said, 'Are you home so early, Joel?' I
heard someone gasp and, I thought, a rustle of
clothing. Very foolishly, I stepped into the study
and said, 'Who's there?' Someone ran straight at
me and knocked me down.

"I went down fighting," Sophia said grimly. "I
tried to seize whoever had, I first supposed, at-
tacked me. I got a handful of dampish cloth; some
material with a hard finish, like an expensive raincoat. That was wrenched from me but I managed
to get my hands on a damp shoe. I clung to the
shoe and tried to up-end its wearer. Then something struck me over the head. I tried to protect
myself; grabbed at the weapon, not knowing what
it was. I got my hands on it and then realized it
was a silk umbrella. Then it was wrenched from
my grasp, too.

"I made a final snatch at it. My hands closed on
something hard; I could hear myself and someone
else panting. Then I went reeling back, flat on my
back. I heard the front door slam before I managed to get up and put on the light. Then—" she
reached under her pillow, "I found myself standing there with this in my hand."

"This" was a horse's head of carved ivory, a
horse with a flowing mane. Chris traced the delicate carving with a thin forefinger.

"Old Dobbin. That's what we used to call it."

"Yes. It was made to fit over the wood or whatever material made up the lower part of an umbrella handle. I held onto it so desperately hard that I pulled it off. The rest of the umbrella went with whoever was carrying it that night."

"The umbrella that you loaned Rowena the night that she disappeared," Chris said.

"This is certainly the top to my umbrella handle. A Chinese artist carved it and you will see my initials in the ivory just below the horse's head. I gave the matter much thought and it was not until after Anice left us—in fact, not until we knew that you would soon be home—that I told the others what had occurred and showed them Old Dobbin. They would rather have laughed off my burglar but they could not.

"For if I had acquired Old Dobbin in any other fashion, I must know what became of Rowena or have some knowledge of her whereabouts, dead or alive. Guilty knowledge. Then, there was no sign that anyone had entered the house that night except by the front door. And Rowena had her keys with her when she left this house for what we have presumed was the last time."

"You've never changed the lock?"

"No. You know that St. George refused to have it changed, wanting Rowena's keys always to fit it. When he died, Daphne wanted the lock changed but I wouldn't permit it. St. George would have been furious; he might have come back to haunt me."

"He'd never have the night latch put on, either," Chris recalled. "I take it you've respected his wishes in that regard, too. That, and his will were two of his few sentimental gestures."

Sophia frowned. "No, as to the will, St. George realized that Rowena 'knew the value of money.' He thought that if she had disappeared voluntarily, that will, which was given some publicity, would bring her back before she could be presumed legally dead, to claim her lion's share of the estate."

"I understand that but— Aunt Sophia, can she be alive?"

Sophia shook her head, looking haggard and old. "I don't know, Chris! I just don't know!"

"But what are we to do now?"

"Sleep on it. You obviously need rest, Chris. We'll talk again tomorrow."

VI

But on the following day he found it impossible to talk, in the way Sophia had had in mind, with any of the family.

He slept as one stunned; breakfasted at eleven. Before he had finished eating, neighbors began "just dropping in to say 'welcome home.'"

Chris was courteous by training and instinct. Nine-tenths of the visitors were women who had known his parents. They were kindly souls and so many of them wore pins on their conservative blue and black silks and some of the stars on the pins were gold stars. Chris dug his best faculty-tea manner from the mothballs and sent everyone home happy.

Then it seemed that two of Daphne's friends were to lunch with them. They were elegant, emaciated females who had, he gathered, quite enjoyed the war, which they had spent encased in smart uniforms behind the wheels of official station wagons so that the gas rationing had not inconvenienced them.

Before dessert appeared, Chris was mentally fondling some startling terms that had been added to his vocabulary during the last three years. He stood up and begged to be excused on plea of his late breakfast.

He went into his father's study and sat down at the enormous old desk that was, now that only Joel used it, cleared of all papers.

"If I could talk to someone," Chris thought. "They're treating me as if I were an atomic bomb. I suppose only Aunt Sophia knows what Anice told me, but all of them heard what I said last night about Henry Hunt. Why did he have to migrate to Los Angeles? I wonder if he may have sold the name and goodwill of his agency? If he did, I might find out where to address Hunt. . . ."

Chris found a telephone directory, leafed through the yellow pages until he came to "Detective Agencies." The Hunt agency was still listed along with the slogan that had caught St. George's eye more than six years ago: "Let Henry Hunt For You."

Chris reached for the telephone. As a matter of course St. George had had the one downstairs phone installed where it would be most convenient for him. A feminine voice said:

"Hunt Detective Agency. Miss Compton speaking."

"I wonder if you could tell me Mr. Henry Hunt's present address?"

"We do not give out Mr. Hunt's home address," Miss Compton said reprovingly. "He isn't in just now. He may be back—"

"Do you mean that Henry Hunt himself is here, in San Francisco?" Chris broke in.

"Oh, I beg your pardon. You thought he was in Los Angeles? No, he reopened his offices here in April. I take it that you desire to speak to Mr. Hunt personally? If you'll give me your name—"

"No, I'll call back. You expect him to be in the office some time this afternoon?"

"He tries to get in a few minutes before I leave, at six o'clock. You can try then—"

Chris looked at his wrist watch. Two o'clock; four hours to kill and Anice had forbidden him to call her. Anice had probably guessed that he had not been able immediately to accept her story without question. Well, just before five he would call her, meet her at 450 Sutter and take her home. Probably he wouldn't be able to see Henry Hunt before tomorrow morning.

And probably, Chris thought pessimistically, ours will be an unsatisfactory interview. I'll be no match for Hunt. It was Father who dealt with him six years ago; I don't believe I saw the man more than twice. But until I've talked with him . . .

The others were leaving the dining room whose door was just across from the study. Chris heard Daphne urging her guests to come upstairs to her own sitting room; caught a snatch of their talk. ". . . simply in rags, my dear, and I'm pathetically thankful to pay any price for anything that doesn't simply resemble sacking, but with wartime fabrics what they are, I cling desperately to some of my prewar Gisele models which are timeless and—"

Chris snapped his fingers. Gisele's—Michael Dundas! The ideal person to talk to: experienced, impersonal, yet knowing all the background. He must, though neither he nor Valerie had ever

mentioned Rowena to Chris or made him feel
that they ever thought of him as Rowena Talcott's
brother.

That, in spite of the fact that he had known
them rather well and seen them quite often after
they first met—how many years ago? A year or
so after Rowena's disappearance, Chris recalled.
Say 1940; not that it mattered. But he'd talk to
Michael though not, God forbid, at that dress shop
of his. Better call Valerie and ask her. . . .

"Getting oriented again, old chap?" Joel said
kindly. "No, don't get up. Naturally you would
want to come here and sit quietly— One doesn't
want to be sentimental but St. George would
have—"

"I know," Chris said curtly. "But you want to
work. How is it coming along?"

Joel grimaced gracefully, looking more than
ever like Basil Rathbone in a society drama. "My
dear fellow! My admiration and awe of St. George
increases as I attack each succeeding volume of his
journal, but one does wish the dear old boy had
not been quite so outspoken and vituperative."

"I can imagine," Chris laughed and got up. He
wouldn't telephone Valerie; he'd just go around to
see her and take a chance that she'd be home. He
would like to see her, anyway.

Joel asked, "Whither away, Chris?"

"I'm going to walk for a while. The doctors advised exercise."

It did not occur to him that he, by nature candid and ingenuous, had grown instinctively wary; that for a long time he would be wary, even when it was not called for as a matter of physical self-preservation.

He added, "I have to have shirts and a sport coat. My chest and shoulders have expanded so that my old things won't do and I'd like to get out of uniform."

Twenty minutes later, having been lucky enough to get a taxi at Van Ness, he was ringing the doorbell of the Dundas' home at Russian Hill Place.

Valerie opened the door, stared at him, said: "Chris! My dear, I am so glad to see you," and kissed him. "Come in. When did you get home?"

She watched him limp over to the chesterfield. He saw her brows pucker and said quickly, "In time I won't limp so much, Valerie. This leg is a poor thing, but mine own, and since I wasn't certain until July that I wouldn't have to part with it, I got to feel a deep affection for it. Of course they gave me a medical discharge, and I got home last night"

"Only last night, Chris?"

Chris turned to look at her and went on looking, more intently than politely. He had always thought her attractive but he did know that other women wrote her off as "good-looking enough." He thought that now they must admit that somehow the good-looking girl had gotten to be a beautiful woman.

He saw that she had not thrown off her old, girlish trick of blushing and said, "I'm sorry but you are—should I say 'out of this world,' or 'in very good looks?'"

"The latter phrase sounds more like you and Miss Austen. And so are you, Chris, considering."

Privately Valerie thought that now he looked more than twenty-nine where at twenty-six he could have passed for twenty-one. He had corn-colored hair, brown eyes, features that were almost too correct. But he had a redeeming, lopsided smile; a hesitant, faintly diffident smile that hinted at an inner conviction that he should not be taken seriously even when he was being authoritative on a lecture platform.

"I am flattered," she went on, "that you have called so soon after getting home, but why have you? Surely, on your first day home—"

It was Chris's turn to flush. "I know I didn't come to say good-bye on my last leave. I saw no one then but my family and fiancée. And now—yes, I do want to talk to Michael, and not at his shop. I'd hoped he might be here, knowing he more or less makes his own hours, and I thought that perhaps—"

Valerie lit a cigarette. She didn't use to smoke, Chris thought, before she said calmly, but with an angry light in her hazel eyes, "Why do you take for granted that Michael is still a civilian? I believe you enlisted in June of 1942 when university was out? Michael went in the next month, July, and I haven't seen him for two years or more."

VII

"Here sits the complete dolt! Trample on me, my dear: I deserve it. I didn't see you after Pearl Harbor but I should have known what Michael would do. But someone mentioned Gisele's and I—"

"Never mind, Chris. I'm a little overwrought," Valerie said, smiling. "I haven't heard from Michael for so much longer than I like that I . . . never mind. He made his manager, Miss Weis, a full partner; so Gisele's is still operating."

"I suppose Michael went into Intelligence? He was a natural for it—"

"Yes, once they decided to let his civilian record pass. They gave him a lieutenancy and he's a major now. Not that I feel I know any Major Dundas. They sent him over before the invasion of Sicily since, besides speaking Spanish, Portuguese, French and Italian, he knows some of the

Sicilian dialects. He picked them up from various brigands he knew here in his younger days. He was in Italy until after the fall of Rome. Then they sent him to France instead of home—"

"They must have considered him a valuable man."

"Oh—" Valerie shrugged. "He broke down and admitted they handed him the D.S.M. in Italy. He said they had either to decorate him or court-martial him. So I take it the award was for service very much beyond the call of duty and that Michael, as usual, was somewhere where he really shouldn't have been.

"Well, he survived the fighting in France and Germany. I had one letter from him after V-E day and then two unsatisfactory notes and that's all. I don't know where he is at the moment—"

She lit another cigarette, walked to the window and stood looking down at the sloping hillside garden below it.

Chris ventured, "He'll walk in some day. I should have known he would go though he hated to leave you and your youngster—"

"Oh, pfui!" Valerie said scornfully and then laughed at the expression on Chris's face. "He loves me and Ricky dearly but he wanted to go and I'll wager he's enjoyed himself. It should have been good for him. Perhaps he'll never mind again

when big he-men patronize him because he designs clothes for women. But why did you want
to talk to him, Chris? Not, after all these years,
about Rowena? I never heard you speak of her—"

"I wasn't forced to, with you and Michael. And
we got so we didn't talk of her, even among ourselves, for common sense, not sentimental reasons."

"Then," Valerie said hesitantly; "you were not
so deeply devoted to her?"

"I've realized lately that I secretly thought
Rowena a little tiresome, partly because she was
given to worthy works and causes. That doesn't
mean I shrugged off what happened or forgot it,
or ever will. None of us will forget so long as we
don't know what became of her. So it was a shock
to come home, and find that . . ."

"I'll get you a drink," Valerie said as Chris hesitated.

She came back with a tall highball. Chris
promptly halfemptied it though he hadn't former-
ly been a quick or proficient drinker.

"Have you time to listen?"

"Yes. Our invaluable maid is spending the night
with an English friend in Mill Valley. She took
our son with her. I'm invited to a tea but I won't
go before five o'clock, if then."

"I won't talk that late. I got home last night, let
myself into the house and then eavesdropped for

some time. Daphne was speaking; what she and Mark said caught my attention. . . ."

Chris told her, accurately and in detail, what had been said in the Talcott house before he went off to Anice; what Anice had told him; what Sophia had had to say to him; that he hoped to get in touch with Henry Hunt this evening.

"What a memorable home-coming," Valerie said and brought him another drink. "I'd ask whether Daphne mightn't just have tried to drive Anice away if that distinctive umbrella handle of your aunt's hadn't turned up—"

"Yes, that tears it. Old Dobbin's turning up won't fit into the theory that it was a stupid practical joke aimed at Anice. Everyone else was at the theater that night so, unless Aunt Sophia lied, some—some stranger entered the house carrying at least the handle of the same umbrella Rowena carried away with her."

"I know. I'd better admit that I detest Daphne. I've encountered her at various literary gatherings and have met her husband, Mark Vibert, several times but don't remember him at all. I've heard of Joel and Bob but have never met them nor your Aunt Sophia. Does she write, too?"

"A few fastidious readers remember her for some polished essays and a penetrating life of Louisa M. Alcott that didn't sell. She's worked for years on a history of the beginnings and development of juveniles. It will be a brilliant piece of work if she ever finishes it, but it won't sell. Your asking that reminds me that we were asked if Rowena had been happy and we weren't certain. We had to consider the possibility of amnesia. We were told that quiet, conscientious, responsible people like Rowena are most susceptible to amnesia; not the gay and frivolous type."

"But there must be some psychological strain to send anyone off the deep end. Was Rowena the only un-literary member of your household?"

"Yes, except for Bob, who is counted as one of us," Chris said. "Rowena may have found her lack of talent humiliating. But she refused to make a fashionable debut so you'd suppose she had no social ambition. She seemed content except for one thing that appeared too trivial to mention to the police. She began taking on weight six months before she disappeared and she wanted to be slim. She was forever dieting yet she couldn't lose weight."

"That can be a deep source of unhappiness to a woman but its not a problem to be solved by walking away from family and friends and two suitors," Valerie said. "Were they really devoted suitors?"

"I doubt that Joel could feel deep affection for anyone. And marrying Rowena would have been a good thing for him. Father would have liked them to go on living at home. Daphne and Mark took over the third floor when they were married."

"You must be a very affectionate family."

"We aren't," Chris said, "but we are close-ly-knit because we usually find one another more entertaining than anyone else we know. Either we absorb people or we spit them out if we can't digest them. We digested Bob and Joel, and Joel and Rowena seemed very companionable. I can't believe she and Bob would have been happy together. He is too—lusty for a woman like Rowena. He didn't need to marry her for her expectations; his father left him a good deal of money. And he acted the part of the bereaved lover to high heaven when she disappeared."

"And she had no intimate friends outside the family circle?"

"No, and was reticent even with us. Did Michael ever discuss the case with you, Valerie?"

"Everyone discussed the Talcott case, Chris. The police questioned Michael because the new dress she wore when she vanished had come from Gisele's. They talked to his manager, Fanchon Weis. Michael told me that, but he never advanced any theories or suggested a solution to the mystery. He did say: 'It seems that I designed a shroud for Rowena,' but it doesn't follow that he really believed she was dead."

"I tried to believe that she must be because that was less disturbing than . . . Is that clock right?" Chris rose abruptly. "Thank you, Valerie. Talking to you has helped. The family wouldn't approve but they needn't know this wasn't just a social call."

"I hope you'll call again when you've seen Henry Hunt. Had you thought Michael might know him?"

"I thought it not impossible, considering what a great variety of characters Michael does know."

"Yes," Valerie agreed, "though he never mentioned Mr. Hunt to me, if he did know him. He might . . . But I suppose I must dress to go to that tea and you want to meet Anice, don't you?"

"Yes. I won't stop to telephone; I'll try to catch her when she leaves the doctor's office. . . ."

Anice, coming out of an office marked "Private," looked at Chris timidly, questioningly. He came forward and kissed her despite a not inconsiderable audience of home-going office workers.

"I've been blue all day because you didn't phone even if I did tell you not to. But it's all right now." Anice tucked her hand under his arm and smiled at him. "Only," she went on when finally they were out of a packed elevator and onto Sutter Street, "your Aunt Sophia did call up."

"You don't seem pleased that she did, dear."

"Oh, she was very nice. She explained how it happened they didn't let me know last night you might be home. Only she just takes for granted we'll both be home for dinner tonight."

"After all, I didn't get home in time for dinner last night and walked out on them almost as soon as I arrived. Do you mind very much if we dine with the family tonight, darling?"

"I do mind," Anice said mutinously. "But it's all right. We'll have dinner with the family because you'll feel guilty if we don't. And you may not enjoy yourself before it's over."

"I'll see that Daphne behaves herself."

"You and what man's army?"

"And now we'll walk over to the Plaza and have a cocktail. I want to tell you what Aunt Sophia told me last night. It may relieve your mind."

Over cocktails in El Prado, Chris told her what Sophia had had to say.

"I remember how Miss Sophia decided not to go to the play with us that night. The rest of us went and we stayed together, too," Anice said. "Well, you can't laugh off a thing like that umbrella handle, can you?"

"You feel," Chris guessed, "that Aunt Sophia should have talked to you?"

"Why should she confide in me?" Anice said tonelessly. "I didn't in her, but I would have spilled the works if anybody had really tried to get me to tell them what really happened that night I fell on the stairs. I was so scared. It's nearly six, Chris, and dinner's at six-thirty. 'An uncivilized hour for dining.'" She mimicked Daphne. "But the cook they have now raises the roof if she don't get cleaned up by eight, sharp."

"Then we had better go."

I forgot about Hunt, Chris thought. Probably he won't be in his office by the time I get to a telephone but I don't want to call from here. I'd have to explain to Anice and there's no need to complicate matters further by telling her about Hunt. If we can get a taxi, we'll be home very soon.

It was ten after six when they entered the Talcott house. Sophia greeted them in the front hall.

"Bob hasn't arrived. I believe Joel and Mark are still in their rooms. Do you want to tidy, Anice? You don't need to. No? Then come into the living room for sherry. Daphne is in there."

Chris excused himself, went into St. George's study and dialed the number of the Hunt Agency. A quick, high- pitched voice admitted to being Henry Hunt himself.

"I am Christopher Talcott; Rowena Talcott's brother. You probably don't remember me."

"That's where you're wrong. I remember everybody. What's on your mind, Mr. Talcott?"

"I've just returned from overseas," Chris explained.

"That so? Been in the Army long?"

"For three years. I was nearly two years in Italy. I got back to the city last night, to stay. I discovered, as soon as I arrived, that there have been certain—developments that I find disturbing and difficult to explain."

Goddamn it, I sound hopelessly pedantic and ineffectual, Chris thought. He cleared his throat experimentally and then heard Bob Lovell bursting into the house in a loud voice:

"Anybody home? Go on with your knitting, gals. I'm going upstairs to wash off the grime of honest toil. Be patient: Lovell will soon be with you. . . ."

Bob clattered up the stairway. Chris realized that Hunt was speaking and said, "I beg your pardon?"

"You don't want to talk to me over the phone, do you?"

"N-no. What I have to tell you will sound fantastic enough under any circumstances. I couldn't meet you tonight conveniently before eight o'clock at the earliest. If you . . ."

"Eight? No," Henry Hunt said slowly, "I wouldn't like to promise to meet you then. I've got—a date and might be tied up for some time. How about ten tomorrow morning at my office?"

"I'll be there. I'm anxious to talk to you."

"Sure you are, soldier. You're entitled to a little peace of mind. I'd like to help out if I can. Only—have you consulted anyone else?"

"No. Of course I have talked to some members of the family but I wouldn't say I'd consulted them. However, I should tell you, Mr. Hunt, that I did call on Michael Dundas, whom you may know, but . . ."

Chris stopped abruptly. There were extensions on the second floor and in Daphne's sitting room on the third floor. He thought disgustedly that his reactions were slow tonight. It had been just before he pronounced Hunt's name that he had heard a faint, clicking sound that could mean someone had taken a receiver from its hook.

"Look, I heard what you heard," Hunt said. "Let's let it wait till tomorrow morning. Take it easy, son."

He hung up before Chris could answer. Chris turned and looked toward the hall and saw that he had left the study door a little ajar. But three feminine voices were still murmuring in the living room and in an instant Bob came leaping down the stairway.

Chris saw him pass, rose and went into the living room. Almost at once, Joel appeared; then Mark, an instant before a frowzy maid announced, "Dinner's ready."

Chris waited at the door for Anice; looked at her closely and thought: Oh Christ, Daphne's had her claws out. For Daphne looked like a kitten who had just caught its first mouse and Sophia was more than usually grim. While Anice, as they went toward the dining room, had little red battle flags flying in her cheeks and her black eyes were stormy. . . .

VIII

It was eight o'clock before Valerie escaped from a hostess who urged her to "stay and talk it over and eat up the sandwiches."

She rather wished, as she climbed the steps at Vallejo and Taylor, that she had stayed. It was always amusing to dissect the departed but not dear guests. And though the surviving sandwiches were pretty well worn out by now, they would have tasted better than a solitary snack was going to.

She'd been foolish to say she must write letters. Of course she did have a great deal to tell Michael since she had seen Chris this afternoon, but lately it had been difficult to feel that she was writing to Michael and not just to "Postmaster, New York."

She reached Russian Hill Place, glanced toward her front door and saw that a smallish, dapper man was waiting there. He smiled ingratiatingly.

"Mrs. Dundas? I wanted to see Michael. I'm an old pal of his. My name is Henry Hunt."

He can't have talked to Chris yet or he would know that Michael isn't available, Valerie thought. He must be an elusive person if Chris hasn't managed to contact him yet. . . .

She said: "Yes, I'm Mrs. Dundas. Michael isn't here just now. Will you come in?" And when Hunt had sat down after one quick, all-inclusive glance about the living room, she added, "I have never heard Michael speak of you, Mr. Hunt, but . . ."

"It's been all of six years since I saw him. And," Hunt said matter-of-factly, "I'm not the sort of guy he'd be apt to introduce to his wife. I'm a private detective."

"Was it you that Michael's grandfather hired to trace him years ago when he first came here? And when you'd found Michael, you two made a financial arrangement that was mutually beneficial."

Mr. Hunt chuckled. "Michael suggested I give him a rake-off if he'd keep in touch with me so I could send his grandpop a regular report without having to do any legwork. I liked his gall and I guess he needed those few dollars then." Again the appraising glance about the living room. "I moved to L.A. six years ago and I've only been back here since February. I did think Michael might be in the Army when I ever thought about him at all."

"He is in the Army. I brought you in here under false pretenses."

Valerie's smile was deliberately provocative. Mr. Hunt's bright, dark eyes were knowledgeable in more ways than one and behind his impudent grin was the certainty that women found it attractive.

"Christopher Talcott was here this afternoon," she went on. "He talked to me, since Michael isn't available. He wants very much to get in touch with you."

"And you thought he hadn't and that you'd grab me for him? But he did get me on the phone a while ago. He wants to see me, but I've got a date tonight so he's to come to my office tomorrow morning. He said he'd called on Michael, and I jumped to conclusions when he didn't get to finish his speech.

"Oh, well, Mother told me there would be days like this. It's as well Talcott didn't go on. I think someone was listening in on us. But when I had something to eat, I decided I'd like to talk to Michael myself, since I supposed Talcott had. I still would like to talk to him, lady."

"Had you considered talking to Nicholas Prevost?" Valerie said. "We know him very well. He's been attached to the Homicide detail for a good many years but I suppose he was still on Burglary when you moved to Los Angeles."

"Yes. His connection with the Talcott case was just that there was a burglary there the night Rowena disappeared. At least there was a kitchen window open and the silverware was out on the dining room table and Rowena's room had been ransacked. Only nothing had been taken from either of the rooms.

"Nick tried to establish a connection between that and Rowena's disappearance," Hunt said musingly. "And he was on the right track. He asked me if I thought it was a bona fide burglary but he gave me an out by adding: 'a professional job?' I told him the truth when I said it wasn't a professional job.

"I didn't," Hunt went on in the same reflective voice, "tell him it was still a bona fide burglary. Or that even if they didn't take the silverware, something had been taken. Only, in one instance, you couldn't call it really stealing."

He stopped and Valerie could not decide whether his little start and rueful smile were genuine or only better than average acting.

"I talk too much to pretty women. Well, I got nowhere on the case, though I knew a few things that the police didn't."

"How did you learn them?" Valerie said baldly.

"My methods aren't those of the police. I've heard rumors that Michael's methods sometimes aren't above criticism though that may just be sandhouse. A private dick can't be scrupulous and get ahead. Its a racket but it's better than taking in washing. No—" Mr. Hunt shook his head. "You've smiled me into talking more than I usually do and you're a friend of Talcott's and Nick Prevost's.

"I'll talk things over with Talcott tomorrow; that's a promise. Could I have a drink? Not liquor; I don't use it. Just water."

When Valerie came back from the kitchen he was looking down at their hillside garden. He nodded toward it, taking the water goblet from her.

"It's nice you left some flowers along with the vegetables. Oh yes," he added with his impudent grin, "I'm not a bad guy. I'm nuts about dogs and kids and I like flowers. Ever try to grow delphiniums? But they don't do so good here. Neither do zinnias. Not hot enough for them. You've got a nice place. I guess you haven't had to worry about the housing situation."

"Have you?" Valerie said cooperatively.

"Lady, do you want me to break down and weep? I had the devil's own time finding a place where I could set up business and it looked like I'd have to sleep there permanently, too. I know the proprietors of plenty of flea-traps south of Market but even they could only accommodate me for three

days or a week at a stretch. No use trying any
first-rate hotels. Well, I'll be going along."

"Did you walk from downtown?" Valerie said.

"Hmm? No, I've got my car. I left it parked at
that stone wall at Jones instead of driving in. It's
been a pleasure to meet you," Hunt said, "and give
Michael my best when you write to him. . . ."

Valerie watched him swing jauntily down the
walk toward the wall that shut this block of Vallejo off from Jones Street. She laughed and shook
her head.

"I wonder who paid him how much *not* to tell
what he knew about Rowena six years ago. But he
is an engaging little crook."

She picked up the empty water goblet and started toward the kitchen. Abruptly she stopped, for
an instant stood stone-still before she dropped the
glass, ran to the front door and jerked it open.

This block was always quiet because of the wall
that discouraged traffic past Jones. It was quiet
now; there was no car moving up the street or
even parked before any house on it.

"And that wasn't backfire!" Valerie whispered.

She began to run. It was a very short distance
to Jones: down her own steps, across the street
where Russian Hill Place meets Vallejo, along a
brief stretch of pavement. Then, stumbling over

bumpy old cobblestones, out to Jones by one of
the twin driveways that curved around the ends of
the wall there.

There was a car standing in front of the wall,
as Hunt had said; already, though this, too, was a
quiet street, there were people gathered about the
car. A large man in house-slippers, red suspenders
hanging down his back, switching the backs of his
thighs, was saying, "I heard this shot and I run
out. I didn't see nobody but this guy in the car. I
hear him groan and I run over. There he is with
this big hole in his back—

"Speak? Yes. He says 'Marg'ret' and then he
dies. That's all: just 'Marg'ret.' So I yell to my
missus to call the cops. I . . ."

He paused, walked dizzily away and was very
sick on the cobblestones.

IX

For a while things went well enough. Sophia had
been trained to make small, impersonal table talk
and Joel was a professional and practiced diner-
out. But Daphne was determined to have the
center of the stage. When it became necessary for
Sophia and Joel to masticate or go unfed, Daphne
began talking about a fur coat she had seen at
Liebes, several days ago.

"It is ridiculously cheap but it simply *is* my coat. Salesgirls can't flatter me but they say so, too. It's a very extreme style but I can carry off anything like that. . . ."

"You have two fur coats, a jacket and twin silver foxes now," Sophia said repressively.

"Oh, auntie! It's original of you to pay no attention to styles but only my leopard is at all new. I couldn't resist it because it was so soft and thick and just like an adorable spotted kitty-cat."

Chris groaned. "Come off it, will you, Daffy?"

Daphne gave him a sweet, sisterly smile. "I know my quaint little fancies seem foolish to others. Of course there is nothing, no matter how trying it is to most women, that I can't wear and look well in. But I don't *feel* right in the leopard and that's important because it makes me unhappy. However, the Persian lamb I was speaking of . . ."

"Yes, Daffy, you have been," Bob said in a bored voice. "So why not just buy the damned thing?"

"Because, pet, I haven't seven hundred dollars."

Bob whistled. "You do go through money like a house afire, don't you, Babe?"

"Don't call me 'Babe,' you big oaf!"

"All right, I won't call you 'Babe,' Toots."

Chris laughed. Bob was one of the very few who could cope with Daphne, mainly because he seemed able to guess just what colloquialisms grated most harshly on Daphne's admittedly sensitive ear.

Mark Vibert, who had been regarding his serving of stringy, overdone roast as if it were a laboratory specimen under a microscope, raised his head suddenly.

"If this is your idea of a tactful approach to the proposition that I buy that coat for you, Daphne, you might as well save your breath."

Daphne looked grievously hurt, fragile and childishly frightened. This was an art she had mastered in her 'teens. When confronted with that look, St. George would yell: "Great heavenly honk, don't cringe, girl!" before letting Daphne have her own way.

But Daphne's once equally indulgent and far more courteous husband now was not only unimpressed but regarded her with the expression of a man who is served leftovers from a sumptuous banquet just once too often.

"You are going to tell me that the war is over. Someone must have told you because you never knew there was a war going on. Please!" Mark raised a weary hand. "I won't buy that coat for you and don't try to charge it to me unless you want your credit cut off immediately."

"Oh, dear, you're feeling badly again, aren't you?" Daphne said. "Would you like milk toast or soft-boiled eggs instead of this horrid roast?"

Mark stood up. There was an anguished yowl and one of Daphne's cats shot toward the door with flattened ears and increased, indignant tail. Daphne forgot her pose of wifely solicitude. She cried, "You kicked Mitzi! You—"

"I stepped on her goddamned tail and if you don't keep her from under my feet I'll kick her into the middle of next week!" Mark threw down his napkin. "I'm going to take a walk. Good night!"

"So say we all of us," Bob remarked stolidly.

Joel declared regretfully, "Mark is not a well man," and Daphne said pathetically, "I am horribly worried about him. If he were well, he couldn't be so unreasonable. I have a certain position to maintain. I'm asked to talk to clubs and organizations. I can't appear in some ratty garment that looks like something a working girl bought on time. Oh, Anice! You know I didn't mean . . ."

"I know what you think of my ratty old caracal that wasn't a good coat to begin with," Anice flashed. "But I went without lunch for several months to buy it. And if you think a seven-hundred-dollar coat is 'ridiculously cheap,' why don't you buy it with your 'own money' you're always mentioning?"

"Not that it is any of your affair, my sweet, but I make very little from my poor little brain-babies. One is not rolling in wealth merely because one turns out an occasional book."

"But you also have some sort of allowance, don't you?"

"Really, Anice, do you think I don't know that you know quite well exactly what my allowance from Father's estate is, since Chris gets the same?"

"I have never discussed my finances with Anice," Chris broke in. "But I want her to know, since it may be some time before I'm earning a salary again, that until the estate is settled, you and I each get two hundred a month from it."

"And a ridiculously paltry sum, considering how much money Father left," Daphne said.

"A great many large families live on less," Sophia said frigidly. "St. George meant the allowance to be pin money for you."

"Pin money!" Anice muttered. "Dear heaven!"

"Oh, perhaps it was enough when Father made his will but he always boasted of his foresight so why didn't he foresee that Mark would be drafted and have to hire a manager for his bookshop at a ruinous wage? And Father predicted a long war so why didn't he realize that prices would double in three years?"

"According to the most reliable statistics, prices have not—" Joel began weightily but Daphne brushed him aside.

"Stat me no statistics. I know what things cost. So does Sophia. By Father's will the estate hands two-fifty a month over to her for household expenses. But isn't it awfully hard to spread that over everything, auntie? Of course you are a wonderful manager," Daphne said sweetly. "Chris thinks so. He must, as you managed his affairs while he was away—and very competently, I'm sure he believes."

X

Sophia looked fixedly at her niece, fingering the cameo pin at the neck of her jumper. "I will give Chris an accounting whenever he wants one," she said without emphasis. "And living costs have soared, but St. George wished me to maintain this establishment as long as any of you wished to live here. He didn't stop to think . . ."

"No, he charged ahead, roaring down all objections and made that ridiculous will," Daphne said. "Not that money, as money, means anything to me."

"We know, chick," Bob said blandly. "White hyacinths are more than bread to you but your white hyacinths cost an awful lot."

"I consider this conversation in very bad taste," Sophia said.

"Isn't it all in the family? St. George treated me like a son and Joel grafted himself onto the family tree many years ago. If Anice is to be considered one of the family, she should be told that if Rowena doesn't turn up before she can be presumed legally dead, Chris and Daphne inherit just twice what they will if Rowena appears to claim her half of the estate."

"You don't need to tell Anice that, Bob," Daphne said. "She knows the terms of Father's will."

"I do not! Why would I?"

"The newspapers devoted some space to his will, Anice dear."

"I don't read newspapers. I only met your Father once, before Chris and I were engaged. I didn't take the liberty of attending his funeral. Chris and I had one day together then, since he only had three days. We didn't talk about wills, but I'm glad Bob explained things because now I see why you wanted to get me out of here."

"Easy does it, my dear," Joel said soothingly.

"You shut up! You just laughed when I told you why I wanted to get out of Rowena's room. You all knew something had scared the living daylights out of me when I fell on the stairs but you wanted to discredit me before I told my story, if I told it.

When I left here, no one tried to find out what it was all about, even though Miss Talcott knew something was wrong when the handle from the umbrella she loaned Rowena turned up.

"You don't," Anice added, "want to admit that either you believe in ghosts or Rowena is alive! And you don't want her to be alive, Daphne! You want your half of Rowena's half of your father's money."

"While Chris takes the other half, my sweet. I think you've always known all about Father's will and to the last nickel what Chris's expectations are!"

"Do you think I'm marrying Chris for his money?"

"What else? And I think you're a nasty little mantrap!" Daphne discarded her delicate stiletto for the bludgeon. "Chris is your best bet, since he's come back alive and has both legs, after all. Otherwise, it would be someone else. I don't care if you make a play for Bob or poor old Joel but you let Mark alone! I've seen you playing up to him, sympathizing with him, turning him against me. . . ."

Anice wadded her fine linen napkin into a ball, flung it on the table and stood up. "You worthless, pampered, yowling little cat! I'm going home!"

Chris caught up with her at the front door. "I'm sorry, darling," he said. And then, because his nerves were jangling, added unwisely, "But you shouldn't have said that to Daphne."

"I should have been a lady and turned the other cheek?" Anice said furiously. "You didn't hear her sniping at me before dinner about my clothes and my 'background' and my education. It wouldn't have mattered if you had, I suppose. So just don't bother about seeing me home!"

"I have my car outside," Bob said. "The maid has stopped listening at the keyhole and is clearing away. Sophia is preparing to land on Daphne with all four feet. Come on, Anice; you'd rather ride than walk any night, even with me."

Anice went out with Bob. Chris stayed where he was, swearing softly until Daphne suddenly burst from the dining room and went running up the stairs, weeping in little gasps of pure rage. Joel followed her, flung his hands out expressively and said, "I'm going to work in the study."

Then Sophia appeared with a glint in her eyes that explained why Daphne had left her so precipitately. She said composedly, "I'm going to read in my room. Goodnight, Chris."

Chris watched her rather wistfully but she went up the stairs without looking back. He glanced irresolutely toward the study door. But he was too weary to deal with the polite evasions he suspected would be his lot if he tackled Joel.

Chris thought: Joel has managed to live with us for fifteen years by being discreet. And he grinned suddenly, recalling Bob's phrase "Joel grafted himself onto the family tree" and Joel's aggrieved, long-suffering look when he heard it.

He realized that he was looking at the old grandfather clock near the front door and that it was only eight o'clock. Suddenly he wanted to be out of the old house. For an instant he saw it as an unclosed crypt to which a lonely, living ghost might return in the dark hours. Chris shivered, left the house quickly and started out to walk himself into a state of exhaustion that would ensure sleep.

He did walk, until he found himself on Chestnut Street in the Marina, realized that his bad leg was aching and went into the first bar he came to. He ordered beer and drank half of it before he thumped the glass down, said, "The hell with it!" and walked out.

He hailed a passing cab with a whistle that was pure G.I. and fifteen minutes later was standing on Anice's doorstep with Anice in his arms, mumbling apologies against her soft hair. . . .

XI

The Inspector from the Homicide detail was named Sterling. He was not stupid; merely tired and unimaginative. Undoubtedly he remembered the Talcott case but he did not immediately connect it with Henry Hunt.

He said, "Hunt had an eye for women and in other ways he got away with murder—till it caught up with him." He accepted Valerie's story that Hunt had known Michael and had come to see him; expressed his regret that Michael was not there; and gone away. Valerie wondered, however, what Sterling might have said if she had not immediately identified herself as the Mrs. Dundas who was Prevost's close friend.

"Nick got caught late in San Jose," Sterling said. "I'll see him in the morning. It was nice of you to tell us why Hunt happened to be up here, Mrs. Dundas. Saved us ringing doorbells to find out. You'd better go to bed. You look tuckered out."

Valerie followed him to the door. "Was someone waiting for Mr. Hunt in his car, Inspector?"

"Looks like it. His car wasn't locked and the keys were in his pocket so it looks like he was fool enough to leave the car unlocked. Anyone could've laid in the back of the car and waited for Hunt. When he got back in the car, it'd take no time for someone to stick a gun against him, blast away and slip out of the car and beat it. Did you say you're alone here tonight?"

"I'll be all right," Valerie said. "I'm not nervous, Inspector."

But she was at least very restless. She pulled the shades to the windowsills in the bedroom, started to remove her dress, got up to walk back and forth.

She glanced at the clock but it was nearly eleven and she thought: "No, I won't call Chris. If he is at home, he's in bed."

It did not occur to her that she could be in any danger tonight. She sat down to brush her hair thinking: "'Margaret.' There's no Margaret connected with the Talcott case. Inspector Sterling said Mr. Hunt had an eye for women. Margaret might be anyone. Oh, damn! I'd better eat something."

Valerie knew her home well enough that she did not trouble to switch on any lights as she went toward their glass-enclosed back porch where the refrigerator stood. She knelt down and looked at its contents unenthusiastically, sniffed and decided that the remains of some chicken au gratin had been around a little too long.

Beyond the porch door was a hilly back yard that had never been leveled off. It was fenced in but Valerie had noticed recently that there were gaps in the fence. Adjoining this yard was a vacant lot, overgrown with shoulder-high brown weeds.

Valerie snaked the dish that held the aged chicken from the refrigerator and stood up with it in her hand, meaning to empty its contents into the garbage can beside the back steps.

And then, with an echoing clang, the lid of the garbage can clattered down across the steps and went rolling away, to thud against the back of the house. Valerie found herself on her knees, sheltered by the refrigerator. She put the covered dish on the floor, because her hands were trembling so violently.

"Just a cat," she told herself. Then: "But could a cat knock that lid off just by walking across it? It fits the can very tightly. Be still; be very still and listen. . . ."

She thought she heard the weeds rustling in the wind—but there was no wind. And it would be so easy for someone to creep into that vacant lot, hide in those tall weeds and wait. The porch walls were glass: a bullet would go through glass.

On all fours she crept toward the kitchen door, got through it; slammed it shut. She stumbled toward the telephone in the hall off the bedrooms, switched on the lights there, picked up the telephone and found herself looking at a length of dangling wire. Someone had hacked it apart just where it went into the bell-box.

"But who?" Valerie muttered. "I did leave the house unlocked when I heard the shot and ran down to Mr. Hunt's car. I was there for quite a while. The house was open to anyone during the time that I was gone. . . ."

The doorbell rang. Valerie took a step toward the front of the house, hesitated and stopped. An angry light came into her hazel eyes.

"The same simple and direct technique that was used with Henry Hunt?" she thought. "I open the door; there's no one there. I step out and present a lovely target. Well, we'll see about that."

Her hands were perfectly steady when she took Michael's loaded automatic from the bedside table. She went back through the kitchen, across the porch and into the back yard, gun in hand. Very quietly she worked her way around the side of the house, through the garden to a clump of shrubbery from which she could see the front steps.

There was no light burning outside the front door and no street lamp near their house. The figure at the top of the steps was vague in outline, but a human figure it certainly was, and for an instant Valerie felt very foolish. Then caution nipped warningly at her heels.

She raised the gun and said clearly, "What do you want? Who are you? Why were you prowling about the back yard just now?"

She broke off and dropped the gun into the shrubbery as a familiar voice, flexible and expressive, said, "*Por Dios, querida!* 'Ben Battle was a soldier bold And used to war's alarms—' but not to being greeted by his loving wife with a deadly weapon in her hand. . . ."

By now Michael was down the steps and had Valerie in his arms. He said contritely, "I'm sorry if you're frightened, my dearest, but I was not prowling about the back yard. I tried to call you but our line is dead. So I came along without . . . Valerie! Don't do that! Remember what you have always said about females who swoon—" But Valerie, who heartily despised swooning females, proceeded to faint, and thoroughly.

PART TWO

I

At seven o'clock Valerie slipped out of bed and began to pick up her clothes which were rather widely scattered about the room.

She had no idea that Michael was awake until he remarked, "You've done the impossible and improved on your figure. How? Gardening, war work, worry and rationing?"

"Rationing, which was not relaxed much until September 1st, put pounds on people. You know nothing of the rigors of civilian life, Major. We ate potatoes, rice, macaroni, creamed gunk and spaghetti. I trust you enjoyed the spaghetti in Italy? But you didn't get that lovely scar across your ribs in Italy. It's too new for that."

"I owe that to a sniper who did not lay down his arms on V-E day. A damned unheroic way to acquire a wound stripe. I wasn't up to writing long letters, only notes, but I didn't want you to be worried about what was only a scratch. And when they started me home I thought you might as well not be tying yourself in knots, waiting for me to get here."

"That was *so* considerate of you, darling. How—how long have you?"

"Several weeks, just now. Don't worry, dear. After that I'll have to sit behind a desk for as long as it takes them to get around to giving me my discharge. They might give me a silver oak leaf and you'd like that, wouldn't you? Even if it's only a farewell gift and token of esteem."

"Esteem? Is that," Valerie said skeptically, "what your immediate superiors felt for you?"

Michael grinned. "It is true that my brigadier once told me . . . No, I believe you're still too young to hear his remarks verbatim. I suspect he spent much of his early life in the company of mule-skinners. He declared himself greatly relieved when he learned I didn't care to make a lifetime career of the Army, and we parted friends.

"Nevertheless," he added modestly, "I earned my board and keep. Sometime I will tell you how I captured Sicily, singlehanded, disguised as a bandit."

"I'm sure you will and I will believe one-half of what you tell me. Perhaps you did and perhaps you didn't. You always wrote me that mostly you sat at a desk 'a safe distance from the firing line' and found it 'damned dull.' Correct me if I haven't quoted you correctly. Have you gotten into the habit of waking early?"

"We went to bed early, my dear—or should I say quickly? You still haven't learned how not to blush. And now tell me why you were wandering around with a gun in your hand and why our telephone wire was cut last night."

"Oh, you saw the wire?"

"Yes. I didn't take time to mention it last night for obvious reasons. But . . ."

Valerie got back into bed. "I have a long story to tell and wish to tell it in comfort, though, as you'll presently see, I mustn't be too long about it. Yesterday afternoon, Chris Talcott came to see me. . . ."

Michael listened without any marked sign of interest until she said, "And then when I got home from that ghastly tea, about eight-fifteen, Henry Hunt was waiting on our doorstep."

With that he sat erect. "Do you mean that Harry wanted to see me?"

"Yes. He thought Chris had already consulted you." Valerie explained how that misunderstanding had occurred. "Did you like Mr. Hunt, Michael?"

"Yes. So do a surprising number of people. Harry will usually give a sucker a break unless said sucker is a heel and has more money than Harry thinks anyone but Harry should have. And if he puts the bee on anyone, even though it's for all the traffic will bear, I think the first payment is the last one and concludes what Harry thinks of as a business deal."

"Frightfully decent of him to blackmail people just once and not for years."

Michael shrugged. "Harry's a crook. He always needs more money than he can make legitimately. And I doubt that he told you what he would have told me, even if he did admire your bright eyes and sweet smile. What did he say?"

Valerie told him, in detail. She ended, "I watched him walk away. A very few minutes later I heard a sound I knew wasn't backfire. When I got down to Jones, Mr. Hunt was dead; shot, sitting in his car which he seems to have left unlocked.

"The blinds aren't down and the people across the way can see in here," she added mildly as Michael abruptly got out of bed. "Your dressing gown is in the closet. Why do you look—angry? Was Mr. Hunt any great loss to the world?"

"No loss to the world, no."

"Then you know who Margaret is?" she queried.

"Yes, I—" Michael opened the closet door. "I'll dress. Have I some old clothes in here?"

"Yes, I've managed to keep the moths out of them. Will you call Chris? Otherwise he'll go to Mr. Hunt's office and—"

Michael nodded. "I'll call him. I'll go to the corner grocery. They'll be less curious there than the neighbors would and won't detain me so long."

He got into an old pair of slacks and an ancient sweater and went off to the nearest grocery, at Leavenworth. Valerie had breakfast waiting on the table before he returned.

Pouring coffee, she remarked, "I thought Nick Prevost wouldn't care to talk to you at any length over the telephone but . . ."

"I didn't call Nick. I called Harry's office. Fortunately one of his old staff went to work for him again when Harry came back here. Harry trusted this fellow as much as he did anyone, so he was able to tell me what I wanted to know. I also talked to Chris and he was inclined to balk."

"At what?" Valerie said.

"At telling Nick everything. Chris is very shocked that Harry was murdered last night but he says he doesn't see that his death is necessarily connected with the Talcott case."

"Chris didn't swear me to secrecy and since I must tell Nick what Mr. Hunt said to me last night, I'll have to bring Chris into it," Valerie said.

"So I told Chris. That staggered him slightly and he agreed, very meekly, to come over here as soon as he can."

"Michael, do you think someone was prowling around the house last night?"

"I don't know. I don't see why Harry's murderer should have had any designs on you. Anyone would suppose you'd tell the police what you knew at once. And the murderer wouldn't necessarily know that Harry had talked to you, even though he must somehow have learned where Harry's car and Harry himself were apt to be around eight-thirty."

"I will try to believe that a light earthquake jarred the lid off the garbage can. My nerves were pretty well shot so I instinctively ran to the telephone. When I found the wire cut, I did lose my head. Did Mr. Hunt cut it when he sent me out of the room to get him a drink?"

"Six will get you ten that Harry did. For one thing, Harry did 'use' liquor and he preferred his water mixed with an equal amount of brandy. Harry must have known someone would like to kill him. I believe he thought that in case he didn't live to see Chris this morning, he would give you something to pass on to your friend, Nick Prevost."

"If he had only said more! But perhaps he didn't care to answer the question: 'Why does X wish to kill you?' And I wonder why he wanted to talk to you before he met Chris."

"I have a notion that he wanted me to act as a go-between, thinking I'd be more broadminded than Chris or the police," Michael said. "I don't know why he cut the telephone wire unless he wanted to give himself time. That is, he'd given you what was virtually a message for Nick and you might have run to the telephone as soon as Harry left—"

"If I had and had really wanted to get in touch with Nick, I'd have gone looking for another telephone. Mr. Hunt would only have gained a few minutes."

Michael shrugged. "He must have wanted to be certain he'd have even a few minutes' running start before you interested Nick in Mr. Hunt's activities. Harry—that should be Chris now. Tell him we're going for a ride if he doesn't mind. I'll get the car out."

II

Chris raised his eyebrows at Michael's costume, or lack of it, but made no comment. He greeted them with a certain formality that made Valerie wonder just exactly what Michael had said to him over the telephone.

When they had crossed Van Ness, Michael ended an unsociable silence by flinging a question over his shoulder to Chris but not one that Valerie would have expected him to ask just then.

"I believe that when Rowena disappeared, the police at first supposed she was the type of spinster who is apt to conceive a hopeless passion for her pastor or doctor or the chairman of committees dedicated to charitable meddling?"

"Yes," Chris said, "The fact that she could have married Bob or Joel didn't fit into that picture. However, Rowena attended St. Jude's on Pacific, as Aunt Sophia always has. And six years ago, the rector was an eloquent orator of not more than thirty-five: Walter Denning.

"The feminine three-quarters of the congregation adored him. I know the police questioned him because Rowena had been an earnest worker in the ladies' guild or Dorcas Society. His wife was a very pretty woman with a streamlined figure. She was competent, too, and she had money. She divorced Denning a year after Rowena disappeared. They'd left St. Jude's a few months before she brought suit. But Rowena's doctor was quite as charming as her pastor."

"Was he married, too?" Valerie asked.

"No. He'd announced his engagement to a Burlingame girl that February. She had a good deal of money, too. But Harold Baird wasn't married when Rowena disappeared. He lived in our neighborhood and had offices in his home, as well as downtown.

"Hal's father was one of my father's lieutenants in World War I," Chris said. "He was badly gassed and in poor health for years. About all he left Hal and Mrs. Baird was the old family home. Mrs. Baird was a plump, nondescript little woman, a great manager, but Hal was devoted to her. I doubt if there was much money left by the time Hal had his M.D."

"Did he marry the girl he was engaged to?" Valerie said.

"Yes. She died in childbirth three years later. I know the police questioned Hal Baird more than once," Chris said. "But Rowena never seemed smitten with Hal or the Reverend Denning. There was no one else for the police to question along those lines except Bob and Joel."

"There was Mark Vibert," Michael said.

Chris looked rather startled. "Well, of course Daphne was seeing a lot of Mark before Rowena disappeared. But Mark is younger than Daphne which would make him much younger than Rowena. Still, I suppose that doesn't signify, though I can't believe that Rowena would . . . Where are we going?"

"Not to San Bruno," Michael said, continuing on out Geary Boulevard toward the beach.

Chris scowled at him. "I asked you a civil question, you know."

"I'm sorry. The answer was a matter of associa-
tion of ideas. And what do you care where you're
going, soldier? You won't know what's going on
when you get there."

Chris blinked and then grinned. "Yes, as far
as a battlefield is concerned, it consists only of
as many feet of earth as you can cover with your
shrinking flesh. What do you honestly think of
Italy, Michael?"

"It stinks," said Major Dundas.

"Incessantly and incredibly," said Mr. Talcott.

Enlarging on this theme they proceeded out
Geary Boulevard to the beach; turned into the
highway that passed the Seal Rocks; the Cliff-
house; the shore, where the waves were beating
themselves to froth on the sands. On the other side
of the highway the little lunch stands and conces-
sions had not yet shaken off their bedclothes.

Leaving those behind, they came to a stretch
where the houses were mostly elderly and rather
widely separated from their nearest neighbors.
Michael stopped before a large, loosely built place
that looked as if it were hugging itself, trying to
keep warm in the raw fog and sweeping wind from
the ocean.

It had a great overgrown yard where sand drifted into neglected flower beds; and a bicycle, a

scooter and several battered sand pails lay on a sickly lawn.

"My remark that we weren't going to San Bruno was not entirely pointless. Years ago, Harry's home was in San Bruno. Few people knew that or that he was married. He took great care to divorce his private from his professional life. When he was at home, their friends were their neighbors who only knew that Harry's business was 'in the city.'

"But he once paid me the compliment of introducing me to his wife," Michael went on. "I'd like you to see why I take more than an academic interest in Harry's death. I'll warn you that he never confided in his wife. I hope that the police have already been here and that they were tactful."

Chris and Valerie followed Michael through the sagging gate that whined fretfully as it swung back and forth on rusted hinges.

The front door was opened by a girl of fourteen with reddened eyes and tremulous mouth. She said uncertainly, "Mamma? Well, I don't know. . . . Oh, if you are friends of Daddy's she'd want to see you. She's in here."

She led the way down a cold, stale-smelling hall. She was a pretty girl with Irish-blue eyes and blue-black hair, but her left leg was badly shrunken though she walked quickly, with only a slight sag in every other step.

She took them into a square, shabby living room. Margaret Hunt rose, removing a boy's sweater and a small drum and two wooden soldiers from the most comfortable chairs before she, too, sat down and said to her daughter: "You'd best run along, Peggy."

Mrs. Hunt had a pale, oval face framed in fine black hair. Her eyes were a deeper blue than her daughter's: quiet, stoical eyes. She regarded Michael gravely for an instant before she said, "Harry brought you to dinner once when we lived in San Bruno. He told me you were just a boy who was having a hard time of it. . . ."

"And so you had an extra good dinner. You've forgotten my name, of course. It's Michael Dundas. This is my wife and this is Mr. Talcott who also knew your husband. Harry did me more than one kindness years ago, Mrs. Hunt. I've been away from San Francisco for a while and didn't know that Harry had come back."

"He did well in Los Angeles but I never liked it there. It was because of me he came back here," Mrs. Hunt said dully. "He came up in February himself but it took so long to find a house big enough for us that we've only been here since middle July."

"Where did he live until then?" Michael asked.

"Oh, around in cheap hotels," Mrs. Hunt said vaguely. "I don't know where-all. I wrote him General Delivery till he got his offices going."

"I see. Do you need money, Mrs. Hunt? I know Harry made a great deal of money but anyone who has seven children needs a great deal."

"Do you really have seven children?" Valerie said.

"Seven living, dear. Too many, Harry always said, but he wouldn't have given up one of them, nor would I." Mrs. Hunt fingered the small gold cross at the neck of her out-of-date black dress. "Only you don't seem ever to have enough money when you have children, even when they're always well."

"I remember meeting Harry one day, six years ago at least, when he was very depressed," Michael said. "You'd had a long run of bad luck then."

Mrs. Hunt followed his lead docilely, almost dreamily. "That was the first year of the Fair when we all had flu in April and I and our oldest boy just kept coughing and coughing. Then Peggy had infantile paralysis. It looked like she'd always walk with a cruel big brace on her leg. She needed special treatment and the doctor said I and the boy ought to live in a real warm, dry place for a while.

"Oh, that was a bad time," Mrs. Hunt said with a rueful smile. "But that July, Harry got a loan from a rich man he'd done a favor for once, and then he was offered a fine big salary to work for a man in Los Angeles who had a good detective agency.

"I never liked Hairy being a detective. When we married he was a special agent—a railroad detective. But that was dangerous work sometimes and didn't pay much. Like Harry said, he was a good private detective and I guess someone has to do that kind of work.

"Well, we moved south. We had an old farmhouse quite a ways from Los Angeles. Harry had to go back and forth and be away a lot but the boy and I got well, it was so warm and dry there. He's in the Navy now though he's only nineteen. Harry was so proud of him. Harry thought nothing was too good for our soldiers and sailors.

"Then," Mrs. Hunt said, "Harry found a real expensive doctor that did wonders for Peggy. You see how good she walks now. I guess there wasn't anything we ever needed or wanted bad, that he didn't get for us. And he kept his insurance up so we won't be too bad off now. But thanks for thinking about it, Mr. Dundas. Harry did have some good friends. And some enemies too, I guess. He'd have to make them in his work, but it's still hard for me to think even a criminal would kill Harry. He was such a good man—"

The sweet, tired voice broke suddenly. Valerie got up, went over and put her arms about Mrs. Hunt.

"You two wait outside," she told Chris and Michael. "Go on. Get out!"

III

It was some time before Valerie came out of the house and climbed into the car. "I know," Michael said, starting it, "I am a first-class heel."

"You would have loaned Mrs. Hunt money," Chris objected. "But were you telling the truth when you said Hunt was kind to you years ago?"

"He fed me when I was hungry—tactfully. He warned me against some dubious characters I came in contact with. Oh, all I have said about Harry is true; and everything his wife says of him is equally true."

"I don't think she knew much about his professional activities, but she may have suspected he sometimes diverted himself with other women," Valerie said, thoughtfully.

"Harry's lights-of-love were only diversions. If one of them had threatened to go to his wife, Harry would have blacked her eye and put the fear of God in her. Harry had a quick temper and no objections to hitting a female—"

"You knew, the year Rowena disappeared, that Hunt needed money very badly?" Chris broke in.

"Yes. At that time I had not met you and my only interest in Rowena was that she disappeared while wearing a dress I'd designed. And I did not have to tell the police what Harry's financial problems were. They knew."

"Oh. That was stupid of me. They would know about Hunt's private affairs."

"Yes, though Harry never gave them any excuse to meddle in his private life. The stupid cops didn't dare, because Harry had too much on those whose records wouldn't bear investigation. Men like Sullivan and Prevost were not blundering bullies and didn't ever think of evening their score with Harry by telling Margaret Hunt the truth about him," Michael went on.

"But I never discussed Rowena with Harry. I did not see him after he worked on the case. It was Nick Prevost who told me that Harry had decided to buy into that Los Angeles agency and somehow acquired enough cash to do so. Harry was never, as he told his wife, offered a job with them at a flattering salary."

"Oh. Then somehow, between April and July—the months that he worked for Father—Hunt got together a good deal of money when he needed money badly," Chris said. "It was July when he told Father he'd better not throw good money after bad. And his fee, we now know, was very reasonable, for Hunt.

"And of course, I see now that even if he was the greatest rogue unhung, Hunt's death matters a great deal more to his family than Rowena's going away ever did to hers. And 'any man's death diminishes me because I am involved in mankind. . . .' I'll tell Prevost the whole screwy story and let him make what he can of it. But the rest of us aren't going to admit, without resisting, that Hunt's death is connected somehow with Rowena."

"I'm sure they won't," Michael said. "It would simplify matters if you haven't told anyone that you tried to consult me and did talk to Valerie."

"Why do you say that? I haven't, though. I don't know why; I'm not secretive by nature."

"'Keep your mouth shut, your bowels open and don't volunteer.' You learned that in the Army, Chris."

Michael swung the car around the wall at Jones and Vallejo and nodded toward another car parked at the juncture of Vallejo and Russian Hill Place.

"There's Nick Prevost, come to talk to Valerie, after having talked to Inspector Sterling who is not as dumb as my wife thinks. I hope you have no late morning or early afternoon engagements, Chris, because I think you will be here for some time."

IV

At one o'clock Valerie produced sandwiches, beer and coffee. At three o'clock the three of them were still in the living room, still talking.

By then Chris felt that he had been mercilessly squeezed and prodded and finally wrung dry and put aside for use at a later date. But he liked the slim inspector with the melancholy black eyes and superbly tailored shoulders. And so he told Prevost more than he had meant to, especially concerning the conversation that had disrupted last night's dinner, which he had intended to dispose of with a hop, skip and jump.

"Well," Prevost said at last, "we'd better be sure we have the timetable straight. Harry had rented an apartment on Pine near Leavenworth for his offices. He preferred that sort of layout to one in a downtown office building, and some of his clients preferred that little extra privacy. We've already been to his office and been over his records."

"Only to find that he didn't keep records on his hush-hush and really lucrative cases," Michael said.

"That's right. Harry was out all yesterday afternoon. None of his staff knows where. He came in just before six and everyone went home and left him there. Mr. Talcott talked to him at six-fifteen. He said then that he had a date later in the evening. But the date wasn't one he suddenly made with himself to come up and see Michael because he mentioned it *before* Mr. Talcott mentioned Michael's name. That's right, isn't it?"

Chris nodded. "And while I was talking to him, Daphne, Anice and Aunt Sophia were together in the living room. Mark and Joel were upstairs and then Bob arrived and went upstairs, too. Any of them could have listened in on one of the upstairs extensions, because none of them came down until I'd finished talking to Hunt.

"Mark, alone on the third floor, could most easily have listened in without being caught at it. But the second floor extension is in the hall so either Bob or Joel could have listened in without the other seeing him, if one of them was in a bedroom with the door closed."

"And at six-thirty you went in to dinner. No one, you said, was called to the telephone during that fifteen minutes or during dinner. You don't know just what time Mr. Vibert walked out on you?"

"I'd guess it was sevenish. It must have been about a quarter of eight when Bob, Anice and I left the dining room. It was just eight when I left the house and the telephone didn't ring while I was standing in the hall, brooding. It was nine-thirty when I got to Anice's place.

"I do realize," Chris went on, "that if someone listened in on my conversation with Hunt, he learned that I was going to see Hunt this morning. But I don't see why you want to know whether any of us was called to the telephone or could have used the telephone between six-fifteen and eight o'clock."

Prevost and Michael looked at each other for an instant; then Michael said, "Harry was killed when he went back to his car which he had left parked and unlocked, Chris. Someone had to know approximately where Harry and/or his car would be, at approximately what time. Since at, or just before six-fifteen, Harry hadn't decided to come up here, when he did decide to, Harry must have told someone what he was going to do. But . . ."

"I see. I'm apt to forget that just now we are your only available suspects. Hunt couldn't have talked to any of us face-to-face—except possibly Mark between six-fifteen and eight. Hunt could only have contacted one of us by telephone."

"And during that period, he didn't," Prevost said. "Harry was in his office at six-fifteen. No one saw him leave it or come back to it. We'll have to find out what he was doing those two hours before he turned up here at eight-fifteen. He did tell Valerie he'd had something to eat which may or may not be true, the post mortem report will show that. At least we know that he was killed almost on the dot of eight-forty.

"It's going to take a lot of time and men to check his movements. I don't have enough to do the job quickly. We're still short-handed. Then we'll have to check on Harry's activities from February on, which will probably lead us nowhere. We knew Harry was back but we didn't have time to keep an eye on him like we would have once. Harry knew that," Prevost said. "His wife didn't know where he stayed before he managed to get a house for her and the kids and they joined him here."

"With hotels so crowded, naturally Harry went to those whose proprietors he'd known well," Michael said. "You have a good idea what hotels those were and Harry knew that you would know. So it's odd that he made a rather special point of mentioning his difficulties along those lines to Valerie. What was it that he said, again?"

"That he'd never slept more than a week in one place though he knew the proprietors of a good many flea-joints south of Market," Valerie said glibly.

"Do you think it matters so much what Hunt's activities were until yesterday or possibly a few days ago?" Chris asked.

Prevost shrugged. "Probably not, but we do try to be thorough. And Harry may have had business dealings with people who didn't want to come to his offices or wanted a private talk with him before he managed to rent offices. He had the place done over at his own expense and bought office equipment, so he didn't lack ready money—in April.

"Of course," Prevost continued, "I'm supposed just to discover who killed Harry, not to dig up a six-year-old mystery."

"A fact that I am sure everyone else in Chris's little circle will immediately point out to you," Michael said. Chris grimaced slightly and did not challenge the statement.

"Yeah. So it's lucky for me I've got a few reasons for insisting on trying to connect Harry's death with the old Talcott case. One: Mr. Talcott was to meet him this morning to discuss Rowena's disappearance. Some of those in the house last night could have learned of that appointment."

"And I had told everyone but Anice, the night I got home, that I'd like to talk to Hunt," Chris said.

"So you did. Then Harry was killed before he could talk to you. Item two: he tried to talk to Michael when he thought you'd already talked to him. When Michael wasn't available, he made some cryptic remarks to Valerie about the Talcott case."

"Were they cryptic to you, Nick?" Valerie asked.

"Damn the slick little crook! He overestimated my intelligence. It wasn't a professional job, he said, but it was a bona fide burglary just the same."

"And even if they didn't take the silverware, something had been taken. Only, in one instance, you couldn't call it really stealing," Michael finished. "And Harry said that you were on the right track when you tried to establish a connection between that burglary and Rowena's disappearance. Why did you?"

"I knew it was no professional burglary. Since it wasn't, I didn't like it happening the very night Rowena disappeared," Prevost said. "It's hard for me to swallow coincidences like that."

"But nothing was taken that anyone remembered should be in the house," Chris objected.

"Or someone lied when they said nothing was missing. Well, it's interesting that Harry not only made cryptic remarks about that so-called burglary but went out of his way to talk to Valerie about flower-gardening," Prevost said.

"But what does that . . . You mean," Chris said, "that you think that when he mentioned zinnias he was making a clumsy effort to plant that name in her mind because our ex-cook was named Zinnia?"

"It was clumsy, for Harry," Michael admitted. "But he didn't talk at random and he certainly was not interested in the little birds and bees and flowers. Harry, like myself, was ready to admire a garden only if someone else planted and tended it.

I doubt if he would have recognized a delphinium or a zinnia when he saw one."

Prevost nodded. "And Harry knew I questioned your Zinnia very thoroughly six years ago. I have a hunch *he* did, too. He had a way with servants. She rolled her eyes wildly when I asked her about the silver and what should be in the sideboard.

"That was natural. She couldn't read or write, she was very ignorant and had an instinctive fear of the police. You remember we found a kitchen window, near to the ground, open? Both she and the cook insisted they hadn't left it open. Do you know where Zinnia is now?"

"No. She left us for a Mrs. Pryor who'd been trying for some time to woo her away. We were only very slightly acquainted with Mrs. Pryor so there was nothing suspicious about Zinnia's change of employers. She would probably have left us before, for higher wages than Father's principles would permit him to pay, if she hadn't been very devoted to Rowena."

"We know that but we've had no reason to keep track of Zinnia. We'll locate her. As to your story, Mr. Talcott—the stories told by your fiancée and your aunt—I don't know what to think. It sounds fantastic—theatrical."

"Good words," Michael murmured.

Valerie said, "I don't want to make you un-happy, Nick, but if you are going to believe Miss Sophia and Anice and you want the woman's view-point—"

"Go on. I can take it."

"You'd better check with all shops that sell expensive and fairly rare perfumes. Jasmine was never a popular or inexpensive scent, and during the war it was hard to get even inexpensive co-lognes that didn't smell mainly of alcohol. If someone is going about wearing genuine jasmine, she paid a pretty price for it and not at the corner drugstore."

"Another routine job that takes men I don't have available. O.K., it will have to be done. But I started to say: I see why your fiancée wouldn't talk, Mr. Talcott. Offhand, it looks like she got a rotten deal. She was frightened but she claims she didn't know enough about Rowena's peculiar char-acteristics to know what it was all about."

"I never discussed Rowena with her," Chris said stiffly. "I hardly imagine anyone else did."

"All right. But Miss Sophia had something tan-gible in her hands: that old umbrella handle. Yet she took her time about telling her story to any of you and when she had, no one came running to the police, wanting us to try to find Rowena, the way I would expect normal people to do."

"You don't consider we are normal, then?"

"To me, all of you but Bob Lovell seem over-educated and over-civilized," Prevost said bluntly. "But I know you were a nine-day's wonder in 1939 and must flinch when you think of headlines again. Do you want us to find your sister for you if she is alive?"

"Certainly I want you to find Rowena if she is alive!"

"I wouldn't know, would I, Mr. Talcott? If she is alive, she must be an amnesia victim. We considered that six years ago, but she apparently wasn't emotionally involved with anyone and had no other reason to be unhappy. Though everyone agreed she was very reserved and didn't confide in anyone."

"That's true," Chris said. "Rowena and Daphne weren't friends and Aunt Sophia is aloof herself. Father was one of the kindest men who ever drew breath but he had so many interests, it was difficult to hold his attention long enough to confide in him."

He added reflectively, "Rowena was no saint, however charitably we spoke of her afterward. When she made up her mind she wanted something, she usually had her way. She was unbelievably stubborn and you couldn't reason with her. She'd make threats and carry them out, to get what she wanted. She went on a hunger strike to force Father, who believed in public schools, to allow her to leave high school for a private school."

"That's very interesting," Prevost said politely. "Well, I'll talk to your people this afternoon. I'm interested to learn if they want me to find out if Rowena is alive. It's a funny thing but though you may not know it, we don't have her fingerprints."

V

"How did you slip up on that?" Michael asked.

"Maybe we slipped up," Prevost said, "and maybe someone put something over on us. When 'Missing Persons' was notified that Rowena had stayed out all night, they didn't take it seriously enough to try right away to get authentic prints. Miss Sophia didn't notify any of us until she talked to St. George Talcott, and he slept late. They had good servants then. While she was talking to him, the upstairs maid was going through her regular routine, dusting all the bedrooms—thoroughly. Miss Sophia says she didn't think to tell her to stay out of Rowena's room; just told her not to touch the dining room.

"I came in, representing the Burglary detail, after 'Missing Persons.' I looked for fingerprints as a matter of routine and didn't find any but the servants' in the dining room and none in Rowena's bedroom. By the time 'Missing Persons' really got the wind up, no one could produce anything with what they'd swear were Rowena's fingerprints on it. So if she's alive, we'll have to depend on photographs. We've got plenty of those but—would you recognize your sister if you ran into her unexpectedly, Mr. Talcott?"

"Even six years ago, she resembled dozens of other moderately good-looking women," Chris said. "If she's aged or changed, I could probably pass her on the street and not know her."

"I was afraid of that. But we'll have to find out if there's anyone in the city who might be Rowena. Your aunt finally did tell her story and did produce that umbrella handle, even though she knew someone might suggest she'd had it in her possession for going on seven years; in spite of the fact that Rowena did walk out of the house carrying the umbrella complete with handle. St. George Talcott testified to that.

"I can't see any reason why Miss King should tell the story she did just for the hell of it," Prevost continued. "What she told points to Rowena's being alive. But Miss King is going to marry you and, as your wife, she'll profit when your father's estate is settled, if Rowena can be declared legally dead then."

"Yes," Chris said, "financially, it matters only to Daphne and me whether Rowena is alive or dead. Father's will doesn't affect anyone else, one way or another."

Prevost was watching Chris and neither of them was looking at Michael. But Valerie saw him sit erect, open his mouth, close it and sink back in his chair without having spoken.

Prevost said, "Though I was supposed only to deal with what you people called a burglary, I was interested in all angles. I read everyone's deposition many times. I gathered that your father had a remarkable memory and very keen hearing."

Chris frowned. "His memory was remarkable, and he was a very accurate reporter, but he didn't have unusually good hearing. It was not too good six years ago, at least."

"No? Yet he said that he was reading in his study on the night in question when he heard 'a slight thud' in the hall. When he went out Rowena told him that she had dropped her purse. But the hall was carpeted so the purse shouldn't have made much noise. Nevertheless, your father heard it."

"Oh. Well, Rowena may have lied."

"Then what did your father actually hear? He commented: 'Never knew a purse to make so much noise.' That detail has always annoyed me. But when Michael and I have discussed the Talcott case he always pounces on an entirely different item."

"Yes," Michael said. "I wonder why Rowena started out to walk nine blocks on a rainy night, wearing a new dress, new shoes and spring hat, when she was going, according to her statement to her father, to do nothing more exciting than play bridge with a husband and wife and the wife's sister—a group you'd think she'd consider that finery would be wasted on.

"She did carry an old purse that didn't match her hat or shoes and wore a raincoat—that wouldn't have protected her hat. She didn't ask Miss Sophia if she might borrow her umbrella. She wore the hat and shoes even though her own umbrella had been wrecked that morning and it still threatened rain."

"That puzzled Aunt Sophia," Chris said slowly. "It wasn't like Rowena to risk having a new outfit rained on, yet Aunt Sophia had to offer her umbrella. Did whoever sold her that dress from your shop remember Rowena, Michael?"

"Fanchon did. She had thought Rowena was sedate, well-mannered and self-possessed. She did think Rowena was not happy about her figure and that she had come to us because she had seen one of our dresses on some friend, admired it, and wanted something along the same lines. That was all Fanchon had to offer and I did not see Rowena, then or afterward."

"Neither did I," Prevost said grimly. "Well, I'll get along if you've no suggestions."

"None that you would accept without argument and I haven't energy enough to try to convince you. It's been a tough war though it was the only war we had. However, going back to the burglary angle that Harry stressed, I like Chris's suggestion that something might have been taken that no one remembered should be in the house," Michael remarked.

"Or something could have been taken that no one but the thief *knew* was in the house. Harry did say there was a bona fide burglary. Of course he complicated matters by suggesting that more than one item had been taken and that the taking of one of them couldn't be called theft."

"Harry was great at complicating things," Prevost said. "And I'd better get to work. I'll be seeing you. . . ."

"And I'd better get home," Chris said when Prevost had gone. "I have Daphne's car and she is probably furious because I've kept it so long. I'm to meet Anice for dinner. This time we dine alone! But we're to meet Bob and some girl later. He insists we do a bit of pub-crawling to celebrate my home-coming."

Michael regarded him pensively. "I also have returned with my shield, not on it, but no one seems to care. No one suggests that I celebrate with song and dance, soft lights and loud music."

"But Valerie said Patton would be arriving with your son around five so I supposed you'd want to stay home tonight," Chris said apologetically. "I'd like to have you and Valerie with us, and Bob is very much of a 'the more, the merrier' type of person. So—"

"So why not ask your sister and Mr. Vibert to join us? And I dare say Mr. Gloster might tag along. I suppose your Aunt Sophia would not?"

"You want to meet the folks? I should have guessed. I'll arrange it though you will have to do without Aunt Sophia. Let's say that we'll meet at the Fairmont around nine. We can go on from there."

"And I'm sure," Valerie said, coming back from seeing Chris to the front door, "that from the Fairmont we will go on and on and on and it will be just too bad for anyone who can't hold his liquor."

"I know you find it dull, drinking coca-cola while everyone else tanks up. But it's the easy, natural way to meet the folks. You never know what will develop on occasions like this."

"No, especially if someone pulls a few strings to make things happen. Michael, what suggestion would you have made to Nick if you had thought he would accept it without argument?"

"I would have advised him to get in touch with one of the older members of the Vice Squad."

"The Vice Squad?"

"Well, at least someone who knows the fringes of the red-light districts—the crummy theatrical boarding houses and hotels, for instance."

"Oh. Well, I suppose there is no better hiding place than a house of ill fame. But—"

"But that wasn't what I had in mind. A screwy idea occurred to me this morning and I can't laugh it off," Michael said, moving toward the bedroom. "These damned ribs ache like hell. I'm going to take a nap before Patton returns with our son."

VI

They met at the Fairmont but Daphne scorned the Cirque Room there and also the suggestion that they go across the street to the Top of the Mark.

"Let's not go where all the trippers and furriners go when they want to 'see 'Frisco,'" she said. "Let's go somewhere off the beaten trail."

"Where they charge high prices for weak drinks?" Bob Lovell said. "However, you lead the way."

As they straggled across the lobby to the street, Chris whispered to Valerie, "I'm afraid Daphne's going to take charge. But at least she is in a good humor and in very good looks tonight."

Daphne was encased in a pale green sheath and wore amber earrings and bracelets. Anice's ivory slipper satin was old but very effective, being a good match for her smooth, dimpled shoulders. Bob's companion was introduced as Fay: Valerie never learned her last name or saw her again.

She was lovely to look at and distressing to hear since she talked through her beautiful nose. Fortunately, she had only three remarks to make and made them at intervals during the evening: "Oh, Bob, you are priceless" and "I see what you mean," or "The same, please."

Outside, where fog swirled about Nob Hill and the little California cable-car went jingling down the steep slope into Chinatown, they got into their cars. Daphne, Mark and Joel led the way and presently they arrived at an establishment on Montgomery Street known as The Copper Kettle.

Bob groaned. "Is this your idea of something off the beaten track, Daffy?"

"This place has atmosphere. You wouldn't appreciate it, being a Philistine, Bob. But look at the paintings!"

The paintings in question were the work of local artists. They covered four walls and were good, bad or merely astonishing.

Bob said firmly, "I'd rather not look at them. I just had a heavy dinner They've had a picture or two of yours here, haven't they, chick? Useful publicity and you might as well throw them a little trade. It's not a bad dump and we can get a table on the balcony that will accommodate nine. Come on . . ."

When they were settled at a long table covered with a dirty, venerable cloth, Bob added, "I'll take your orders down to the bar. One thing that makes this joint so deliciously quaint is that the waiters are pushing ninety. Valerie?"

"Pepsi-Cola. I mean it. With ice."

"The same with a double shot of rum," Mark said.

"Oh, darling, should you? You know," Daphne said, "that the doctors said no drinking and—"

Mark removed his arm from her soft, solicitous hand. "Then why did you force me to come with you tonight? What are you drinking?"

"Brandy and plain water. Cold water but no ice and whatever brandy they have that's not too bad. I suppose they have nothing imported—"

"You suppose right, Babe," Bob said, "Anice?"

"Just brandy, unimported, with water, will do. Chris wants Scotch and soda—"

"And so does the girl friend. You too, Joel? And you, Major Dundas? O.K., kiddies. Ol' Uncle Bob will provide—in time."

Valerie had Mark Vibert on one side, Joel on the other and Anice and Chris across from her.

She turned tentatively toward Mark. She thought she might like this man with the wide, tolerant mouth and cockatoo crest of dark hair. But he continued to stare haggardly at the table, digging at the cloth with a fork left behind from the dinner trade, while Joel was ready and inclined for conversation.

"Perhaps we all feel a bit defiant tonight and mean to prove to the world that we have not a care—"

"'Defiant?' Why?" Valerie asked.

"Oh, come now. You know that we have been questioned by the police this afternoon regarding our whereabouts at the time of Henry Hunt's death."

"Do I?"

Joel fitted the tips of his long white fingers together and smiled at her reproachfully.

"Dear lady, you must not suppose I am entirely impractical even if I am bookish. I'm not so shrewd as Bob but . . . Incidentally, where did he acquire that wench and why? Bob ordinarily is a squire only of dames who have money of their own, or fathers who have money, or connections that could be useful to Bob."

"Like the admiral's daughter," Anice murmured.

"Eh? What's that?"

"I shouldn't have mentioned it. I know people who know Bob and I heard that during the war he was that way about some admiral's or captain's daughter," Anice said. "They made the snide remark that Bob never misses an angle when it comes to getting ahead. But it's only sandhouse and probably not true because I've seen Bob out mostly with girls like Fay."

"Even a conscientious self-seeker must have his little relaxations," Joel said. "But, returning to our original topic, I will guess that Chris confided in you and your husband, Mrs. Dundas. And I know that Major Dundas is a very good friend of the very courteous Inspector Prevost who questioned us. Odd customer, that Prevost. Quite the gentleman in his manner and speech. The latter is usually quite impeccable according to our rather slipshod American standards, but at times—"

"Nick was left by someone on the steps of an orphanage," Valerie explained. "It was in the Mission. He was brought up there. When Nick is angry or disturbed, he reverts to South-of-Market-ese. Now that that very important matter is settled—"

"You don't think it's important? I will admit that all of St. George's household except Bob has a great regard for the niceties of speech."

"That's all very well if you don't think too much about it. If you do, it's one of the worst forms of intellectual snobbishness," Valerie said flatly.

Chris grinned. Joel shrugged and threw his hands wide in a favorite gesture.

"You mean that what Prevost said is more important than the accent in which he uttered it? Well, I was able to tell him that Mark left us about seven and that he came home around ten o'clock last night." Joel lowered his voice and Mark gave no sign that he heard him. "He said that he 'just walked.' I doubt that he told Prevost more than that. Daphne and Sophia remained in their rooms all evening and can't prove that they did. They didn't see each other and I didn't see either of them. Bob took Anice home and left her there—"

"But that was only about eight o'clock," Anice said. "Bob told me he was going home—"

"He says he did but as he no longer has a house-boy, he can't prove that any more than I can prove that I worked in St. George's study until eleven o'clock, going over his diaries."

"That must be a gigantic task," Valerie said.

"Yes. I've been at it for three years. St. George specified they should not be published before 1946. He began his memoirs in 1920 and often wrote ten large pages at a sitting. You can see what that adds up to. The Talcotts seem to be diarists born. Sophia has always kept a journal and Chris admits that he brought back a diary from Italy."

"I promise you," Chris said, flushing, "that I will not publish it. Father frankly wrote his diaries for publication. Even most of his letters read as if he rather expected they might be published."

"They shall be," Joel said. "They will need editing, too, since St. George was amazingly indiscreet. But his letters must be published and I can soon begin collecting them. It may be a long task but it will be a rewarding one."

"Oh, will it?" Chris said bleakly. "I know little about the hundreds of letters he wrote to the great or near-great. But you'll have to make up your collection minus Father's personal letters: to me, or Rowena or Aunt Sophia."

"Sophia can be persuaded and you will look at it differently, in time," Joel said blandly. "We must not allow St. George to sink into oblivion."

"He's not apt to if they start hunting for Rowena and find her," Anice remarked. She shrugged off Joel's look of well-bred distaste. "Chris told me about everything while we ate tonight. Anyway, I had a policeman asking me questions after I got home from work."

"I asked Aunt Sophia about Harold Baird, the doctor, you know, Valerie?" Chris said. "He's dead. He developed cancer and when he reached the stage where he would have had to stop working, he took an overdose of morphine. That was just after last Christmas. His mother sold their house, went to live with a sister, and died in February. And Walter Denning ended as a Navy chaplain and was killed in the South Pacific. Not very promising, is it?"

"No," Valerie agreed. "What about Zinnia?"

"Oh, she's kept in touch with Aunt Sophia. She married a Pullman porter and lives in Oakland."

"I could have told you that," Joel said "I knew something of Henry Hunt, too."

"You did?" Chris said.

"My dear man, certainly. Your father chose Hunt at random. One didn't argue with St. George but when I met Hunt he seemed to me rather a bounder. I wished to protect St. George against his own impulsiveness—"

Chris interrupted, "Father would not have thanked you for that."

"As I knew. But Sophia agreed that we should try to find out what Hunt's reputation was. We asked Bob and Mark to institute a few discreet inquiries."

"That is," Chris said, "everyone was consulted but me."

"You were only a boy, my dear fellow."

"Yes. But Father was no fool," Chris said curtly. "He was, for instance, impervious to the wiles of the most talented con men. He didn't know what a private detective's fees could be but he wanted a competent man. I'm sure he thought Hunt was competent."

"We were assured that he was," Joel said, "and let it go at that. Bob knew insurance detectives who knew a good deal about Hunt. St. George wouldn't have cared that, according to the information we received, Hunt was—uh—a chaser. We were told Hunt might not be above blackmail, but he didn't blackmail St. George so we kept that item to ourselves, too. I don't see why the police aren't trying to locate the woman scorned, the jealous husband or lover, or. . . . Ah, here's Bob with the cup that cheers."

Bob put down a large tin tray and began distributing drinks. Valerie was very thirsty since one item of the impromptu banquet Patton had provided had been a luscious chowder. She picked up a tall glass of Pepsi-Cola; drank a good half of it without really tasting it, grimaced and finished it in two more gulps, thinking: "What an odd taste this has."

She stared at the two emaciated ice cubes in the glass. They, the table, Chris's and Anice's faces began to flicker as Mark said truculently:

"Was this your idea, Daphne? There's no rum in this drink."

VII

Mrs. Dundas has a superb digestion—"you and an anaconda" Michael sometimes remarked enviously—but her allergy toward liquor is even more spectacular. She did not pass out of the picture, but for some time the picture passed away from her.

She heard herself saying: "I'm afraid I took your drink by mistake, Mark," and supposed that Mark demanded and obtained another glass of Pepsi-Cola with something added.

She was dizzily aware that suddenly he was inclined to talk to her. Some sentences penetrated the fog and she knew that he was discussing a lifelong interest in the theater, telling what she felt were probably amusing stories of actors and actresses he had met. Now and then she made some comment and hoped that her faraway voice sounded normal to others.

Presently she got down the dirty steps from the balcony without stumbling. The foggy air outside was a blessing that lasted only a few minutes. For they went a very short distance up Montgomery and settled themselves in the Black Cat.

All she ever remembered clearly about their sojourn there was an unidentified man who recited "Boots" with great fervor and loud stampings. "Drunk as a hoot-owl," Valerie thought pityingly and drank ginger ale. It was at this point that she began to feel abused and bereft as she realized that Michael was devoting himself to Daphne.

Finally they moved on. The walk back to the cars was helpful; so was the ride to Chinatown. She always thought of their third bar as "Clementine's" since, if it was not exactly "in a cavern, in a canyon," it was in a cellar, in an alley somewhere off Jackson.

When she had managed to clamber onto a stool there, she was no longer dizzy, only soddenly sleepy. She succeeded in keeping her eyes open, feeling that they were propped apart with small sticks. She concentrated on a huge, dusty Chinese lantern that hung from the center of the ceiling and in this fashion dozed with her eyes open.

She was lucid enough to know that Daphne was talking incessantly. It also occurred to her that Daphne was the most difficult type of cheap drunk, being herself completely convinced that she was a good, two-fisted drinker. "And who are you to cast stones?" Mrs. Dundas reflected, bending her energies to the task of keeping awake.

There was a dance floor the size of a small doily, and the inevitable juke box. Bob and his Fay, Michael and Daphne and then Michael and Anice, tried dancing. Valerie was sober enough to reflect maliciously that even Michael, extraordinarily good dancer that he was, had some difficulty in keeping Daphne on her feet. And when they left "Clementine's," it was to the tune of Daphne's disapproval of her husband.

"It isn't as if you had a head for liquor, Mark. People who can't handle it shouldn't drink. I certainly would not if I were that sort of person. Besides, the doctors told you—"

"Will you," said Mr. Vibert, slowly and distinctly, "shut your yap, my jewel? My little jewel in an expensive setting that must be renewed frequently at great cost. My little jewel who—"

"Ride with us, Mark," Chris said persuasively. "Bob's car will hold five and I've hardly seen you since I got home."

Mark let himself be nudged into Bob's car. It came to Valerie as the blurred impressions of a dream return in the morning hours, that Mark had been putting down drink for drink with Daphne without appearing to like what he drank. And that Chris had taken to plain fizz long ago, while Joel was a cautious sipper and still sober.

Bob was pleasantry elevated but his Fay wobbled when she walked. Anice appeared to be, in fact, the sort of drinker that Daphne fancied herself; while as for Major Dundas, "I suppose," his wife thought resentfully, "that he's poured it down that hollow leg of his and still steady and staunch he stands."

At the moment Michael was saying, "We'll have a nightcap in some quiet neighborhood place and then we can get something to eat. I'll lead the way."

He chose a bar on the corner of Polk and Sutter. A fairly large restaurant had once been housed there, so the cocktail lounge was spacious. Suddenly, when they had put two tables together and were seated, Valerie was alert and interested in her companions.

Everyone was watching Daphne apprehensively except Michael and Anice, whose red mouth was curled in scornful amusement.

Daphne demanded and got another brandy and water. She downed half of it before she began, "Yes, our quarters must be done over. Dear heaven, we've lived with the same decor for five years! One isn't expected to wear the same clothes and hairdress for five years so why should one be required to exist in the same surroundings for so long a time?"

"Isn't she just full of quaint fancies tonight?" Anice murmured sardonically.

Daphne lowered her drink and went on, "We must redecorate at our own expense. Aunt Sophia won't have the work done and charge it to upkeep. Aunt Sophia is such a wonderful manager, but I don't think dear auntie has managed any too well."

"Daphne! I know," Chris said austerely, "that you're tight but nevertheless . . ."

Daphne regarded Chris with the unwinking stare of a cat disdaining foolish mortals. She had control of her consonants; only her usually faint hint of a babyish lisp was intensified.

"You're swacked, lamb. You never could drink. I'm the only one of us who could. I'm sorry for you because you're so sure that our auntie is upright and righteous. Not that she would ever spend one cent of her own on the house even if she still had a good private income. Mark and I will have to pay the outrageous prices these horrid presumptuous workmen ask and . . . Won't we, darling?"

"No," said Mr. Vibert, "we will not!"

Daphne pouted. "Oh, Mark, you want your Daffy to be happy and you wouldn't be cross if your horrid old tummy wasn't every-which-way—"

Mr. Vibert rose, leaned across the table and slapped his wife's face, audibly. He knocked half the glasses from the table as he brought his arm back. Daphne screamed once before she settled to steady, high-pitched weeping.

Some of the onlookers laughed. The more apprehensive edged toward the door. A chivalrous gentleman in his cups declared that he would never be able to face his dear old mother if he allowed a man to strike a lady. His companions restrained him and a bartender whisked out from behind the bar to say soothingly, "Now! We run a nice, quiet place here."

Anice put her head down on the table and laughed. Bob's Fay stared blankly about and finally remarked, "The same, please." Chris's face was flaming. He got up and pushed Mark, not too gently, into a chair.

Mark struggled to rise. Joel did rise to Chris's aid when Mark declared that he hadn't begun to talk yet. Bob got out his billfold and asked the bartender, "What's the damage?"

Midway of these proceedings, Michael murmured to Valerie, "Get out to our car, dear." Then he, too, rose, went to Daphne and said coaxingly, "I'm going to take you home. You want me to, don't you?"

Chris caught up with them at the door. "Look here, I don't want you to—"

"Someone must take her home," Michael said coolly. "One will get you ten she'll be very ill in a short time. You deal with Mark."

"Yes, but—" Chris followed them out to Michael's car. Michael put Daphne in the back beside Valerie, got in and closed the door rudely in Chris's face.

"Remember, you must see Anice home, too," he said, and drove away.

"Dundas and Dundas, kidnappings a specialty," Valerie said caustically, steadying Daphne against her shoulder. "Have you enjoyed yourself tonight?"

"I only plied Mrs. Vibert with brandy and water and compliments. Oh, I did agree that she should have her rooms redecorated since a lovely jewel deserves a perfect setting."

"Michael! You didn't?"

Major Dundas had the grace to look rather shamefaced. "She is insatiable and my ears are numb from her girlish prattle. But with one ear I listened to you putting Joel in his place at The Copper Kettle. Rather on the precious side, isn't he?"

"Yes; and he does consider himself one of the family and seems determined to be St. George's Boswell. I suspect he's making his job of editing last as long as possible."

"Naturally. Daphne told me that several publishers are already bidding for the diaries. So, if he doesn't find other employment connected with St. George, by next year Mr. Gloster will have no excuse for lingering on in his soft nest and . . . Blast that female!"

Michael had been driving slowly and now he throttled the car down to the point where it coughed complainingly. "Has she passed out yet?"

"You should have fed her one drink more or one less, my hero. If she is ill, I'm going to shove her head out the window. I wonder—"

Daphne stirred and began to whimper. "Mark's changed. He doesn't love me now."

"Of course he does, if he ever did," Valerie said unsympathetically. "Why should he have changed?"

"That's it. He loved me before and I haven't changed. Anice . . . But it isn't her fault. She only sympathized with Mark. She wants to marry Chris; she wouldn't bother with Mark. It's some other woman; that's what's wrong!"

Daphne dripped maudlin tears into Valerie's Persian lamb jacket. "He's treated you abominably," Michael said soothingly. "And—*Gran Dio!* Valerie, don't look at me like that. I want to be convincing. You have other worries, haven't you, Daphne? You have been horribly frightened lately, but you have been brave and haven't told anyone. . . ."

"Oh, heavenly days! I'll be ill before Daphne is. Have you no conscience?"

"Less of it, love. She's a nasty little show-off and if I were Mark I'd have hung one on her jaw years ago. You didn't tell anyone that you were frightened, Daphne, because you are so high-strung and sensitive that people don't understand you."

"No, no one does," Daphne sobbed, "and I've been so frightened I was afraid I was going mad. But ghosts don't write notes, do they? Or smell of jasmine scent?"

"What?" Michael was sufficiently startled that he narrowly avoided collision with another car before he turned from Fillmore into Broadway. "No, of course not. There are no ghosts, Daphne."

"Then why doesn't Rowena stay in her grave? She has to be dead after all these years! But she didn't like me and she won't let me alone. She was always so stubborn. When she wanted anything, she *would* have it."

"What does she want now, Daphne?"

"I don't know. She set her heart on odd things sometimes. What could she want that I could give her? So why won't she stay dead? Why does she leave notes pinned to my pillow? She—I—I feel ill. . . ."

Valerie held Daphne away from her. "This is where I came in! Don't drive by the house. Stop!"

Michael stopped, very quickly. He extracted Daphne from the car and steered her up the front steps.

"She's good for a few minutes yet. Have you her purse? She should have a latchkey."

Daphne broke loose, rang the doorbell, giggled girlishly and rang it again before he could stop her.

"This will make us popular with Sophia," Valerie commented. "Here are some keys. If we let ourselves in, we may save Sophia a trip downstairs."

When he had the door open, Michael struck a match and located the light switch in the hall. Daphne drooped over his arm. There was an alarming greenish hue about her mouth. Michael regarded her with an expert eye.

"We'd better get her to her own bedroom. Third floor, isn't it? Pray God she isn't sick over the banisters."

He hustled Daphne urgently up two flights of stairs and into a bathroom done in sea-green, even to the sunken tub. A Siamese curled up on it leaped to the floor, looking at Daphne knowingly.

Michael took her coat, said, "I think you know what to do," went out and closed the door. Subsequent sounds indicated that Daphne did know what to do and was doing it.

Michael found Valerie surveying Daphne's gray and fuchsia bedroom while she stroked a yellow Persian that was curled up in the center of the lustrous quilted spread that covered Daphne's bed. The cat yawned disdainfully and went back to sleep.

"Remarkable resemblance to Daphne, don't you think?" Valerie glanced at Daphne's drawings, the only pictures in the room. "She draws sublime cats, I give her that. But I feel as if I were in the middle of a very gooey French pastry. Isn't this setting luxurious enough for our precious little jewel? All this gray furniture was made to order."

"Yes," Michael agreed absently. "Where would Daphne hide a note from Rowena?"

"She probably destroyed it."

"She would want to have proof her story was true if she ever had to tell it." Michael cocked an ear toward the bathroom. "Dear me, the little lady is having a strenuous time of it. Well, here's a desk. . . ."

He pulled down the lid of the fragile gray escritoire and swore softly as a stack of letters and bills cascaded to the carpet.

"Not tidy, no," Valerie said provokingly. "Michael, this house is too quiet! Why hasn't Miss Sophia appeared? Don't the servants sleep here, even if they might not answer the doorbell this late."

"Um-hum," Michael said inattentively. "This sort of desk often has a so-called secret drawer."

"That's really no secret at all," Valerie agreed, diverted. "Don't you think there's space above that little center drawer? Try pressing or turning one of those useless knobs on either side of it . . . . See!"

"I see," Michael said as the knob clicked and a space showed in the satin gray wood. He pulled the hidden drawer out and turned over its contents rapidly. "Hmm. Some quite ancient love letters—and this."

VIII

He showed Valerie a piece of paper that seemed to have been torn from a small note pad. On it was written in a squarish, distinctive handwriting:

> *Daphne, I forgot it's my turn to take flowers over to St. Jude's. It will take me some time to arrange them so tell Father where I am if he should want me. R.*

For an instant Valerie and Michael stared at each other. "It—it does sound like the sort of note a person like Rowena would leave so that no one would worry about her," Valerie said. "And this must at least closely resemble her handwriting. Though it might be an old note Daphne happened to keep."

"It is written in ink and blue-black ink doesn't look like this after more than six years. But," Michael said, frowning, "one doesn't usually write a note of this sort in—"

The bathroom door opened and Daphne appeared, watery-eyed, swollen-faced. She just did manage to reach the bed and collapse across it. The Persian hissed indignantly and took himself off to the gray brocade and fuchsia cushions of Daphne's chaise longue.

Michael eyed her disgustedly. "We'll get nothing from her now. You'd better put her to bed."

Valerie prodded Daphne tentatively. "Oh Lord, she wears a girdle. Did you ever try to get a limp female out of a girdle? Roll her over for me."

Michael turned Mrs. Vibert over on her back. The green gown slid from her shoulders, uncovering a fading bruise roughly the shape of four fingers.

"How intriguing. Does Mark beat her regularly? You had better retire now but I wish you'd see if Miss Sophia is—is just sleeping soundly."

"Since you mention it, I think I'd better," Michael said and went down to the second floor.

But Sophia's room was empty. It was evident enough that it was hers since her knitting was on a table while a roomy pink flannelette nightgown and the hug-me-tight Chris had mentioned lay across the disordered bed.

Michael whistled softly; then backed from the room as he heard a door opening and closing downstairs. Presently Sophia appeared, spare and upright in an old tweed coat, with a shapeless felt hat riding the back of her head. She was panting slightly and her harshly colored face was redder than usual.

She started when she saw Michael and tightened her grip on the old redwood walking stick she carried. Then, after looking at him more closely:

"Mr. Dundas, isn't it?" she said in her dry, well-bred voice. "You have been pointed out to me. To what do we owe this honor? Or, I should ask, who have you had to pour into bed?"

"Your niece, Daphne. We were beginning to be uneasy because you hadn't appeared. Nor have the servants."

"They sleep at the back of the house and don't get out of their beds, once they are in them. But I couldn't sleep so I dressed and went for a walk," Sophia said with a take-it-or-leave-it air.

Michael smiled skeptically but he took it. "You were prepared for the worst," he remarked, nodding toward her stick.

"It's best to have some sort of weapon late at night nowadays. Is my dear niece very drunk?"

"Very. So is her husband. Perhaps Chris and Mr. Gloster are trying to sober him up a trifle before bringing him home. He got rather out of hand and slapped his wife."

"No doubt he had some provocation," Sophia said impersonally. "Well, I'm for bed now, Mr. Dundas."

"Will you answer two questions before you go? When Rowena bought that spring outfit in February of 1939, did she buy a matching coat, too?"

"She had a matching blue coat she had bought late the previous autumn. The style doesn't signify since she didn't wear the coat that night."

"No. But didn't she have a blue purse, too?"

"Why—yes, certainly. She had blue gloves, too. She wore them that night but didn't carry the purse. It was a blue cordé bag."

"Large or small?"

"Quite—small," Sophia said slowly. "It was a very expensive bag."

"But it matched her hat and shoes which I fancy were expensive, too, while the bag she did carry did not match them. Neither did her raincoat tone in with the rest of her carefully chosen ensemble."

"She'd take the raincoat off and lay her purse aside—"

Michael nodded. "That's the point. But if she really meant to play cards with the Lymans, so would she have removed her hat on such an informal occasion with only three others present. But still she wore the new hat though she had no umbrella of her own to shield it from rain and apparently didn't intend to ask for yours."

"Yes—yes, I offered it and Rowena seemed reluctant to take it. She was very careful of others' belongings. What are you driving at, young man?"

"I think you know, Miss Talcott. Chris spoke this morning as if his father fought in the last war. Is that true?"

"Yes. Though he was in his thirties he never willingly passed up a fight. He was captain of a California company and in the thick of things in France. Though I don't see why that interests you and—hmm. The rest of the toss-pots have arrived."

Mark was able to walk without assistance but he was quietly morose. He sank into the first available chair in the lower hall and rested his head in his hands. Chris, pale and tired, limped over to the stairway and sat down on the bottom step.

Bob closed the front door very carefully and it was left for Joel to say, "Don't take it too much to heart. Daphne may think more highly of you because you—uh—asserted yourself. I don't condemn you."

"Who the hell would?" Bob said. "The ladies, God bless 'em, don't seem to realize that if a guy has a chronic bellyache, he'd rather not have it discussed publicly. Tell Daphne so tomorrow."

"Yes, but Daphne is a spoiled brat and it's partly your fault that she is, Mark," Joel said temperately. "You have always indulged her so she doesn't
take you seriously when you refuse her a fur coat
or to have your rooms done over."

"Oh, for God's sake!" Mark sat erect, regarding them stonily. "Haven't you guessed the truth
or are you just so persistently well-bred that you
don't want me to know you have?"

"I don't know what you mean, my dear man,"
Joel said.

"I mean, my dear feller, that I'm broke: flat,
busted, out of funds! If I wanted to indulge my
dear little child-wife's whims—and I don't!—I
couldn't because I haven't the money."

Bob whistled. "But your father left you well-off
and the bookstore is a flourishing concern. . . ."

"My father did not leave the comfortable for-
tune everyone supposed he did. He was a sucker
for oil stocks. The bookstore and its goodwill
would have been an adequate inheritance if I'd
had any sense or any guts. Haven't you two a vague
idea how much money Daphne and I have gotten
through since we were married?"

Joel and Bob looked at each other; then Joel
said, "Well, Daphne has had an allowance but—"

"But! When Daphne graciously consented to
marry me there was nothing money could buy that

I'd refuse her. I spent every cent of my income and borrowed money besides. Then when I went into the Army I had to hire someone to manage the shop. I chose a woman I thought was a competent and agreed to pay her an absurd salary.

"I came back to private life to find she'd bought unwisely and alienated our old and most valued customers. And—well, I won't go into detail but Vibert's is barely paying its own way and I have creditors snapping at my heels. In time I may pull through but some capital would be a godsend."

"Things go like that where businesses are concerned," Bob said sagely. "But next year Daphne will come into a lot of money and—"

Mark laughed unpleasantly. "And then she will allow me pocket money for carfare and cigarettes? Don't be a fool, Bob. Daphne's motto is: 'What's yours is mine and what's mine is my own.' And I am not asking favors, financial or otherwise, from my dear wife."

He got up, adjusted his tie and coat and added, "I'm not as swacked as I wish I were. Everyone in the trade knows about Vibert's. I'm surprised you haven't heard rumors. You should know, Bob, what effect the war had on some excellent prewar incomes. I've heard you tried to live like an admiral on a lieutenant's pay. That wouldn't do your private income any great good. . . ."

He started up the stairway to the second floor. By unspoken agreement, Sophia and Michael stepped into her bedroom until Mark had passed them. In an instant they heard Valerie's clear, low voice:

"Daphne's in bed, Mark, and I want very much to go to bed myself. I don't know why we do this sort of thing—"

Mark made some response that Valerie accepted with a pleasant, "No, none of us is getting any younger. Good night." Then she came on down to the second floor.

Michael introduced her to Sophia and said quickly, "We'd better be going. We'll see you again."

"Undoubtedly," Sophia said with a grim smile. "Tell Chris to go to bed and Bob either to go home or to his old room here—at once. Good night!"

She closed her bedroom door vigorously. On the ground floor another door closed. When Valerie looked over the banisters, Bob had disappeared. Chris was still sitting on the stairs, but Joel met them when they were halfway down the stairway. He stopped and looked Michael over deliberately.

"Major Dundas, you are supposed to be remarkably clever in more ways than one. But I think I am expressing the wishes of this family when I say that we would be grateful if you would interest yourself in other matters than those at present engaging our attention. It would be a pity if anything occurred to tarnish your excellent Army record."

"Is that a threat?" Michael asked gently.

"And if it is?"

"Just tell it to the chaplain, Mr. Gloster. I suspect, Old Faithful, that you are speaking for yourself, not for the family that has provided you with a soft living for many years. I've done nothing except talk to my old friends, Chris and Nicholas Prevost, and join in a party gotten up to celebrate Chris's home-coming."

"You're making a bloody ass of yourself, Joel," Chris said. "Sound off and go to bed."

"Thank you," Michael said when Joel, his narrow shoulders expressive of resentment, had passed from sight. "But I have been meddling."

"Didn't I virtually ask you to?"

"Not quite. I've no right to this and you'd better have it. You may decide if you will show it to Nick. I believe Daphne found it pinned to her pillow some time or other."

"And if she hasn't shown it to any of you, she wouldn't show it to the police," Valerie said as Chris sat staring at the bit of paper Michael gave him. "She thinks she's seen Rowena. She was muttering while I was putting her to bed and I gathered that she believes Rowena has been in her room several times, very late at night."

"Yes? This looks like Rowena's writing," Chris said stolidly, "and it's very typical, except that Rowena seldom left this sort of message for Daphne because Daphne was apt to forget to deliver them. Tomorrow, I'll check this against some of Rowena's letters. Right now—"

"Right now we should all be in bed," Valerie said. "If you don't mind, Michael—"

"I seem to be tired," Chris said apologetically. "We walked Mark around the block five or six times before we took Anice and Bob's girl friend home. I'll see you tomorrow, I suppose? Good night. . . ."

Outside, Major Dundas handed Mrs. Dundas into the car and said as they started home, "I must congratulate you on a remarkable recovery, my love."

"What? Michael, did you know I was very nearly under the table and you just left me to struggle along as best I could?"

"I know that two tablespoonfuls of whisky cause you to see pink elephants. You'd downed two slugs of rum before I knew it. You had my heartfelt sympathy but if I'd expressed it, you would have collapsed ingloriously. As it was, you put on a damned good show though I did not risk asking you to dance."

"I could have done as well as Daphne did in that respect. I hope she stepped on your toes. However, you probably did the best thing and I've completely recovered. I mean, I know what's happening now and—"

Michael laughed; put out an arm and drew her close. "Yes, I know what you mean, *bell' alma innumorata.*"

IX

Valerie woke abruptly and for a minute lay blinking at the unexpected pale sunlight before she realized that Michael was out of bed, fully clothed, shaking her gently while he chanted,

"'Beautiful dreamer, lash up and stow. The cooks to the galley has gone long ago. Show a leg! Show a leg! Make a move!'"

"Oh, dear," Valerie said sleepily. "I've been so glad that you and Chris at least have returned still speaking English instead of an incomprehensible service jargon. Where did you learn that?"

"It's part of the invitation to rise that you still hear on British ships."

"You did get around, didn't you?"

"I can cope with the British," Michael said modestly. "For one thing, I truly admire them and for another, I can be just as goddamned supercilious as they are. I must be off."

"Have you already had breakfast? Dear heaven, has the Army made a man from a dormouse?"

"The telephone rang and continued to ring and I answered it. I've had a morning romp with our son," Michael shuddered gently. "You were right to speak of 'the rigors of civilian life.' Patton has let him get out of hand."

"So have I, dear. He likes me now but when he's been very naughty, he snuggles up to me and says, 'Nay mamma.' He reminds me of you and I melt. You'll have to take him in hand. Who telephoned?"

"Marcia Prevost. We're to have dinner with her and Nick tonight and I want to go down to Gisele's while I can."

"I wondered whether you remembered you still had a business here. Fanchon's done her best with wartime shoddy and shortages, but she's no designer and she's never found one who didn't work just by rule-of-thumb. Gisele's did maintain a standard but you'd turn green if you saw some of the garments that were sold with your precious label on them."

"Would I? I spent two short leaves in Paris. If American women wish to return to Paris styles, they will. But they won't get anything that remotely resembles the current atrocities from Gisele's when I'm in the saddle again," Michael said.

"Fanchon won't argue with you. She'll fall on your neck and weep and want to dump her troubles in your lap. So I'm surprised that you—"

"I know. But I want to consult our old records," Michael admitted. "I'll be back as early as possible. Marcia said we were to turn up around seven and pray that Nick will get home at a reasonable hour."

And Prevost would have reached home in time to mix the cocktails if, just as he was reaching for his hat, Detective Costello had not stumped into his office.

"My feet hurt," he said, sitting down. "Any of the rest of the boys had any luck, Nick?"

"Not much. Harry Hunt got a sandwich on Polk Street Tuesday night about seven-thirty. He didn't use the pay phone there. It was easy to locate about six hotels he stayed at, off and on, till his family moved up here in July. But they don't keep tabs on their guests in those joints.

"Harry had been a good enough friend to some of the old-time clerks and the proprietors that I think they'd talk if they knew anything that'd help us. Apparently they don't. Harry seems to have been a good boy lately. And why are you looking so self-satisfied?"

"That perfume business you put me on this morning. There was all kinds of black markets so finally I worked on that angle," Costello said. "And I tried this little shop in Chinatown. I'd heard it wasn't always strictly on the up-and-up. Besides, jasmine made me think of China, see?

"Well, when I mentioned murder, the guy that runs the place talked. He had some of this jasmine stuff though not many dames used it. That's why he remembered selling some of it in early March. He didn't know the exact day.

"The stuff sells for fifty dollars an ounce. So he didn't forget the dame that come in and bought an ounce, in two bottles and paid for it without batting an eye when she didn't look like she had five bucks to spend, let alone fifty."

"Could he describe her?" Prevost said eagerly.

"Pretty well. She was short and fat, not bad-looking, but just ordinary features: blue eyes and brown hair, light-complected. Her hair looked like she did it herself; and she was neat, though her clothes was cheap. But she had a scar that slanted acrost her temple onto her forehead. She pulled her hair forward but that didn't cover all the scar. It was white and looked pretty old."

"That's better than I expected," Prevost said. "Did you ask the proprietor of this shop if he had thought the woman might be a prostitute?"

"Sure. I know how some will wear any old kind of clothes when they ain't working but blow money on fancy underwear and perfume. This Joe Fong said he thought about that but her clothes were neat and clean; she wasn't painted up and she had a nice, educated voice. And when he come back from wrapping the bottles in a back room, she was sort of staring into space with her lips moving like she was talking to herself. When he spoke to her, she acted like she didn't know who he was or where she was. He says she looked sort of lost."

"Oh." Prevost was silent for several minutes before he said, "You'd better call it a day. Tomorrow I want you to start trying to find that woman. Is Barnett still attached to the Vice Squad?"

"Beginnin' his twentieth year on the detail. You want me to team up with him? I'll talk to him now if he's around. Then I'll go home."

Prevost was late enough that Michael had mixed Manhattans and was pouring them when he arrived. He had time, while they were still in the living room, to give Valerie and Michael a resume of his conversation with Costello.

"So the lady was nondescript except for a scar on her head and she had fifty dollars to spend for perfume?" Michael said.

"Yes, but unless Costello is a fool for luck again, it may take a long time to find that woman. The Talcotts don't want publicity."

"No, neither the Talcotts nor their hangers-on want publicity," Michael said. "But Chris cannot bring himself to ignore facts."

"You're right. He brought me a note this afternoon that he said Daphne had found pinned to her pillow—he didn't know when—and an old letter of Rowena's so we could compare the handwritings."

"Have you?"

"The experts are working on it."

"But your experts at routine didn't turn up anything helpful when they covered the hotels Harry stayed in from February until July," Michael said thoughtfully. "They had no difficulty in locating the hotels in question. It's odd—"

"No, it isn't. Naturally we knew Harry's old haunts," Prevost said. "He knew we would."

"And so it's odd that he bothered to tell Valerie about his difficulties finding a place to rest his head. Are you perfectly certain, my dear, that Harry didn't—"

But Valerie was looking toward Marcia Prevost who had just appeared in the doorway. "Soup's on, as I've already said in a more polite tone of voice. Come and get it or I'll throw it out."

Prevost rose hastily. "Chris told me he hadn't been able to talk to Daphne today," he went on, in the dining room. "Do you think that's true?"

"Yes, and Michael brought that about," Valerie said. "We all went pub-crawling last night. . . ."

Her story lasted well into a noble prime rib roast complete with Yorkshire pudding. "That's all I have to offer," she ended. "Michael says I didn't miss anything when I was in an alcoholic haze."

"You didn't miss anything that would have meant any thing to you. But she didn't hear what Mark Vibert said to the other men when they brought him home."

Michael told them what Mark had said to Joel, Bob, and Chris in the lower hall the night before, adding, "Sophia wasn't in the house when we got there. She came in while Valerie was putting Daphne to bed. She said she'd been walking because she couldn't sleep."

"Had she been to bed?" Prevost said.

"Yes. But she'd dressed and armed herself with a stout walking stick."

"Oh. I'll have to talk to her about that. You know," Prevost said abruptly, "I find it hard to

believe a room would smell of perfume just because a person wearing it had been in a room for
a while."

"Jasmine must be terrifically sweet, Nick," his
wife said. "And you remember that horribly expensive perfume you gave me one Christmas?"

"Yes. You spilled some on the bureau scarf and
the bedroom did reek of it even with the windows open. The scarf still smelled of it after it
was washed, you said. Did you meet your match
in Miss Sophia, Michael?"

Michael grinned. "I did. Well, in time it may
help to know the true financial circumstances of
all these people."

"Maybe. You say Daphne hinted Miss Sophia
isn't as well off as she is supposed to be. But she
doesn't get much from old St. George Talcott's
will whether Rowena is dead or alive."

"I think you'd better make an all-out effort to
find Rowena, Nick."

"My God, do you suppose I don't intend to?
But that's not going to be easy."

"Not if she doesn't want to be found," Michael
said.

"*If* she doesn't. What the hell do you mean by
that?" Prevost said.

"Just what I said. And what about Zinnia?"

"I found out where she lives. In Oakland and I haven't had time to go over there. And it'll do no good to shout at her, 'What did you tell Harry that you didn't tell the police?'"

"No, but she might tell you if Rowena had been given to snacks in the kitchen between meals or late at night."

"Well, I'll be—"

"I'd thought of that," Marcia said quietly. "As a nurse I had some experience with people who were supposed to lose weight. Valerie told me in the kitchen that Chris said Rowena kept gaining weight in spite of dieting. But people who really do diet, do lose weight. Those who say they are dieting and still gain weight are usually eating on the sly."

"So what?" Prevost said. "I know Rowena was unhappy because she was too plump but—"

"But perhaps she was too plump *because* she was unhappy which is a little different. Some people eat too much when they aren't happy just as others drink too much for the same reason. And Valerie said that Chris told her Rowena began getting stout only about six months before she disappeared."

"I get your point; that Rowena had some real reason for unhappiness. We tried to follow that line six years ago. Have you anything more to offer, Michael?"

"I went down to Gisele's this morning and looked over our old records. I was surprised to learn that the Reverend Walter Denning's wife patronized us for several years, off and on. I didn't—"

Michael stopped and looked at Marcia.

"The lot of the policeman's wife is not a happy one. What would you like to do, Marcia?"

"Oh," Marcia said with an apologetic smile. "I'd like to have you concentrate on my lemon pie instead of talking shop and then we might play blackjack."

They were still at the card table at midnight. Marcia went into the kitchen to get the coffee she had started a few minutes before. Her husband looked disgustedly from the two pennies before him to the stack of dimes in front of Michael.

"I'm glad we aren't playing for real money. Did anyone ever take you at twenty-one?"

"Not that I recall. I've told you, Nick, to stand on seventeen and leave it to the dealer to beat you. In the long run . . . Is that the telephone?"

"Let Marcia get it and if it's for me, she'll stall them off. She's very good at that and . . . What is it, Marcia? Is it important?"

"I'm afraid so," Marcia said. "That was Chris Talcott. Patton told him that Michael is here. He wants you two to come around at once. He said it was urgent and then he hung up."

PART THREE

I

The day—Thursday—had dragged. Chris woke with a taste of brass in his mouth. Daphne and Mark did not appear at the breakfast table. Sophia read the newspapers and the set of her shoulders discouraged conversation. Joel chose to be dignified.

Chris did not attempt to woo him from this attitude. He drank two cups of muddy coffee and went back to his bedroom and looked up a small bundle of Rowena's letters to him written in 1938.

Chris had been in England then and a trifle homesick and Rowena had been a conscientious reporter of small family matters. Glancing through the letters, Chris came across a reference to Mark.

"Daphne met him at the Knopf party last week and seems quite smitten. She's been like that about other men but she might marry Mr. Vibert. She's older than he is though she'll never tell him. He treats her as if she were fragile and precious and that's what she wants most. He'll be a fool if he marries her. He deserves better. . . ."

Chris laid that letter aside and picked up another in which Rowena remarked, "Bob's taken to dropping in frequently. We're always glad to see him. He knows all the family history and catch-phrases and jokes and fits in. He is terribly extravagant. I suspect he's already gotten through a good deal of his father's money. Daphne doesn't like it because Bob's taken me dancing several times lately. Neither does Joel but that's very good for him. . . ."

"I'd forgotten that Rowena was more voluble and outspoken on paper than she was in person," Chris thought. "Well, these aren't important. . . ."

Still, after skimming the rest of the letters he returned them to his desk except for a page filled with trivialities. He put that in his billfold to give to Prevost with the note Michael had handed him last night. Then he went out into the hall just as Mark came down from the third floor.

Mark looked ill and tired but he managed to smile. "Don't ask me if I want breakfast. No, no, a thousand times no! But I must be at the shop this morning."

"You have my sincere sympathy. I suppose Daphne will stay in bed all day?"

"She usually does."

"Usually? Does she do this often?"

"This is her third binge in the last eight months—that I know of and not counting V-J night. She did better before she decided that brandy and water is a good tipple. You might as well give up any idea of talking to her today."

"Do you know if she thinks she has . . . well . . ."

"'Seen' Rowena?" Mark finished. "Yes. She was so frightened one night in May that she spent it in my room. She said she'd had a nightmare; dreamed someone was standing by her bed, bent down, took hold of her ears and shook her head gently. What's the matter? That seemed such an absurd detail to me."

"No. Daphne always slept late and Rowena often tried to get her out of bed. That's a way she had of waking Daphne when they were younger and fonder of each other. That's all Daphne told you?"

"Yes. The next morning she insisted she'd forgotten her 'nightmare.' And Rowena had not honored me with a visitation, Chris. I'll see you later."

Chris let him go. He looked at his watch, saw that it was already eleven o'clock and decided to wait until afternoon to see Prevost. He had turned to go downstairs when Sophia appeared, carrying a stack of long brown envelopes and two account books.

"Come into my room, Chris." She sat down at her desk. "Draw up a chair. I have balanced my accounts but you will find when you look over these bank statements," she tapped the envelopes, "that I borrowed money from you for six months. Your checks from the estate kept coming in and you'd unwisely given me a free hand. . . ."

"'Unwisely?' I can't think that I was unwise to turn my affairs over to you. I—"

"But you are embarrassed and a bit shocked to learn that I juggled funds that were entrusted to me?"

Chris flushed. "Well-l-l. You couldn't maintain this establishment on the sum allotted to you for that purpose from Father's estate?"

"I didn't. Daphne will point out that you've only my word that I used your money to help maintain this household. I've the household accounts here but I could have falsified them."

"Don't be foolish. And why should Daphne be so malicious?"

Sophia shrugged. "She can't bear criticism and I have criticized her lately. She ignored the war and she has utterly failed Mark. Secretly she is aggrieved because he, her property, was unheroically discharged from the Army and didn't get to be an officer."

"Yes, she would rather he had been heroically killed in action. Daphne looks so well in black and would quite enjoy the role of war widow."

Sophia raised her heavy eyebrows. "I believe you are learning, Chris. Well, I suggested that if Daphne wished to continue living in the lap of luxury, she should contribute something toward the upkeep of this place. Considering that she entertains here—and on a lavish scale—and that even the supplies for her cocktail parties appear on the household bills, I thought that was not unreasonable.

"She proved to me that she spends every cent she has: her allowance and her royalties, even before she receives them, having unlimited credit. However, when Mark came home, he began paying what's known as 'a nominal sum' for their board."

"What about Joel?" Chris asked.

"He also pays a nominal sum for his board. St. George gave him a hundred a month and 'found' as resident secretary. He gets the same salary as St. George's literary executor, but he'd need an additional hundred a month to live anywhere else as he's lived here."

"I'd forgotten. Father's death was a shock and I was numb during the ceremonial reading of a very complicated will. Also, my feet hurt. I'd been in the Army such a short time, and I felt that the terms of Father's will weren't going to matter much to me. He meant well, as he always did, but it's turned out to be a very troublesome document. But you said you'd balanced your accounts, Aunt Sophia?"

"I have received certain dividend checks."

"What? Oh—" Chris uttered an unprintable five-letter word. "I beg your pardon, Aunt Sophia. But I think Father was unwise to want this household to remain in status quo. I know he thought Rowena might have come home. But I'll wager you would have preferred having an apartment of your own."

"I would have, but being able to go on living here has been a godsend to me. Because I am not the well-to-do woman people take for granted I am."

"But Aunt Sophia—"

"You think your aunt is a hard-headed business woman. But your grandfather was a gambler who happened to die during a prosperous period in his affairs, and I resemble my father. I've always speculated and always been unlucky. I haven't been a wealthy woman since the big crash of 1929. Even that did not teach me a lesson. Not that I am destitute. But we are all used to having money and don't like to be without it."

"You didn't tell Father," Chris guessed. "Or he would have left you more than five thousand."

"No, I didn't tell St. George. I very foolishly valued his high opinion of my abilities."

"Well, as to repaying what you borrowed from me, that's foolish."

Sophia shook her head. "No, I want to balance my accounts. I might have dismissed the maid, sold the family car, been firm with Daphne, and practiced a hundred small economies that other women would think of at once and don't occur to me even now."

"You'll forget what you borrowed from me," Chris said decisively. He added with his sidelong smile, "I'm the titular head of the family now. Until the estate is settled I'll contribute what you need to keep up this Noah's Ark that the allowance from the estate doesn't cover."

"Well—, at least check these over."

Chris hesitated and then accepted the bank statements and account books. "When I get around to it, if you insist. I'm going downtown after lunch."

In the early afternoon he had his brief interview with Nicholas Prevost. He killed several hours in Roos Brothers and Hastings, then, encumbered with a parcel of shirts, sat in Lefty O'Doul's on Powell Street and nursed a drink along until he could meet Anice in front of the Medico-Dental Building on Sutter.

Anice was pale and tired. "Mother told me there would be days like this. An old man had a heart attack and we thought he'd die before Doctor came in. Would you eat spaghetti with Marion and me? The restaurants are so crowded. Marion is very tactful. And she really likes to read lying over her bed. She'll excuse herself when the dishes are done."

Marion did, with a blunt, "I've had a hard day and I'm not up to making polite conversation while you two cast yearning glances at each other."

Chris grinned. "You might be diplomatic and say that you have letters to write."

"I wish I did," Marion said and left them abruptly.

"Did I drop a brick then?" Chris asked.

"You couldn't know, honey. Marion's boy friend has been missing for a year. She doesn't admit he must be dead. She goes out with some nice fellows but it just doesn't take. I can guess what it's like. I had over a month of it when you were missing. I couldn't take much more."

Chris sat down in a big chair. "Come here. I have one good knee and you're a featherweight. One should be glad the War Department doesn't make more mistakes than they do, I suppose.

Somehow I lost my dog tag—maybe it was blown off—and it was a long time before I could say who I was."

"Don't!" Anice threw her arms about him and for some time said nothing. Then she murmured, "How is dear Daffy today? It was mean of me to laugh last night, but I was high myself; so when Mark slapped her, I wanted to shout, 'Three cheers!'"

"You think she had it coming to her?"

"Don't you? Some men are more sensitive than women about certain things," Anice said shrewdly. "Most men don't like to have their stomach trouble referred to in public. You've never said one word about Daphne saying I made a play for Mark."

"Don't be foolish," Chris said shortly.

"But I was sorry for Mark and I encouraged him to talk to me. He never talked down to me like the others did. And I wouldn't be surprised if he'd met someone he fell in love with while he was in the Army."

"Well, God knows that happened frequently. But if that's the way it is, Daphne and Mark will have to work it out for themselves. I decided I'll catch up with my living and the hell with my relatives. So let's get married right away."

"Chris, it wouldn't matter if it was a hasty wartime marriage, but it won't be; and Daphne will sneer if I don't have a decent trousseau. No! You aren't going to buy it for me!"

"Who will care and who needs to know if I buy your bridal lingerie?"

"Daphne might guess. No," Anice said stubbornly, "I need at least another month's salary. Don't be mad, Chris. You can give me a present every day when we're married and I won't scold. Your folks all think I'm a little mercenary, and I am."

"Hmm? Do you honestly expect me to believe that when—"

"Oh, as to not marrying you tomorrow without a trousseau, a girl has her pride, to coin a phrase. But I'm glad we won't have to worry about money. Daddy was absolutely impractical and I always had to make one dollar do the work of three. One reason people around San Rafael still make snide remarks about me is that I tried to collect his bills when he died. And all of you people think money's important, but you don't really know how important. You never look at the price list on a menu. You just order what you want, regardless."

Chris sighed. "Well, then, let's talk about what sort of home we want when we're married."

"For a while, we'll take what we can get. But we can dream, can't we? Kiss me first."

Chris kissed her. He went on kissing her at intervals while they planned the home they would build.

"A vast living room but a dining room that cannot accommodate more than six dinner guests," Chris specified.

"Yes," Anice agreed, "and a study for you; and a sewing room for me; and a nursery, though not too large a nursery. . . ."

It was at this point that Chris found himself kissing Anice practically without intervals; pushed her off his knee and rose abruptly.

"I'm going home," he said rather grimly, "and don't ask me why, my sweet."

Anice faced him, breathing rapidly, pushing her hair back into its natural wave. Even the tips of her ears were crimson but she said mutinously, "After all, I'm not a—an Ice Maiden!"

Chris grinned. "No, you are delightfully co-operative. But having established a beach-head, I think I will go home. It's after nine and the doctors told me to retire early and avoid undue excitement."

Anice giggled; then said unexpectedly, "I think you've changed, Chris," and made no objection when, having implanted a chaste peck on her forehead, he left her.

Chris was agreeably surprised to discover, when he was in bed, that he was pleasantly drowsy. He drifted into sleep almost at once and it was some time before he began to dream.

He was in a strange yet familiar land where the sun was too bright and the sky too blue. Yet when he walked it was very slowly, in deep, sticky mud. He had had companions; their weary monotonous cursing was the refrain to which he slogged along.

But they seemed to vanish, those other men of his platoon and for an instant he was alone. Then he saw a blond Aryan head and the grenade in the German soldier's hand before the earth went to pieces before his feet. . . .

Chris sat up in bed, trembling; sweat running down his neck onto his chest. He switched on the bedside lamp, shaking his head ruefully.

He muttered, "And I was so smug because I hadn't been troubled with dreams. That was too realistic for comfort. I'd almost swear I actually heard—" He broke off, passing a hand over his damp forehead. "But was that entirely a dream? Perhaps . . ."

He slid out of bed and stumbled across the room. As he reached his doorway, Sophia spoke from hers, standing there in her flannelette night-gown, her eyes dull with sleep.

"Chris, did you hear . . . Something woke me. A shot, I thought. Or was I only dreaming?"

"If you were, I dreamed it, too. I'll look downstairs."

The front door stood a little ajar. Outside, in the old-fashioned outer vestibule, a woman lay dead. She was in her late thirties, short, fat, a whitish scar slanting across her temple into her brown hair. Under an old raincoat she wore a blue silk dress with white bowknots scattered over it and her fingers were still clasped about the strap of a large, worn suede purse.

II

Joel rose and poured himself another drink—his third since they had been herded into the living room and told to stay there.

All of them, that is, but Daphne. Daphne, having looked at the dead woman, had become violently hysterical. Prevost banished her to the third floor, sent the cook to minister to her, and one of his men to watch both of them.

The door opened and Michael came in with Bob Lovell. Bob went like a homing pigeon straight to the decanter. He poured himself a stiff peg and looked questioningly at Michael. Michael nodded.

"Please. Prevost won't keep you out of your beds much longer. He's been waiting for Mr. Lovell."

"It took you long enough to get here, Bob," Joel said.

"I came as soon as I could after Chris called. I had to dress. I was in bed and I don't suppose any of you have a better story than that to offer."

"We were all in bed by ten," Sophia said. "Chris and I were waked from sound sleep by the shot. Joel was sleeping on his good ear and didn't hear it. Daphne had taken some sleeping tablets. Mark heard the shot but not so plainly as Chris and I did, being on the third floor. At that, we were all assembled in a very short time."

"Prevost will deal with that angle," Chris said, "but in another matter, he is more or less dependent on us. You've seen her, Bob. What do you think?"

"I don't know, boy," Bob said slowly. "If Rowena were nearly seven years older and twenty pounds heavier, that woman could be Rowena. What do the rest of you think?"

"Daphne said nothing coherent," Sophia told him. "I agree with you. Rowena looked so much like so many other women, and fat makes a great difference where facial expression is concerned. That woman's features and hair are like Rowena's. What do you think, Mark?"

"It's Rowena," Mark said briefly.

Joel hesitated before he said, "I suppose it is
Rowena. She was gaining weight six years ago. It's
difficult to tell, looking at one who—who is dead,
what her expression would be if she were living.
But despite that there is something disturbingly
familiar about that woman's face."

"And we don't know what that woman has done
or how she's lived during the last six years," Mark
said. "She may have had to live a sort of life that
would change her greatly."

"That's the hell of it," Chris said. "Michael,
if that scar on her head is the result of an injury,
has the police doctor said whether it might have
caused loss of memory?"

"Nick asked him that and his snap judgment is
that the scar indicates a rather serious head injury
some years ago, and that it might have caused loss
of memory, especially if the injury did not receive
the best possible medical attention," Michael said.

"Well, suppose that after she left here, Rowena
was injured. Whoever was responsible for that did
not take her to a hospital or she would have been
identified. . . ."

Chris paused as Prevost came into the room.
"Go on," the Inspector said. "Only you should
have said that she was not taken to any reputable
hospital."

"I hadn't thought of that. Yes, and if any reputable doctor had treated Rowena he would have notified the police. No doubt Henry Hunt knew more than one doctor who wouldn't ask questions and would keep silent if he were paid a sufficiently large fee. Perhaps that's the sort of lead that Hunt followed when he came on the case."

"We investigated that angle in 1939," Prevost said. "We are thorough and we have a little list. But Harry knew his fair share of shady medicos and he might have gotten the truth from another crook where we couldn't. I think that we must assume that Harry knew what had happened to Rowena. Otherwise, why was he killed?"

"Presumably because he was going to 'tell all,'" Michael said. "But why? He'd kept his knowledge to himself for six years and we assume that he was well paid to do just that. So why did Harry suddenly decide to talk to Chris?"

"I don't know," Prevost said irritably, turning back to Chris. "You were saying, when I came in—"

"Oh, that Rowena must have had some sort of care after she was injured. But when she recovered, she didn't remember anything. It's hard to believe; it sounds like a third-rate thriller. But she might even have been taken out of San Francisco and only returned recently."

"Returned instinctively because she was beginning to recover her memory?" Mark said.

"That's not impossible, is it? We do know she's been in this house," Chris said. "We have the note Daphne found, and we have Old Dobbin—the umbrella handle. You can't disregard those. And—did she let herself into the house tonight?"

"There was a key in her purse that opens your front door," Prevost said. "Also a ten dollar bill, compact, comb—and this."

He showed them a fine linen handkerchief, scented with jasmine and pointed to the hand-worked initial "T" in one corner.

"That is a handkerchief Rowena had initialed to order," Sophia said. "She always had spandy nice pocket handkerchiefs and of course she would not have gone out without one in her purse. And it was her old purse I saw tonight, her raincoat and the dress she wore the last time I saw her. She didn't wear a hat tonight and the shoes are cheap brown ones, not Rowena's blue gabardines. But shoes wear out. As to undergarments—"

"The doctor said, when I asked, that she's wearing rather new, inexpensive rayon underthings," Michael said. "Lingerie wears out too. Pearls don't."

Sophia looked at him sharply but he went on, "A raincoat of that type lasts forever. So does the quality of pure silk that we used in that dress. The dress was well cared for, too. She'd had to let out all the seams but we have never skimped on material so she managed to alter the dress and get into it, though it was a tight fit."

"I suppose she instinctively clung to the coat and dress," Joel said. "And a purse wouldn't wear out—" Suddenly he banged his glass down on a table. "My God! We sit here talking calmly and academically yet Rowena's come home and we know little more than we ever have."

"You know someone killed her," Prevost said dryly. "She was shot through the heart at close range. There was no gun beside her body. We have searched the house and found only an old Army service revolver, vintage of the last war, in a desk drawer in St. George Talcott's study. The thing hasn't been fired for years."

"St. George brought that home as a souvenir of the last war," Joel said. "I'd forgotten it's in the study now though I use that room more than anyone else does."

"It doesn't matter. I started to say that Rowena's murderer must have been waiting for her in this house at the front door. That doesn't let Mr. Lovell out," Prevost said. "He has a key to this house. Anice King had one once; she could have had a copy made before she returned her key to Miss Sophia when she left here."

"That's true," Chris said wearily, "but why drag Anice into this?"

"Because you'll be a much richer man since your sister is dead. We know you couldn't have killed Harry. You were seen walking in this neighborhood the night he was killed and we located the bartender on Chestnut where you had a beer and the taxi driver who picked you up there after Harry was dead."

Michael grinned at Chris's startled look. "Did you expect Nick to take you entirely on faith? And it's true that Anice, through you, will gain by Rowena's death."

"And I will profit through Daphne," Mark said. "And Daphne herself will gain greatly and that ends the list of people who will."

"Yes," Chris said, "but people do not kill only for hope of financial gain."

"I wouldn't have expected you to bring that up," Prevost said, "but it's possible there's another motive for Rowena's death than the fact that she'd have inherited half your father's estate next year if she was alive."

"You mean Rowena may have been killed because one of us knows, and always has known, the true facts behind her disappearance and killed her before she could talk," Bob said stolidly. "That theory would eliminate Anice but none of the rest of us. But how could any of us know that Rowena was going to come home tonight or approximately what time she'd be here?"

"One possibility is that Rowena had regained her memory to the extent where she got in touch with one or more of you and announced that she intended to come home tonight. Or one of you urged her to. But that's pure guesswork and we all need rest. Now that we have an up-to-date picture of her to print in the papers, we'll find out where she's been living recently. I'm leaving a man here tonight. Tomorrow I'll want to talk to Mrs. Vibert. You may call in her own doctor if you think she isn't well enough to talk, but—" Prevost paused.

"Our family doctor won't take much stock in Daphne's hysterics," Bob said bluntly. "I think I'll bed down in my old room here, Inspector."

Prevost nodded. "All right. I'll be back tomorrow. Good night."

When they were outside, he added, "I'll take you home since you left your car for Valerie, Michael. I need sleep so I didn't go on hammering away at those people. Any of those living in the house could have shot Rowena at the front door, beat it along the hall to the back stairs and been back in their rooms before Chris reached the front door."

"Joel, Mark or Daphne probably would have used the back stairs," Michael said. "Mark and Daphne would have had an extra flight of stairs to climb to get back to their rooms."

"Yes, but when the alarm was given, they could claim it naturally took them longer to get down to the first floor than it did Chris and Sophia. Mark did point that out. Chris said he went down by himself and found the body. Sophia said she thought she had better rouse Joel, and when she had, she joined Chris at the front door," Prevost said.

"Chris says he wasted no time getting to the telephone and that by then Joel had come down, closely followed by Daphne and Mark. Any one of those four had ample time to shoot Rowena and get back to their rooms. Lovell and Anice would have had even more time to get away. Lovell was at home when Chris thought to call him. He has a swanky apartment on Jackson near Presidio Avenue. It's some distance from the Talcott house but he has a car. Anice King would have had to get home by walking, or taxi, or streetcar. But no one thought to telephone her until enough time had passed that, even walking, she'd have been home. Sophia's the only one who'd have been hard pressed for time."

Michael nodded. "She was standing in her doorway, in her nightgown, when Chris got to his bedroom door. But if someone who lives in that house killed Rowena, he or she certainly took the precaution of undressing and getting into night-clothes before going downstairs to wait for Rowena."

"That would be the only smart thing to do," Prevost agreed. "Nobody's clothes were warm when we searched their rooms and their beds had really been laid in for a while. And though Sophia would have had little time to spare, she could have made it back to her room, using the front stairs. I didn't tackle her tonight but I still want to know why she was out walking so late last night."

"And when are you going to talk to Zinnia?"

"Zinnia?" Prevost frowned. "I don't know if I'll get over to Oakland today. I'll have more import-ant things to do than talking to Zinnia. Maybe later—"

"I'm sure you know your job," Michael said with what Prevost would have recognized as suspicious docility if he had been less weary or preoccupied. "Chris told Valerie that Zinnia married a Pullman porter."

"Hmm? Oh, yes: Thad Hampson," Prevost said abstractedly. "They own their own home and have a couple of kids. Six years ago, Zinnia was a slim, high-yaller gal, very jittery. I hope I'll find that matrimony has calmed her down when I do get around to her."

He stopped his car at Jones and Vallejo before the wall where Henry Hunt had parked on Tuesday night.

"If it's all right with you, I won't drive in."

Michael nodded, got out of the car and then stood leaning against it for an instant.

"I want to look at that dress Rowena was wearing tonight, Nick, if you don't mind. I know you will file it away with the usual exhibits but—"

"But why are you interested in it? It had your label at the back of the neck all right."

"Women have been known to sew our labels into dresses I didn't design. But that dress did come from Gisele's. And naturally I am interested because I did design it—a shroud for Rowena. Good night, Nick."

III

As soon as he had rounded the wall at Jones, crossed the cobblestones and started slowly toward Russian Hill Place, Chris saw that Michael already had his car out of the garage. A second glance showed Patton, gazing anxiously down at Master Roderick, who was happily kicking the car's tires.

Michael looked up at Patton and said heartlessly, "This parting is not for years or even for a day. I will return your idol intact. I have reason to believe I fathered this brat and I won't let him come to grief. So go back in the house, woman. Your big, sad eyes distress me."

Patton went back into the house and very nearly slammed the door behind her. Michael scooped his son from the dust and plunked him down in the middle of the car's front seat.

"You may sit here just so long as you behave yourself. Otherwise you will ride alone in the back. *Comprendes, mi angelito? Pues bien. Vamos!*"

Chris got into the car. "Does he understand Spanish?"

"Quite as well as he understands English," Michael said dryly. "Like most small animals, it is a certain tone of voice that he comprehends. I had a serious conversation with Patton this morning. She's given us the sort of service you can't buy, but I'm not going to have my son grow up thinking he can always have what he wants if he screams loudly enough. Fortunately she believes a man should be master in his own home so she will forgive me—in time."

Chris smiled diffidently at Master Roderick. He liked children and was very shy with them. Dundas Junior, a dark, wiry child, stared at him unwinkingly for several minutes. Then he grinned delightfully, settled himself against his father and appeared to slumber.

"You convinced me this morning that I should come here to accompany you on some sort of trip, but why are we taking your son with us?" Chris asked.

"Because Zinnia has children."

"Does Prevost know we're going to see Zinnia?"

"No, Nick will be very busy today. It was all right for me to answer your S.O.S. last night but I can't go tagging after Nick in uniform. I did risk going to see Margaret Hunt more or less in a state of undress but—"

"You're in full regalia now, you know."

"That will impress Zinnia but it might have made Mrs. Hunt uneasy. Besides, I am merely driving you across the Bay because you wish to talk to your old family retainer."

"I do admire your ingenious scheme and I only hope Roderick won't raise his voice to high heaven when he is confronted with a little pickaninny."

Michael chuckled. "Patton tells me disapprovingly that 'Master Ricky,' has a passion for Chinese infants and small colored 'persons.' And if Zinnia's offspring appear to be swarming with germs, I will personally disinfect Roderick this afternoon."

"I don't fancy there's any danger of that. Zinnia was forever scrubbing, and she was very neat."

And so, when they reached it, was Mrs. Thad Hampson's small yellow cottage. Its lawn was well combed and curried and the flower beds along the front walk were rigidly confined within rock borders. There was a vegetable garden at one side of the house and here Zinnia, slightly hampered by the demands of two entrancing tar-babies, was hoeing corn.

She had gained weight since Chris had last seen her and if she was not actually placid, at least she was no longer strongly and instinctively on the defensive.

She said warmly, "Mr. Chris! It's mighty nice to see you. Miss Sophia, she tol' me about you bein' wounded, las' time I went to see her. I sure am glad you got back safe. Won't you gent'men come in the house?"

"Can't we sit on the porch?" Michael said. "It's a fine morning and I'd better keep an eye on my son."

He released Roderick who immediately plopped happily down into the dirt between the rows of corn. Zinnia regarded the three children doubtfully.

"My boys might play a little rough, sir."

"If he gets his ears pinned back, so much the better. It is your sons I wish to protect, not mine.

Mrs. Hampson, I'm a friend of Chris's and Henry Hunt's. Chris had better tell you what's happened."

"What? Oh—well."

Chris stopped to think. Then he told Zinnia, very succinctly, of Hunt's death and Rowena's home-coming. Although he had, as a popular lecturer, learned to hand out information briefly but comprehensively in capsule form, he was surprised that Zinnia seemed to understand him without difficulty.

"Back when I was with you folks, I couldn't read or write," Zinnia said, echoing Chris's thoughts. "I was fresh from the Old South an' didn't know my rights. Just talkin' to police scared me most to death. It ain't that I'm dumb. My husband was bo'n right here and he says I was silly to be scared. I'm sorry to hear about Mr. Hunt and Miss Rowena. You know how I liked Miss Rowena; an' Mr. Hunt was a gent'man though I reckon he had a eye for the ladies."

"He did," Michael said, "yet he had a wife and children for whom he would have made almost any sacrifice."

"Sure 'nuf? I know men like that in Thad's line of work. Nothin's too good for their fam'lies but they got a fancy woman in ever' division point, too. Not Thad. I'd take a razor to him if he ever started cheatin' on me," Zinnia said placidly.

"Mr. Hunt didn't pay me money to talk; no, sir! The police hinted later he might have. But he just kep' comin' back and comin' back and we talked slow and easy and so I don't know if I told him anything important. Well, maybe one thing I told him was, but I never heard no more about it so I ain't certain, even 'bout that!"

"I'm sure you aren't," Michael said. "But shall we see what you remember? First, though it's not too important—was Miss Rowena given to eating between meals or late at night?"

"She certainly was. Or she got to doin' that. When I first come there she was pretty slim. I used to say to her, 'Miss Rowena, honey, why you starve you'self at the table and then eat my icebox down to the bone at night?' She'd just shake her head and say she can't seem to help it. I never tol' on her—not once. And I wasn't goin' to embarrass her by shootin' off my big mouf."

"Did you ever do things for her that weren't really part of your job?"

Zinnia nodded. "I ironed her real nice waists and underwear sometimes. The laundress we had then wasn't a real good fancy ironer. I am and so was Miss Rowena though you wouldn't suppose so. She was so particular and neat she wanted things ironed right even if she had to do them herself."

"Would she allow you to put the clothes you ironed away in her bureau drawers?"

Zinnia frowned. "Miss Rowena was mighty fussy 'bout her bureau drawers. She kep' them in order herself, wouldn't let none of the maids do it. But you wouldn't know that—"

"He was told so, Zinnia," Chris said. "And he didn't forget."

"Well, she got so she'd let me put things away. She didn't mind havin' me aroun' her bedroom. She'd go on with whatever she was doin'—"

"Like writing at her desk?" Michael asked.

"Yes, lots of times she'd be doing that and she wouldn't stop. I told Mr. Hunt that one time. He didn't say it was important but he did ask me—"

"Let me guess?" Chris said. "He asked you if Rowena ever wrote in some sort of book, probably a rather small book—"

"How'd you know? Only, like I said to Mr. Hunt, he didn't have to describe the kind of book it was even if I couldn't read what was printed on it. Because two or three months before she went away, I says to Miss Rowena, 'Seems to me you doin' a powerful lot of writing in that little book lately.' Then she says it's a diary and tells me what that means. I says, 'Like your Papa writes ever' night.' She smiles and says it seems like it runs in the fam'ly to keep di'ries."

Chris nodded. "It does. So it might have occurred to us, six years ago, that Rowena might have kept one. You thought there was a chance she might have, Michael, hearing what Joel said to Valerie the other night at The Copper Kettle? I knew she had a diary when she was around sixteen. I kept one, too. I felt that no one understood me. . . . I'm sorry, Zinnia. I didn't mean to interrupt."

"Your comments aren't pointless," Michael said. "Various people turn diarist for various reasons and one common reason is a desire to get something off your chest that you hesitate to tell anyone."

"Miss Rowena kind of sighed and says diff'rent people keeps di'ries for diff'rent reasons," Zinnia recalled. "And she asked me not to tell anyone. She says once Miss Daphne got hold of a diary of hers and read it, when she was younger. . . ."

Chris nodded. "Daphne memorized portions of Rowena's 'teen-age outpourings and quoted them in public. Daphne never found my journal. Of course Rowena wouldn't want Daphne to know that she had turned diarist a second time."

"That's it, Mr. Chris. Miss Daphne rummaged in Miss Rowena's desk for stamps and things so Miss Rowena kep' the little book in her bureau under her underclo'es. I did wonder what-all she wrote in it. I took the liberty of sayin' to her, 'Miss Rowena, you ought to get married.' She just smiles and says, 'I'm very fond of Mr. Lovell and Mr. Gloster but I'll never marry either of them, Zinnia.'"

"Oh. As definite as that?" Chris said.

"Yes, sir. But I never thought 'bout that diary when Miss Rowena disappeared. I s'posed you all found it and it didn't help you none. Wasn't my place to speak about it. Only when I found myself tellin' Mr. Hunt about it, I thought he was interested. He asks me didn't anyone mention that Miss Rowena kep' a diary or that it was missin'? I had to say that no one ever did and I didn't know was it missin' or not."

"You couldn't know," Chris said. "And we didn't know there was a diary so we didn't know that it had disappeared. It must have because, since someone had turned her bureau upside-down that night, we checked her belongings very carefully and there was no diary in her room. Well, Michael, that's what Hunt meant when he said there had been a bona fide burglary."

"Perhaps. Oh, Harry was a smart little crook but he had his Achilles heel and he wasn't quite smart enough. But I think Harry learned something a good deal more important than that from you, Zinnia."

"W-what's that, sir?" Zinnia said, for the first time during the conversation, uneasily.

IV

Michael got up and deprived his son of a beautiful dirt-encrusted pebble but allowed him to retain a long green cornstalk.

"Will it hurt him to chew on that?"

"I don't reckon it will. I'm keepin' an eye on them, Mr. Dundas. It do beat all what babies puts in their moufs," Zinnia said, at ease again. "You was sayin'?"

"Why, I have thought a good deal about the purse Rowena was carrying that night. It was shabby, it was black, and it didn't match her blue ensemble. But it was a very large bag and the purse that would have matched her costume was quite small."

"Who told you that?" Chris said.

"Your Aunt Sophia. I thought it possible that Rowena had special need for a very large bag that night. When she dropped it in the hall outside your father's study, he heard the thud it made though you say his hearing was not particularly acute."

"Y-yes, but—"

"And I believe that when Rowena left Sophia's bedroom that night, she closed the door after her?"

"Yes," Chris said. "Aunt Sophia didn't hear Rowena go on downstairs, if that's what you mean.

There is a small gap between the time Rowena left Aunt Sophia and the time when Father spoke to her in the lower hall."

"So Rowena did not necessarily go straight down the stairway and toward the front door. She could have gone into the dining room first."

"Certainly. It opens off the lower hall, too. The door is opposite that of Father's study."

"When I wondered why Rowena carried such a large purse that night," Michael said, "I thought of something that could not be carried in a small purse; something that Rowena wouldn't want anyone to see. And last night Prevost told us that your father's service automatic is still in his study. But did he always keep it there? Because Joel Gloster said that he had forgotten that it was in the study 'now.'"

"Why—I remember. Father kept the gun loaded; he said there was no point in having an unloaded gun if you wanted it for protection. Aunt Sophia objected to his keeping it in his desk. When Father started looking for elusive notes or manuscript, he'd make a wild grab at the entire contents of a drawer. Aunt Sophia said that one day he might manage to seize the gun, too, and manage to discharge it. So he put it in the dining room sideboard. Zinnia—"

"Y-yes, Mr. Chris?"

"It's all right," Michael said quickly. "I know that when the police questioned you about the contents of that sideboard, you were afraid that they believed you had pocketed some of the silver."

"Yes, sir! And there could've been some spoons missin' on account of they gets throwed out with the garbage. That night Miss Rowena disappeared, I was putterin' aroun' the kitchen and I finds these two real silver spoons the maid that tended to that had missed puttin' away. I didn't want 'em to get mixed in with the kitchen silverware so I starts to the dining room to put 'em where they belonged.

"There's a swingin' door to the dining room that never made no noise," Zinnia said. "Miss Rowena didn't hear or see me. I stopped where I was. She was all dressed; even had her gloves on. She closes one of the small sideboard drawers under the big top one where we kep' the silver. Then she goes out, still not seein' me. I remember she was carrying that big old black suede purse, and how stuffed it looked.

"I put the spoons back and I hears Miss Rowena talkin' to her Papa. But she hadn't closed that underneath drawer quite tight so I pulled it to. An' that was the drawer ol' Mr. Talcott put that gun of his in. I know, 'cause the maid that set the table was always sayin' she was scared it would go off and shoot her. And Mr. Chris, that night aroun' eight, when I closed that drawer, there wasn't no ol' pistol there at all!"

"I believe you," Chris said. "But the next morning—"

"It wasn't on account of being scared that I didn't tell the police about that," Zinnia said quickly. "I never thought that maybe Miss Rowena took that nasty old gun away. Why would I, when next mornin' the gun was there? The policemen had it out on the dining room table—"

"As I was about to say," Chris broke in, "I saw it there. Well, Hunt said there was a bona fide burglary though not a professional one. Rowena's diary must have been taken from the house the night she disappeared. But Hunt also said, roughly, that though the silverware hadn't been taken, something had, but that in one instance you couldn't call it 'really stealing.' And if Rowena took Father's gun away with her, you could hardly call that theft. But I know the police examined that gun of Father's and wouldn't they know if it had been . . ."

"Let that go for now," Michael said hastily. "You told Mr. Hunt what you've told us, Zinnia?"

"He sort of wormed it out of me. I didn't tell him ever'thing all at once. He kep' coming back. I knew he was int'rested in what I says about the gun. And I asks him, 'Should I tell the police?'

"He says, 'They'd want to know why you didn't tell 'em sooner.' Because it was June or maybe July before I told him that. Then he says the police might not believe me on account of the gun was back in the sideboard that next mornin'. So I kep' still."

"Harry was an unscrupulous little bastard," Michael, said reflectively. "Of course he wouldn't care to share any lead he'd stumbled onto with the police." He got to his feet. "Thank you very much, Mrs. Hampson. Chris—"

Chris's manners were equal to this demand. He praised Zinnia's home and her children; promised to "remember" her to Sophia. But when they were in the car he did not speak again until they had passed the tollgates to the Bay Bridge.

Then he said, "Hunt must have gotten his first leads from Zinnia. But she didn't tell him about Father's gun until June or July. Father paid Hunt off in July so he must have progressed rather quickly."

"He may already have stumbled onto other leads that dovetailed with the information Zinnia gave him," Michael said, "I doubt if we'll ever know, now."

"No. But I know that the police examined Father's gun the morning Rowena was missing. And if that gun had been fired the night before . . ."

"The police would have known if the gun had been fired at all recently."

"But they asked us no questions about it; just dismissed it from the calculations. So—"

"So," Michael said, "either the gun they examined was your father's but it had *not* been fired recently. Or the gun in question was not your father's and it was not—nor is the one now in his study—the Colt .45 he brought back from World War I. And we'd better talk to Nick as soon as possible."

"Do you think he'll resent what we've done?"

"He couldn't forbid you to pay a morning call on your ex-cook," Michael said. "We've saved him time. His morning probably has been well-filled with routine matters." Chris smiled. "Yes, he is fond of saying, 'At least we are thorough.'"

"He picked that up from Sullivan when Sullivan was head man on the homicide detail."

"I remember Sullivan. Well," Chris said, deliberately turning to trivialities, "most of us pick up our pet phrases from our friends or our reading. And few of us realize what our pet phrases are. Do you?"

"I'll let you tell me."

"'If you don't mind' and 'six will get you ten.' Even merely as a manner of speaking, you never give long odds, do you?"

"Not willingly. I once spent a good deal of time around the race tracks. There is a special and distinctive argot or jargon connected with many professions or lines of work, you know. Well, we must take Roderick home before he begins to howl for food.

"And," Michael said, "perhaps we had better eat, too. We can't get to Nick before noon, now, and he goes home for lunch when he can. We'll be more apt to find him in his office at one o'clock."

V

"That was damned nice work, Michael," Prevost said generously. "You weren't just guessing; you did have some facts to go on and you made them count. Of course, it would help if now and then you'd explain in words of one syllable that a poor, hard-working cop can understand, what you have in mind. You know I was always interested in the fact that St. George heard Rowena's purse hit the floor. But when you discussed the ensemble she was wearing you only said that her purse didn't match it."

"What?" Michael frowned. "But if you are referring to our conversation on Wednesday afternoon, I *was* interested primarily in the fact that Rowena went out on that rainy night wearing a new ensemble. Have you anything interesting to tell us, Nick?"

"No. Same gun used to kill Rowena and Harry Hunt. No one in the Talcott's neighborhood happened to look out quickly enough, even the few who heard the shot, to see anyone leaving the house—if anyone did. I tried to talk to Daphne Vibert."

Chris grinned sympathetically. Prevost went on, "Daphne insists the woman who was killed last night isn't Rowena. She says she found the note you gave me pinned to her pillow one night in May but that it's a forgery."

"Is it?" Chris asked.

"Our expert thinks not. It's not a tracing and the note was written recently. They can tell that from the ink."

"Experts would, wouldn't they, from examining ink?" Michael murmured. "Never mind, Nick. Go on."

"Well, the letter of Rowena's that Chris gave me for comparison was written in 1938 so she would be seven years older now. That would help account for any slight differences between the writing in that letter and the note Mrs. Vibert had. Not that experts are infallible and I didn't try to reason with Daphne," Prevost said grimly. "She didn't have hysterics . . ."

"But she lay there looking lost and tiny, and you felt you were an uncouth brute," Chris said.

"Well, I talked to Anice this morning. By now you probably know that she has no alibi since she and Marion were in bed by ten, too."

"I saw her early. She insisted on going to her job though she said she'd probably be fired when the doctor saw the papers. But I doubt if—"

Prevost broke off and said, "Come in," as someone knocked. "Oh, Costello? What—"

"While you were at lunch a Mrs. Sawyer called up. She's got a rooming house on Pine near Fillmore; respectable neighborhood—or used to be. She seen the picture of Rowena Talcott in the early afternoon papers when she went to the groc'ry. And she was already wonderin' why one of her roomers hadn't slept in her room last night. I took it on myself to go out to see her. No use wastin' your time if it was a bum steer. I went over this dame's room—"

"What did she call herself?" Prevost said.

"Rose Tanner. There was no little knickknacks or pictures to make the room homelike. Not many clothes; all of them cheap ones."

"Did she have a coat?" Michael broke in.

"Yeah, a brown sport coat and one pretty new suitcase, about half cardboard," Costello said. "And a little bottle of this jasmine perfume on the bureau and in one corner an old silk umbrella with no handle on it. So when Mrs. Sawyer described this Rose Tanner to me, I asked would she mind comin' down to the morgue. She didn't fuss and we just been there and she says our body is Rose Tanner."

"Then show Mrs. Sawyer in," Prevost said impatiently.

Costello brought in a thin, willowy female of fifty whose drooping form was draped with funereal garments that smelled of mothballs. However, her features were intelligent and her voice less lugubrious than one would have expected.

"You won't mind talking before these gentlemen?" Prevost asked. He gestured toward Chris. "This is Rowena Talcott's brother."

"I don't mind. I read all about Rowena Talcott years ago but it never occurred to me my Rose Tanner could be her. Well, poor thing." Mrs. Sawyer took off her darned cotton gloves and folded them carefully. "I guess she didn't know herself who she was. She came to me the fifteenth of February. You know how she looked and she had nice, ladylike manners. She said she had a job in the Just-Rite Laundry between eight and four o'clock."

"According to Zinnia, Rowena was a 'fancy' ironer," Chris muttered.

"Hmm? Well, she always went off early and come back around five. I didn't ask where she lived before she came to me. It was no use asking anyone that, during the war. Rose was quiet and neat, only sometimes she made me feel kind of funny."

"Did she? Why, Mrs. Sawyer?" Prevost asked.

"I never saw much of her except when she'd pay her rent. I'd feel like she hardly really saw me, at times. She wouldn't hear what I said and she'd look like she was staring past me, trying to remember something, if you know what I mean?"

Prevost nodded. "And you never asked her friendly questions: how long she'd been in the city, where she was born, if she had parents living?"

"No. Except one night when I took clean towels in, Miss Tanner was lying down and said she had an awful headache. I asked if she had many head-aches. I'd noticed that scar on her forehead. She stared at me the funny way she did and said, yes, it seemed to her she'd had headaches forever. So I said I guessed she'd been in an accident once. She said, slow and hesitating like: 'Yes, a bad accident a long time ago.' Then she said: 'I never could re-member much about it' and changed the subject. That was the only time she said even that much."

"But you do know whether she had any visitors that came to see her often?"

Mrs. Sawyer shrugged. "Some roomers do have friends I get to recognize, Inspector. Not Miss Tanner. I've seen her come home late enough that

I thought she'd eaten dinner out, or seen her go out around seven, the time most people go to movies in the neighborhood."

"We can check on that, Costello. I suppose you don't know, Mrs. Sawyer, what time Miss Tanner would come home when she'd been out in the evening?"

"No. I'm dead beat by ten o'clock. But this last week my oldest roomer had the flu," Mrs. Sawyer said. "I'm fond of her so I did for her while she was sick. Her room's right across from Miss Tanner's. Well, this is Friday, ain't it? Then it was Monday that Miss Tanner had her first visitor."

"You came home on Monday night, didn't you, Chris?" Prevost said.

"Yes, but I didn't reach home until after eight. The train was late. I presume the others had dinner at the usual hour; six-thirty. I . . ."

"Six-thirty?" Mrs. Sawyer echoed. "No it was about five when I took some broth to my sick roomer. And there was someone in Miss Tanner's room. I could hear her voice and a man's voice but not a word they said. I didn't approve but I've given up trying to make the roomers leave their doors open when members of the opposite sex visit them.

"I gave my sick lady her supper and when I left her, in half an hour or so, I didn't hear anyone talking any more in Miss Tanner's room. Well, that was Monday. Tuesday night about seven—"

"You're sure of the time?" Prevost said.

"Yes, because my sick lady was real bad that day and wouldn't eat earlier. When I'd had my own supper, I went upstairs again with the soup. That was right around seven. And when I heard voices in Miss Tanner's room. I thought: 'What, again?'"

"There was a man with her again?"

"Yes, Inspector. The same man, I supposed at first, but now I'm not so sure. Whoever was there Monday had a low voice, same as she did, though deep enough that you guessed it was a man. Except for one time Tuesday this man didn't talk so I could make out words, but afterwards I realized his voice was higher; a man's voice but not a deep one. And he'd brought a woman with him."

"You mean two people visited your Miss Tanner on Tuesday evening?" Prevost said.

"Yes. My sick lady still wouldn't eat so I wasn't with her but a few minutes. When I come out of her room again, all of a sudden this woman spoke up loud and clear. Cursed a blue streak, she did and her voice wasn't ladylike at all. Then the man raised his voice, too, and says, 'That won't get you anywhere, sister. I've told you how it is and that's how it's going to be.'"

Prevost and Michael looked at each other. "Harry Hunt?" Prevost said. "He had a high-pitched voice."

"Harry to the life," Michael agreed. "Did the woman with the unladylike voice and command of language speak again, Mrs. Sawyer?"

"She swore some more. Then she said, 'All right, at least you did warn me. I'll say that for you.' I admit I stuck around a few minutes. I wasn't going to have anyone shouting like that and disturbing sick people. But the man lowered his voice then, and then I heard Miss Tanner murmuring, low-like. The other woman kept still so I guessed it was all right and I went on downstairs."

Prevost sighed. "And you didn't try to get a look at Miss Tanner's visitors when they left?"

"I don't say I wouldn't have tried but my own phone was ringing when I got back to my rooms and it was a friend of mine that talks forever. So I never had a chance to try to see Miss Tanner's company."

"Mrs. Sawyer, do you know whether or not Miss Tanner left the house later that night?" Chris said.

"Yes, she did. I met her in the hall at twenty-five of nine. Ordinarily I wouldn't remember, but my sick roomer should've had some medicine at eight-thirty and I was late getting up to her and had it on my mind. Miss Tanner said she had a

headache and was going out for a little walk. She
went on and I don't know what time she got back."

"Oh. Then she couldn't have . . ."

"No, Chris, she couldn't have killed Harry,"
Prevost said. "He was killed at eight-forty. Go on,
Mrs. Sawyer."

"Nothing out of the way happened Wednesday
night. Miss Tanner come home the usual time and
so far's I know, didn't go out again. I saw her come
home yesterday afternoon, too. I didn't see her
again. Last night I took for granted she was home.
But this morning when I took clean sheets in, she
hadn't slept in her bed. When I saw her picture in
the papers, I guessed I'd better call you."

"Were there ever any telephone calls for Miss
Tanner? Did she use your telephone often?"

"I've got a phone in the hall for the roomers to
use. It's to the back and my rooms are in front.
I never saw Miss Tanner at the phone. When it
rings, I answer it after a while if no one else does.
Mostly the roomers know about what time someone's going to call and try to answer it themselves.
But no one ever called and asked for Miss Tanner
that I know of."

"Miss Tanner didn't make friends with any of
your other roomers?" Prevost asked.

"No. Maybe those on the second floor where
she was could tell you something about her but

I doubt it. Till the war was over, lots of them worked nights. My sick lady that was right opposite Miss Tanner hardly ever saw her for more than to say 'hello,' to her."

"I see." Prevost turned to Costello. "You'd better talk to the other roomers but first check on Rose Tanner at the Just-Rite Laundry. And try to scare up a taxi and see Mrs. Sawyer home."

"Pine near Fillmore," Chris said reflectively, when Costello had escorted Mrs. Sawyer from the office. "That's only about twelve blocks from the old homestead."

"It was very stupid of me not to have thought that Rose Tanner would be living in some fairly respectable, if down-at-the-heels locality—for the last seven months," Michael said.

Prevost looked at him sharply. "Why 'for the last seven months?' I told you last night that I intended that Barnett, who's an old-timer on the Vice Squad, should help Costello comb the—uh—slightly disreputable districts for a woman who could be Rowena. But when she was killed last night, I needed Costello for other jobs this morning. Barnett started on the assignment alone and he hasn't reported progress yet."

"I can't," Chris said abruptly, "imagine Rowena working in a laundry, living in a second-rate rooming-house and before that, God knows where."

"God knows where, and so far he hasn't taken Barnett into his confidence," Michael said.

Prevost grinned but Michael went on, "Chris, have you seriously considered what Zinnia told us?"

Prevost looked at him thoughtfully.

VI

Michael managed to appear comfortable in a most uncomfortable chair and, except for the uniform, which became him, was as Prevost had always known him—swarthy, black-haired with a blunt nose and chin, features that made him the ideal poker player. Even his eyes, which were a vivid and startling blue and his mouth, arrogant, expressive but self-controlled, seldom gave him away. They did not, now.

But Prevost, like others who knew him well, listened to Michael's voice without looking at his face. And he recognized the tone as one reserved for children; the aged; dogs and cats; and those for whose peace of mind Michael felt, however reluctant he was to do so, he must assume responsibility.

"Of course I've given some thought to what Zinnia told us," Chris said irritably. "No doubt it is helpful to know that six years ago she told Hunt what we know now. But it complicates matters."

"In what way?" Michael said.

"Oh, it wasn't too difficult, considering that scar on her head, to believe Rowena suffered some sort of accident on her way to the Lymans' house. I know that Mrs. Lyman said she had not asked Rowena to play cards with them that night. But she could have forgotten that she had. Father said that she had oatmeal mush where her brains should be."

"So," Michael said, "Rowena went off to play cards with the Lymans, wearing her newest ensemble, even to the hat, which she'd remove as soon as she arrived? However, you mean that you can't fit Zinnia's testimony regarding your father's gun and Rowena's actions at the dining room sideboard into the theory that she was, we will say, struck by a speeding car or hit over the head by some undesirable character? And the disappearance of Rowena's diary needs to be explained. Your Aunt Sophia was able to look through Rowena's bureau drawers at her leisure. I can easily imagine her, or your father, or even some other member of the family circle deciding that Rowena's diary need not be public property and simply suppressing it—permanently. However—"

"However," Prevost broke in, "Harry said that there was a bona fide burglary even if it wasn't a professional job. The term burglary involves illegal entry; it's housebreaking at night. Harry knew that as well as I do."

"That's the drawback to settling on the simplest explanation of the diary's disappearance," Michael said. "Zinnia told Harry that there was a diary. She also said that Rowena wrote in it frequently during the last several months before she disappeared. Chris told Valerie that Rowena didn't begin to gain weight until six months or so before she vanished. Zinnia told us that she did diet at the table but gorged herself privately and said she 'couldn't seem to help it.'"

"You agree with my wife's bright idea that Rowena kept gaining weight *because* she was unhappy?" Prevost said, "Well, so do I. And Zinnia gave evidence that backs up that theory."

"And the fact that Rowena was gaining weight steadily before she disappeared is important now."

Prevost looked at Michael with inquiring eyebrows but Chris brushed the remark aside. "I'll concede that Rowena was unhappy and tried to ease her unhappiness by spilling it onto the pages of a diary and by overeating. And apparently her relations with Bob and Joel weren't important to her. She told Zinnia she'd never marry either of them. Though I would have thought, since I believed her feelings were not acute, that she'd rather be married than not be married."

"I would have believed she would have, all other things being equal," Michael said.

"'All other things being equal,'" Chris repeated testily. "That's a slipshod phrase made up of
weasel words."

Michael grinned. "I agree with you. Well, Rowena
told her father, when he said that she couldn't
keep Joel and Bob dangling forever, that she had
come to a decision. She didn't tell him what it was.
Then she went away, carrying the outsized black
purse with her carefully matched blue ensemble;
a purse into which we will presume she'd smug-
gled your father's service automatic. No, Chris.
If you don't mind, let's forget the gun for a few
minutes. I went down to Gisele's yesterday morning. I talked to Fanchon Weis about Rowena. She's
always remembered Rowena because she bought
the dress she was wearing when she disappeared
only a few days before that date. Fanchon got the
impression that Rowena had seen one of our dresses
on a friend and wanted something along the same
lines. But she did not mention the friend's name.
Nick, you know St. George's deposition nearly by
heart, you told us once—"

"Yes. I guess I know what you want. St. George
said that when he commented on Rowena's outfit, she said she'd wanted something rather special
that spring and had thought her dress was slenderizing when she'd seen it on someone else who was
too plump. Is that it?"

"Yes. File that away for future reference. I'll have to tell you a few trade secrets," Michael went on. "We've always kept records, even of cash sales, with a description of the garment purchased and the name of the purchaser. In that way we knew where we were with all customers. It's always paid me to cater to a certain class of women who dress well, but conservatively. They will pay for line and material. Though they only buy one suit and one dress every year, they will pay through the nose to get precisely what they want."

"You might be speaking of Rowena," Chris said.

"She was younger than the majority of that type of customer is. Well, in the early fall of 1938, I designed a dress with that type of customer in mind. It was made up in a small, blue-and-white print. There were only five of those dresses; sizes 34 to 42. They were so well liked that in February of 1939 we turned out five more. It was one of that second lot, size 38, that Rowena bought in February and, according to your aunt and father, was wearing when she disappeared. But," Michael finished casually, "it was the size 38 of the first lot of those prints which were all sold in the fall of 1938, that Rowena was wearing last night."

"Why, damn your soul!" Prevost cried. "You knew that last night! Or did you? I saw you testing the material between your thumb and forefinger."

"Yes. The silk in the first lot of dresses was of slightly better quality than we could get for the second batch. Also, though both prints were made up of small white bowknots on a blue ground, the bowknots in the dress we know Rowena bought were slightly smaller than those in the first prints. Oh yes," Michael added as Chris made a slight, dissenting movement, "I'm quite sure of that, even after all these years. Besides, I changed the cut of the yoke slightly when we decided to make a second lot of those dresses. The yoke on the dress we know Rowena bought was wider than the yoke of the dress she was wearing last night. And there was a slight difference in the cuts of the sleeves of the two dresses in question."

"How can you be certain—" Chris began unwisely.

"*Chiccherichi!*" Michael said, a sound like the derisive crow of a rooster. "You will concede that it is my business to know and remember such details."

"I'll accept you as an expert witness," Prevost said hastily. "But now tell us—"

The telephone rang. "Don't you go away, Michael," he said as he picked it up. "Hello . . . Oh, Barnett. Did you . . . Then why haven't you brought her to . . . Oh. Well, maybe you're right, at that. Four-thirty isn't far off but you keep an eye on her until then. And then bring her here whether she wants to come or not. . . . O.K. Be seeing you. . . ." He hung up.

"Barnett finally landed at the Vine Hotel on Turk," Prevost explained. "The place is a dump though it's never been raided. The manager-clerk says that for six months, until this February, they had a woman there who called herself Rose Tanner and looked like our pictures of Rowena, taken last night. Barnett didn't take this guy down to the morgue because he insisted he'd never spoken a dozen words to her.

"And also because he said his Rose Tanner knew no one in the hotel except a waitress who calls herself Billye La Grayce. Her room was across from Tanner's. They were the only two on the floor who weren't transients. Barnett questioned what guests he found in and got nowhere; then went off to this greasy spoon where La Grayce slings hash, on Kearney. She doesn't get off until four-thirty and they're shorthanded. She didn't want to leave until her relief showed up. Barnett said she was good-natured but capable of raising an ungodly row if he tried to bring her down here right now, by force. You heard what I told him. Now, Michael—"

"Speaking of hotels, may I use your telephone?" Michael dialed a number, said: "Valerie? I've had a bright thought regarding something that's been bothering me. I started to ask you about it last night and then Marcia sidetracked me. When Harry was talking to you about . . ."

He paused, smiled provokingly at Chris and Prevost and dropped into Spanish. Chris thought he had acquired a passable knowledge of that language during a long vacation in Mexico but Michael's liquid Castilian with its soft "c"s was too much for him. He and Prevost exchanged glances of deep mutual sympathy.

Chris murmured, "Can she understand him?"

"Valerie? She's shy about speaking Spanish but she must have had to learn to understand him, in self defense. . . ." He stopped and listened as Michael began speaking English.

"Why shouldn't you forget one small detail when you remembered so much else?" Michael said. "And it may not be important. Harry might have been talking at random just then and, even if he wasn't, my guess as to what he had in mind may not be correct. . . . Yes, I'll try to be home for dinner."

"Something important?" Prevost inquired with an exaggerated air of courtesy.

"Perhaps. Is there no resident manager in the apartment house where Harry set up his offices?"

"No. A real estate firm handles everything."

"But surely there is a janitor?"

"Surely?" Prevost smiled sardonically. "Major Dundas, one of these days I'll tell you about wartime San Francisco. For three years, I washed our windows in my spare time. . . . But they had a janitor once. His name is Albert Sheely and he's more or less of a wino. He acted as janitor and occupied a very crummy basement apartment. He still does because they couldn't evict him. But he stopped janitoring and got a job in the shipyards. However, when Harry rented the top apartment, Sheely agreed to clean Harry's offices during his spare time, in the evenings."

"In the evenings," Michael repeated. "Yes. Nick, may I take a tour of Harry's offices?"

Inspector Prevost studied Major Dundas for several minutes while Chris tried to analyze the Inspector's expression. It occurred to him that Prevost looked, briefly, as long-enduring as only a Slav can look, and then that his expression was that of one confronting an infant prodigy who is irritating but cannot be lightly brushed aside.

He said mildly, "Why, Michael?"

"Shall we say, because I doubt that from February to July Harry was quite such a good boy as you have supposed he was?"

Prevost linked his fingers loosely together, rested his chin on them and stared at his desk.

Suddenly a sound escaped him that was half grunt, half snort, at once rueful and amused.

"Could be," he said. "Go ahead. I won't go with you; I've too much paper work to do. Here—" He took a key from a desk drawer and gave it to Michael. "This will open Harry's offices. His secretary worked there this morning but she won't be there now. Al Sheely's already been laid off so he may be around. Don't forget to come back. Are you taking Chris with you?"

"If he will come, he'll be useful as a front."

"O.K. Be careful," Nicholas Prevost said with what seemed to Chris astonishing calm, "and don't use my name."

VII

The apartment house was gray, long-faced, doleful. Half the ground floor was occupied by a timorous delicatessen whose stock in trade consisted of pallid pies, anemic cakes and rolls, unhealthy-looking potato salad, and pale beans slightly tinctured with pinkish tomato sauce. Henry Hunt had been permitted to put up a small sign that urged the passerby to "LET HENRY HUNT FOR YOU."

The house was one that had needed doing-over before Pearl Harbor. Its hall walls and light fixtures would have interested a geologist. On them were represented five distinct ages of grime:

prewar, early war, just plain war, medium late war, and "pretty soon we'll have to do something about this."

However, the top front apartment was light and airy and its wallpapers and paint had been recently applied. A small, square hall opened into a square room intended as a living room but used by Hunt as a reception room.

There was one impressive desk here; telephones; numerous filing cabinets; several large, relaxing chairs. In an adjoining room were two smaller desks, several small filing cabinets, more telephones.

"This," Michael said, "was where Harry's operatives hung out. He evidently still has useful connections, to get these telephones installed in wartime. Harry interviewed clients if his receptionist couldn't handle them. This room was originally meant to be a dining room, with wall bed added."

"There's a wall bed in the front room," Chris remarked, merely to say something, because he was exasperated with Major Dundas but did not want to risk being accused of sulking.

"Yes. Plenty of beds if one wanted them. And a bathroom, I suppose, and a kitchen."

Michael stalked quickly through these rooms, then paused to consider a fifth room, a small one off the main hall, detached from the rest of the apartment except for a door into the bathroom. It was meagerly furnished with an ancient desk, a decrepit safe and a very wide, old couch.

"Harry's private office," Michael said. "Let's go down to the basement and talk to Al Sheely."

Before the war and Italy, Chris would not have believed that basement apartments—three tiny rooms whose windows had not been raised for years; incredible filth in what must be called both living and bedroom; cockroaches, unwashed dishes in a greasy sink, odorous garbage in the kitchen—existed. There was a dirty glass on the drainboard with a few inches of sherry in it, an eighth of a bottle of an obscure brand of sherry beside it. And no one, though the front door was unlocked, in the apartment.

Michael lifted the wine bottle absently. His slim, strong brown fingers tightened unconsciously about the bottle neck. "I don't like this," he said. "Let's go."

They climbed the dirty steps from which paint was peeling in obscene brown flakes, to the first floor. Here it was quiet, except that the smell of pork and cauliflower, dust in ragged carpets, stale cigarette smoke and onions, struck like a harsh noise on one's senses.

"No resident manager," Michael muttered. "Nick implied, if he did not say, that people here keep themselves to themselves. His men have certainly interviewed all the tenants."

Chris had been peering down the front hall. "There's a boy of about eleven or twelve sitting on the front steps."

"A boy? We're in luck. Ask him if he knows Albert Sheely. Try to find out where Sheely might be at this time of the day."

The boy was freckled, alert and completely skeptical. Chris was in civilian garments and had not thought to wear his honorable discharge insignia. The boy eyed him warily.

"Yeah, I know Al, but what's it to you?"

"See here, my lad," Chris began stiffly.

Michael sighed and turned to face the boy. "Don't be difficult," he said. "We want your help. When did you last see this man Sheely?"

The boy's war-wise eyes swallowed the gold oakleaves, the campaign ribbons and decorations in one gulp. He said respectfully:

"Al's a pal of mine but Mom and Dad don't approve 'cause Al hits the bottle. Not that I ever would. I'm going to be a flyer in the next war."

"'The next—' *No permita Dios!*" Michael said with an involuntary passion that surprised Chris though his own reaction to the boy's blithe words was exactly that of Major Dundas.

"But Mom and Dad work the swing-shift," the boy said uncomplainingly. "Al worked from eight to four till they laid him off. So we eat together a lot. And he's a wiz at building model airplanes. We're working on one now. That's why I've been waiting around for him to come home."

"Come home from where?" Michael asked him.

The boy frowned. "Since he was laid off, I don't know where he goes in the afternoons. He always comes home by night because he cleans the detective's offices. Only Mr. Hunt has been killed, so—"

"Yes, I know. And would you know at about what time Sheely usually cleaned Hunt's offices?"

"Al had all night to do his work in so most of the time he did it pretty late. Sometimes he'd work on airplanes with me till I was supposed, to go to bed, at nine, though he hadn't started his cleaning. He hadda habit of putting things off, I guess. But he's probably on a binge right now."

"Why do you say that?"

"Well, I wanted to see Al so I went down to his place early, about seven-thirty, after I'd got my breakfast. He never locks the door, so I went in. He never makes his bed so I can't tell by the looks of it if he slept in it. Only he hasn't been getting up early since he was laid off; and he hadn't made any coffee, either. But I can't think where he could've been because the beer-parlors don't open that early."

"And neither can I."

The boy's freckles darkened apprehensively. Michael smiled and put his hand in his pocket.

"However, it doesn't matter," he said convincingly. "We are friends of Mr. Hunt's and we must wait here until the police arrive for another check-up. That's dry work. Is there anyone who would sell you beer, even if you are a minor?"

"Oh, sure. I get it for Mom and Dad all the time. I'll have to go three blocks, Major, but I'll be back before you know it. . . ."

"But Michael, you don't like beer," Chris said.

"No. I wanted to get the boy out of the house."

Already Michael was running up the stairs toward the third floor. Following him, Chris smiled in gentle amusement. Michael always insisted that he was "hopelessly unathletic" but he was nowhere near panting as he said, "Sheely's own quarters are unsightly, to put it charitably. If he was going to talk to a—to someone who professed to be sensitive to surroundings and odors . . . Well, Sheely certainly had a key to Hunt's offices."

By the time Chris had limped up the last flight of stairs and into Hunt's reception room, Michael was tugging at the knob of what pretended to be

a wide door and was actually the front for a wall
bed. The bed came out reluctantly, creakingly;
then suddenly fell to the floor with a crash.

Chris had supposed that for the rest of his life
he and his stomach would be quite impervious to
dead men. He had seen so many, on beaches and
hills and roads; mostly young men, too many of
whom he had known. But this was different.

This man was old, slight and unkempt. His sort
slumped on benches in parks and asked you for
"a dime to get a cup of coffee." It was not fitting
that he should be violently done to death. He did
not belong on the dusty mattress of an unused
wall bed with a knife handle between his shoulder
blades.

VIII

Barnett was a devoted husband, a loving father to
six children, a pillar of the church. A moral man
was Barnett, perhaps because he had served twenty
years on the Vice Squad. Ladies of easy virtue were
apt to call him "Pops," and when he invited them
to come quietly, more often than not, they did.

But by five o'clock Barnett was beginning to
look more harassed than usual. He made a second
trip to Prevost's office and entered as the Inspector was speaking to Chris and Michael.

". . . only had time to skim the surface so far but I'm not hopeful that we'll know any more by tomorrow. Sheely wasn't in his own place at seven-thirty, according to the boy you talked to. He must already have gone up to Harry's place. Nobody in any of the other five apartments saw him go up but he had a key to the back door and could have used the back stairs.

"Harry's secretary told me, when I called her that she got to the office a little after nine and worked until one. Saw no signs of a struggle and had no reason to investigate the wall bed. No one else in the house saw a stranger enter it or leave it before nine though some of them saw the secretary arrive. What is it, Barnett?"

"That dame I've got waiting to see you is getting pretty mad, Nick."

"Oh, let her . . . No, since I know you're given to understatement, you'd better bring her in," Prevost decided. He turned back to Chris and Michael.

"The doctor says Sheely was killed between five and eight this morning. He favors the in-between hour of six-thirty. There are no fingerprints; we don't know if anyone got in touch with Sheely before coming to see him. He had no phone, and if he got a letter, it's not on him or in his place. If he telephoned anyone, it was probably at some bar. We can work on that angle but we might as well see La Grayce."

Miss La Grayce was large, smooth, violently blonde with a flat pink-and-white face that normally would be blandly cheerful. Now she was flushed and angry. Prevost promptly rose, placed a chair, was solicitous for her comfort and deliberately so charming that Miss La Grayce capitulated.

"It don't matter: I haven't anything to do till six-thirty. But I don't like to be shoved around. And 'Pops' here took me to look at a dame on a marble slab that turns out to be Rose Tanner and I could do with a snort. It was kind of upsetting even if I didn't know her very well."

"How long did you know her?" Prevost asked.

"She was at the Vine about six months. The Vine is a dump," Miss La Grayce admitted cheerfully. "But the guy that runs it is a good egg and I've been there five years. Mostly people come and go. Rose came about August of last year and left this February. Our rooms was opposite so I'd speak to her and finally we visited back and forth a little."

"At night? That is, did she have a job?"

"She didn't seem to stick to any job. She worked in a dime store a while; she quit and waited tables and quit that. She seemed restless and like she had a grudge against the world, if you get me?"

"I'm afraid I don't, exactly," Prevost said.

Miss La Grayce frowned, pulled up her stockings and adjusted her round garters.

"Well, she said she got that scar in a bad auto accident. She said she guessed she was lucky to be alive; she'd rather be alive than dead; but she used to think she'd be somebody in the world before she was sick a long time, got that scar and got fat.

"I don't know just what she meant. She wasn't a talker but most of us girls can go just so long without woman talk. When we settle down to a good gab we usually say more than we intend to, especially over a bottle of—I mean, a cup of tea." Miss La Grayce made this correction with an unabashed grin.

"Then Miss Tanner wasn't a teetotaler?"

"Who're you kidding, Inspector? Rose could lap it up with the best of 'em. She had a natural head for liquor so she never got tight enough that she talked much; never told me where she was born or if she had folks living or anything like that."

"Did you think she'd been born here or lived here for some time?" Michael asked.

Miss La Grayce eyed him thoughtfully. "I'd like to know what you've got to do with this, Major, with all your ribbons and so on, but I won't ask. No. Rose said 'Frisco' too often and she was surprised, when she first came to the Vine, that it's almost as cold here in August as it is in winter. And that was funny, come to think of it."

"Yes?" Prevost said encouragingly.

"When Rose said good-bye in February, she kept looking through me like I wasn't there. And seeming not to get what I said right away. When I asked her if she didn't feel good, she said she'd been having bad headaches lately and her memory wasn't so hot; that she'd forget people and places she'd ought to know. Yeah, and then she said she didn't think the Vine was the kind of place she ought to live in. And she hoped that she hadn't acted queer. . . ."

"Had she, until then?"

"No. I'd've said she knew what the score was all the time and could look out for herself. There was never anything queer about Rose till she said good-bye. She didn't tell me where she was going."

"What sort of perfume did she wear, if any?"

"'Evening in Paris,' when she wore any."

"Nothing like violet, lavender or carnation?" Prevost said. "A flower fragrance, that is?"

Miss La Grayce shook her head. "I never smelled any on her. That's stuffs old-fashioned. She had a bottle of 'Evening in Paris' on her dresser but she didn't use much of it. She didn't have many clothes and nothing she paid more than ten-ninety-five for. She had a figure like a sack of beans, whatever

VIRGINIA RATH

she wore." Miss La Grayce glanced complacently downward at her own voluptuous curves.

"Did she have a raincoat?"

"One of these transparent things that looks like cellophane. I remember that: we had plenty of rain in December and January."

"And she carried an old silk umbrella?" Prevost suggested.

"No. Who has a silk bumbershoot now? Times have changed since they moved Cousin Willie to dig a sewer. Rose didn't have any umbrella; her raincoat had one of these hoods. I'm not too proud to do a little chambermaiding when the manager is short of help. I never tell anyone I ever pinch-hit for a chambermaid. Rose didn't know. But if you want to know what she had in her closet and so on . . ."

"We do. You've said she had no umbrella and only the raincoat you've described, not an English import of a greenish-brownish material?"

"One of them ugly things that never wears out? No. She had a brown sport coat, brown shoes to match, and a brown purse strictly from oilcloth. I looked in her suitcase."

"What sort of suitcase?"

"It was old but it'd cost plenty once; one of these kind out of leather that has little bumps on it. Only expensive thing she owned. She had some cheap rayon dresses: two browns, a green and a red."

"No blue-and-white print; white bowknots on a blue ground?" Michael said.

"No. Blue don't go with a brown coat good. She didn't have no jewl'ry." Miss La Grayce dislodged a flake of dandruff from her blonde wave and regarded her talon-like fingernail pensively. "Funny; she had a nice low voice and talked refined—unless she was mad. One night a drunk bumped into her in the hall and almost knocked her down. You should've heard her cuss him out! I wouldn't've known her voice, she went so high and shrill. Usually she talked nice but like an actress, not like it came really natural to her. So I wondered if maybe she'd been an actress once."

"She had no other friends at the hotel?" Prevost said.

"No. Even I and her didn't visit much. I'm out a lot. I know she went out nights, too, but I never saw her go out or come in with anyone."

"Well, thank you, Miss La Grayce. You've helped us a great deal."

"It's been a pleasure, Inspector. I like to play ball with the cops. Though," Miss La Grayce added candidly, "I don't say I'd have come to you if you hadn't come for me. Maybe I might, though, seeing's it's as serious as murder. Be seeing you. Going my way, Pops?"

Prevost grinned briefly as Barnett, with a long-suffering look, escorted Miss La Grayce from the room, and then seized the telephone on its third ring.

"Prevost speaking. . . . Oh, Costello. Well, tell me about it."

He listened for some time to what Costello had to say; then told him, "That's fine; keep it up," and turned to Michael. "Costello talked to the manager of the Just-Rite Laundry. Rose Tanner went to work for them on February fourteenth. She told him when she made out the usual papers that she was a foundling; didn't know who her parents were. That made no difference to him but he told Costello he 'felt there was something queer about her.' In just the same way that Mrs. Sawyer felt she was queer. She 'looked through him,' seemed to forget who he was or where she was. But she did her work well though none of her fellow workers got to know her. They felt she was 'stuck-up,' but agreed with the manager regarding her other peculiarities. Meanwhile, Costello will—"

Chris broke in. "She didn't—Miss La Grayce— say how Rose Tanner managed to live when she wasn't working at some job. She probably didn't know."

"I wouldn't worry about that," Michael said. "Wherever Rose Tanner lived or whatever she did before she took a room at Mrs. Sawyer's, I think you may say that all the brothers were valiant and all the sisters virtuous. Because one will get you fifty that the woman who was killed at your front door last night was *not* Rowena."

IX

Prevost sat back in his chair, whistling; a soft, contented sound.

Chris said, "You aren't surprised, are you, Inspector? Even before we went off to try to see Al Sheely, you'd begun to guess what Michael had in mind?"

"Well," Prevost said, "consider some things he's kept harping on, and consider all the evidence that won't fit in with the theory that your sister came to grief quite by accident after she left your house. I mean that whatever happened to her didn't involve premeditation or plans by anyone— even Rowena.

"There's Zinnia's evidence which we have already discussed. And contributing evidence that Rowena was not at all happy. Cause of unhappiness not known but presumably she stated it at length in her diary. The diary never turned up. Harry Hunt knew that; Harry said there'd been a bona fide burglary, not a professional job. Of course he ran true to form and confused the issue by saying that something had been taken only in one instance, it couldn't be called really stealing. Having in mind, we'll guess, your father's gun.

"So," Prevost continued, "Rowena went out on a rainy night, wearing a brand-new outfit, even a new spring hat, as Michael kept saying. That is, she was dressed to look her best. She did wear a raincoat but you take off a raincoat, wherever you go, without even asking anyone's permission. And even I know a woman doesn't take off her hat unless she's paying a very informal call."

"In which case she doesn't bother to wear a new hat on a rainy night when she doesn't expect to have the use of an umbrella," Michael remarked.

"Exactly. And though the rest of her outfit was blue, she carried a very large, old black purse. And, if we believe Zinnia, she carried your father's gun away in that purse."

"Yes, considering that Rowena took Father's gun with her and yet there was a gun in the sideboard the next morning, though Rowena had vanished, you must argue that whatever happened to her involved a gun," Chris smiled deprecatingly. "This matter of withholding evidence must be contagious."

"You've been holding out on us?" Prevost said resignedly.

"Not for long. When we were waiting for you after we found Albert Sheely's body, Michael remarked, 'The knife looks like any ordinary butcher knife. But it wasn't necessary to use a gun on Sheely.'"

"Yes, I did say that," Michael agreed.

"And then—I don't know why it was then and not before—I remembered something. I'll tell you what it was when Michael has told me if it wasn't Hal Baird's mother who bought a dress that was so nearly the same as the one Rowena was wearing when she disappeared." Michael nodded.

Prevost said, "You're smart, Chris. I'd thought it was the Reverend Walter Denning's wife since Michael admitted she was an occasional customer of his."

"No. It would have been a waste of time for Rowena to try to ape Mrs. Denning. She had a streamlined figure. But Hal always seemed sincerely to admire his mother and her taste."

"Let me guess what you have to tell us," Michael said. "You are going to say that you have remembered that Harold Baird's father, who was one of your father's lieutenants in the war to end all wars, also brought home his side-arms as a souvenir."

"Yes. Hal had offices in his home. I used to consult him about minor ailments. Patients weren't too plentiful in those days and one night he'd had time to clean out his desk. There was a Colt .45 on it and I said, 'Did your father bring that back as a souvenir?'

"Hal laughed and said: 'What officer didn't?' and put the gun back in his desk. I don't know why I should remember that that gun had a little gouge on the butt, roughly the shape of an arrow—"

Prevost whisked open the desk drawer and produced a Colt .45.

"I brought this with me last night, not wanting to leave any lethal weapon in your household. And here is your arrow-shaped nick. I know that a good lawyer could make mincemeat of your story but it'll do me. I'm sure this gun belonged to Dr. Baird's father. We will try to find out. It's a pity you didn't examine it the morning Rowena disappeared."

"But I didn't. I saw it lying there with the rest of the contents of the sideboard that the police were examining. This looked like Father's gun; his gun should have been in the sideboard, so . . ." Chris shrugged. "I wonder who used Father's gun the night before?"

"It would be a waste of time to indulge to any great extent in pure speculation," Michael said. "But you have given us a few facts. Baird announced his engagement to another girl just before Rowena disappeared. You have said Baird was a charming fellow; that he and Rowena naturally saw a great deal of each other.

"You have said she was secretive and confided in no one. You thought she was the type who would prefer to be married to anyone fairly eligible than to remain a spinster, yet she refused to marry Bob or Joel. And she went out that night dressed in her best despite the weather. She carried a gun with her and you have said that Rowena sometimes made threats when she wanted her own way and sometimes carried out those threats; that she was unbelievably stubborn and one couldn't reason with her."

"Yes," Chris said wearily. "She might have threatened to kill Hal or herself. I know: we are not to theorize. But it is a fact that Hal and his mother may have encouraged Rowena, to coin a phrase. Then the other girl, with money of her own where Rowena had only expectations, came along. She was an appealing little thing besides. And whatever happened, involving Father's gun, in—we presume—Hal's offices at his home, any sort of scandal would ruin him. He was just keeping his head above water then. His wife's money was a great help to him. And Hal's mother had pinched pennies to put him through university and medical school.

"Besides, Aunt Sophia once said that there was no commandment Mrs. Baird wouldn't break if by so doing she could further Hal's interests. She would have given Hal any help he needed and kept silent forever. Though I cannot imagine how those two managed to dispose of—of a body—"

"Don't try," Prevost advised. "If they did, they played in luck. The first bit of luck would have been that they had no servants then, to see or hear anything. And though we don't advertise cases where we're sure murder was done but can't prove it because we can't turn up a body, we have a little list. Forget about what may have happened to Rowena except as it's related to Rose Tanner and a conspiracy to pass her off as Rowena."

"Thank God for La Grayce and good, competent routine police-work," Michael said. "La Grayce is shrewd as they come and after listening to her it was evident that Rose Tanner wasn't Rowena. Rose was a good, two-fisted drinker and I'd guess Rowena was not, because Daphne remarked 'I'm the only *one* of us who *could*—' drink, she meant."

"Rowena seldom finished even a glass of sherry," Chris said. "Liquor made her ill."

"Very well. Rose didn't use jasmine perfume before she left the Vine Hotel. She didn't have Rowena's purse, dress and raincoat or Sophia's umbrella in her possession then. Though her voice and diction were usually above criticism, La Grayce felt that Rose spoke like an actress. When she lost her temper her voice was shrill and high and her language anything but ladylike. And in that connection—"

"Yes," Prevost said, grinning, "In that connection, there were *not* three people in Rose's room Tuesday evening. What Mrs. Sawyer heard were Rose and Harry talking, until Rose lost her temper and spoke in a voice and language Mrs. Sawyer didn't recognize. Then Rose got control of herself and went back to her usual low tones."

"Rowena might have managed the language but her voice was naturally so low that it never could have been high and shrill," Chris added.

"Good," Michael said. "Then La Grayce thought Rose hadn't been born in San Francisco. She never acted like a person who suffered lapses of memory until she said goodbye. And in February Rose moved to Mrs. Sawyer's respectable establishment, got a job and stuck to it and set about establishing a background that would be entirely different than hers had been until then. She even discarded her old suitcase and bought a new one; the old suitcase being the only thing she'd had in her possession for any length of time."

"Establishing that background, to help prove she could be Rowena if anyone investigated, would be the first step in the conspiracy," Prevost said. "And nothing happened until after she'd moved to Mrs. Sawyer's place."

"No manifestations occurred until a woman answering Rose's description acquired some jasmine perfume. Two bottles, one of which was found on her dresser at Mrs. Sawyer's. What became of the second bottle?"

"She'd used one whole bottle," Chris said.

"Do you think so?" Michael said politely. "Perhaps. But one can't believe that it is merely coincidence that so many things happened shortly before February and in February. Mark Vibert came home for good just before Christmas. Harold Baird killed himself just after Christmas. Mrs. Baird died in February; Rose Tanner took a job in the Just-Rite Laundry and moved from the Vine Hotel; Harry Hunt returned to the city without his family; and you were reported missing, Chris."

"Is that last important?"

Michael ignored the question. "Did you make a will?"

"No. I made Anice the beneficiary of my insurance but I didn't feel she had the right to share in Father's estate unless we were married. If I'd really died in February . . . Well, Daphne is my next of kin. She would have profited considerably and so would a real or fake Rowena if she'd turned up before the estate was settled and I'd been dead."

"Yes," Michael said smoothly, "if you had died in February, there would have been more money involved."

"Yes," Chris agreed absently. "A minute ago you came back to the Bairds. . . . You still must explain why Rose Tanner was wearing a dress that Mrs. Baird once bought instead of the one Rowena wore when she was last seen."

"I've said I designed a shroud for Rowena," Michael remarked. "Before she left the Vine Hotel, Rose didn't have the dress, purse and so on; very valuable stage-properties."

Prevost snapped his fingers, "'Stage properties!' That's what's bothered me all along. The business always had struck me as stagey without my realizing it. But that's a thought in passing. What Michael means is that what remains of Rowena's dress is probably wherever Rowena is. Sorry to put it so bluntly, Chris. Her pearls never turned up, either, though as Michael remarked, pearls don't wear out.

"But Rowena would lay aside her coat, purse and umbrella when she got wherever she was going. Since those things have turned up, we have to suppose someone's had them all these years. And if we are going to argue, on the evidence of the two service automatics, that the Bairds knew what happened to Rowena, who but the Bairds could have had her belongings? And Baird died in December and his mother in February. So—"

X

"I see," Chris said slowly. "I can't believe that Mrs. Baird would ever willingly have parted with such incriminating articles. And we can only speculate as to why they didn't destroy those things years ago. At least we do know that if Hal had Rowena's purse, he also had her front door key and could easily have entered the house to take away her diary and leave his father's gun there. As to Mrs. Baird's dress that seemed to most people the twin of Rowena's, I can suggest how it got into someone's hands.

"The ladies of St. Jude's have a big rummage sale every year in January. Mrs. Baird may have parted with some of her old things then. Yes, that's not above half bad because she would go into mourning for Hal. And she'd be clearing things out of their home, which she sold after he died. You can check with Aunt Sophia. She's been a guiding force in the Dorcas Society for years and I suppose they had their usual sale this year."

"We have been presuming that only the Bairds and Harry, who was paid for his silence, knew what happened to Rowena," Michael said. "If that is true and I believe it is, someone else had to learn the facts for an attempted imposture to be halfway practicable."

"I can't imagine that anyone would dare set such a conspiracy in motion so long as Hal and his mother were living," Chris said.

"And Baird died in December, his mother in February and the plot was set in motion. But—"

Prevost grinned. "You'd consider it a weakness to make a deathbed confession, Michael. You'd die with your sins on your soul rather than hand them over to someone else to worry about. But I've known some very tough customers to unburden themselves when they were dying. Since Baird killed himself, it was a matter for the police, so I know his mother was away on a visit and he sent the servants away. He could have had a visitor that night before he went to bed with an overdose of morphine. He could have written a letter. He did write one to his mother that we saw. So, which of you would he have been most likely to confide in, Chris?"

"Must it have been one of us?"

"Could anyone outside of your circle have enough knowledge about Rowena to plan this business—unless you want to except Mark Vibert?"

"No one, and you can't except Mark," Chris said. "When Rowena disappeared he stuck by us and we talked a great deal about her at that time. We'd keep recalling incidents of her girlhood and childhood; her personal peculiarities and so on. He heard us then and he married into the family afterward. By now he must be familiar with all of our family stories and we are given to anecdotes along those lines. Mark could have coached Rose Tanner and he could have helped himself to some of Rowena's letters to get samples of her handwriting. Her letters to me were left in my room while I was away; I wouldn't know if any of them are missing.

"As to which of us Hal might have confided in. He'd always known Aunt Sophia and seemed to like and admire her. He seemed rather to like elderly women in general. Then he and Bob and Joel were of an age, eligible bachelors who got around. They played tennis and golf together and met at dinners where there were extra men. Mark is younger but he and Hal belonged to the same frat. And during part of Hal's short married life, Mark and Daphne were married and saw a good deal of the young Bairds. Before that Daphne made rather a play for Hal for a time but I don't think they took it seriously. And so I don't at all know which one of them Hal might have confided in."

"Well, at least the scheme was put in motion," Michael said. "First by Tanner's beginning to establish a background. Then what we will call the 'manifestations' began, to prepare the family to accept the idea that Rowena, though slightly deranged, was alive. The manifestations didn't begin until Rose had acquired some jasmine perfume. And Nick said last night that he didn't think it reasonable that a room should reek of perfume merely because a woman wearing it had been in the room—"

"But Michael!" said Prevost who for an instant appeared not to have been listening to him, "it was in—" He stopped, looked at Michael warily before he finished with an effect of anti-climax, "It was a detail that bothered me. The perfume probably was scattered on the carpet in Rowena's room so that people couldn't help smelling it."

"Yes," Michael agreed. "The ghost haunted Rowena's old room until Anice left it. In May a note was left on Daphne's pillow, one that might have been written by a confused Rowena. A note written in ink so that analysis would show it had been written recently. That was an error; most notes of that sort are hastily scribbled in pencil."

"Rowena's thoughtful little notes always were," Chris said. "I should have thought of that. Then in June, Rose Tanner was in the house and encountered Aunt Sophia. Since they'd all planned to go to the theater that night and it was only at the last minute that Aunt Sophia decided to stay home, Rose must have believed that she would be coming to an empty house."

Michael nodded. "Undoubtedly, though, since whether she meant to or not, she left Old Dobbin in your aunt's hands, it turned out to be one of their most successful manifestations. The entire scheme, fantastic as it appears when you discuss it in cold blood, was rather well handled, I think. At least the family was beginning to believe that Rowena was alive. I was halfway ready to believe she was when I'd heard the story. As far as I know, the manifestations ceased in June. Because, I suppose, by that time Hunt had been approached."

"Yes, if we're going to agree that Harry knew the truth about Rowena, Rose Tanner couldn't be passed off as Rowena, unless Harry cooperated," Prevost said. "And I'd guess that for his own sake, he didn't want to expose this proposed scheme unless he had to. He'd have too much explaining to do. It would be enough for him if the scheme was given up because he wouldn't be a party to it. But then Chris came home and began asking questions."

"Now that I think it over, Hunt did not seem at all surprised that I wanted to talk to him," Chris said. "And he was solicitous and promised to help."

"Yes, Harry, who dearly loved his own skin, decided to spill the works to Chris," Michael said slowly. "Well, he was an odd mixture. I wonder— But the scheme might have succeeded."

Chris nodded. "Since we've had more than our share of the limelight and dread it, we'd have accepted Rose in the eyes of the world and given her every chance to prove that she was Rowena. The estate won't be settled until next year so we need not have acted hurriedly. We would have expected to encounter gaps in her memory; that sort of thing. We'd have called in doctors but I know that the best psychiatrists may be deceived. Then if we had accepted Rose, she would have gotten half of Father's estate. But how would the person who found and coached her and planned to foist her on us have benefited?"

"Joel or Bob could simply have married her," Michael pointed out. "If it was decided that 'Rowena' was competent to handle her inheritance she could have paid off the originator of the scheme gradually, in cash or securities. If you had decided that she must have her inheritance but needed a trustee, whoever was appointed in that capacity would have benefited financially."

"Aunt Sophia? Because I trust her, I'll tell you that she needs money. And I'll tell her when I get home, what was said here this afternoon."

"You do have a rather deep regard for your aunt, don't you, Chris? And even for Daphne—"

"Oh," Chris said rather sardonically, "I am by nature an affectionate little feller. Aunt Sophia would consider any undue display of affection ill-bred, but yes, I am very fond of her. And, much as Daphne irritates me and as little as I approve of her, I have been her brother too long not to care for her, as one does for a difficult child. But we have not discussed Rose Tanner as Rose Tanner, or Albert Sheely's death."

"There's nothing complicated about Sheely's death," Prevost said. "We've agreed Harry must have been asked to cooperate. We know none of your gang went to see him at his offices in the daytime; we checked on that. So someone met Harry elsewhere."

"And Harry made a point of telling Valerie that he'd had great difficulty finding sleeping quarters until his family moved back here," Michael said. "He seemed to direct attention toward hotels where he'd stayed. But that was unnecessary; Harry knew Nick would know what hotels he'd be most likely to stay in and would check with them as a matter of routine if anything happened to Harry.

"Then it occurred to me that since Harry converted an apartment into offices, he could have slept there after April. I wondered if Valerie had forgotten to tell us something. She had—the fact that Harry remarked that it had been difficult to find offices and that it had looked like he might have to sleep there *permanently*, too. If Harry sometimes slept in his offices, he might also have seen anyone who wished a private meeting there, late at night. The janitorial work in offices is usually done in the evenings."

"So when you learned there was a resident janitor you tried, to see Al Sheely," Prevost finished. "We did talk to him before we knew enough to hammer away at him with any very definite questions. And Sheely did know something; let it go at that. I doubt if he'd have told us anything for free if he thought he had a chance of cashing in his information elsewhere.

"As to the Tanner woman, we know she resembled Rowena, was conveniently stout, had that useful scar. Someone must have been sure she had nerve and was a competent actress. If she'd been an actress, she was never well-known. Also, she can't have had a criminal record because fingerprints would give her away. Probably she had a little talent for forgery. Certainly she was unscrupulous but I'd guess she drew the line at murder and tried to give the show away the night she was killed. And perhaps we'll manage to find out where it was she met the person who planned all this. They had to meet and they had to keep in touch afterward. Meanwhile I'd like to go home with you and talk to your aunt, Chris. It's getting late."

"Six-thirty—our dinner hour. But I doubt that there is any dinner so that doesn't matter. The cook was wanting to resign this morning and I fancy Aunt Sophia allowed her to. I'm to meet Anice at seven-thirty for a latish dinner."

"Would you and Anice care to drop by tonight?" Michael asked.

"Anice and I? Why Anice?"

"And why so suspicious? Valerie told me after lunch that Joel and Bob both telephoned and asked if they might call on us very soon. We are popular. I'd like to ask Anice a question or two about various members of your sacred circle."

"In that case, we will turn up after dinner tonight," Chris said. "I take it I'm going with you, Prevost? Where is your car?"

XI

Michael took time to walk over to Portsmouth Square where, on weathered benches under ragged trees, park habitués and tired passers-by sat in the pale sunlight. He stopped to gaze, as on an old friend, at the Stevenson monument where forever the *Hispaniola* sails toward Treasure Island.

He turned and looked toward Kearney; at the Hall of Justice hovering over its disreputable brood of bail-bond offices; and, turning again, at the sky line: Nob Hill, Russian Hill, Telegraph Hill, punctuated by the exclamation points of the Fairmont, the Mark, Coit Tower, and tall apartment houses. He drew a deep breath and murmured, "Ugly, vulgar, adored in her wallow beside the bay, she knows that her lovers return—"

He drove home, glad for a time to be alone. When he reached Pacific and Leavenworth, it occurred to him that it would be well to take home a few bottles of soda. He stopped at a small grocery whose proprietor he had known for five years.

The man gave a surprised shout and at once slipped into his native Sicilian. Having expressed his immense happiness at beholding Mr. Dundas again and spoken admiringly of the great beauty of Mrs. Dundas and the alarming intelligence of Master Dundas, he produced a newspaper that apparently had been used for wrapping garbage.

He pointed to a small, smeared picture of Henry Hunt.

"You see this? People were talking about a man being killed near where you live but no one described him to me. I sell the papers but I don't read English much. I didn't notice this picture till yesterday and the more I look at it, the more I think this man came here and used my phone Tuesday night."

Michael snapped his fingers disgustedly. "We should have made inquiries in this neighborhood. What time did the man stop here?"

"I try to close by eight and I was about to lock the front door when this guy came along and asked to use the phone. So it was probably eight, or maybe a minute or two after."

"You didn't hear what he said, Luigi?"

"No. The telephone's in back and I was sweeping out the front of the store. I saw him dial a number and then he waited and finally swore and hung up. He stood a minute, kind of frowning. I noticed because I wanted him to go so I could lock up before someone else came in.

"He started to walk away but then he shook his head and went back to the phone and this time he got his number. Maybe he talked five minutes, maybe not. I didn't hear what he said; I was sweeping into the street by then. But I'm glad you came by. You know the police and now you can tell them what I told you and that I am your friend. If they want to talk to me, I'm always here," Luigi said comfortably. "You tell them I'm a busy man. . . ."

"I will," Michael promised. Then he marched back to Luigi's telephone and left word both at Prevost's office and at his home that Major Dundas wanted the Inspector to get in touch with him as soon as possible.

Sophia Talcott said, "Yes, Florence Baird did donate a bundle of castoffs to our January rummage sale. But it was a bundle and though she brought it here and left it, I didn't look through it. We had the sale in a vacant store on Sutter. I'll give you the name of the woman who had charge of sorting and pricing old clothing. She can tell you who her assistants and saleswomen were. But the bundle, with several like it, lay in the upper hall for several days, until finally Mark loaded the lot into the car and took them down to the store, since Daphne couldn't find time to do it for me.

"I've never been clothes-conscious but I remember that dress of Florence Baird's now," Sophia went on. "I did look well at the dress Rowena wore the last time I saw her because she seemed anxious that I should admire it. I thought then that it looked like something Hal Baird's mother would wear."

"And you think Mrs. Baird might have kept that dress for nearly seven years?" Prevost asked.

"Yes. She spent little on herself and when she bought a dress, she got an expensive garment and wore it to shreds."

"Then you think that she may have donated that dress to your rummage sale, Miss Talcott?"

"Yes. She was wearing new black for Hal and she had sold her home and was stripping it of personal belongings. She brought an unusually large bundle of castoffs where once she would have waited to see if she could find some use for her old things."

"And you think," Prevost said, "that we may have come somewhere near the truth, trying to guess what happened to Rowena?"

Sophia fingered the cameo pin that today did service for a missing button at the neck of her blouse.

"Yes, I am afraid that Rowena was determined that at least Hal shouldn't marry the girl to whom he was newly engaged. Rowena could be deaf to reason. I don't think she'd understand that Hal loved that girl even if Hal's mother promoted the match for more practical reasons. Just as she had, until a better prospect came along, been quite willing to forward a match between Hal and Rowena.

"And Florence Baird could have done what must have been done: carried out the grisly details, upheld by her determination that no harm should come to Hal. When he died, to all practical purposes, Florence Baird died too.

"And now you mean to ask me, Inspector, why I chose to take a stroll on Wednesday night," Sophia said with her grim smile. "And now I'll tell you.

"I was alone here; I woke suddenly and believed I heard some sound in the hall. Recent events had made me cautious. I got up in the dark and very quietly opened my door. The light had been left on in the hall because the others would come home late and probably in liquor. I saw a woman going toward the stairway—"

"And didn't call out?" Prevost said skeptically.

"To whom?" Sophia retorted. "Our servants sleep very soundly at the back of the house. I could see the woman's profile. She was frowning; she looked angry, and my impression certainly was that she was in full possession of her faculties. She was wearing a tan sport coat and carried a brown purse.

"I got into some clothes as quickly as possible. I didn't care to confront a woman to whom I

might have much to say, garbed in a nightgown.
I had to risk having her leave the house while
I dressed but I doubted that I could detain her
by force if she chose to go and I certainly could
not follow her out of the house in the aforesaid
nightie. I presume she lingered downstairs after
she reached there since the front door closed just
as I started downstairs. When I was outside I had
no difficulty in picking her out, walking toward
Fillmore Street.

"My education," Sophia said ruefully, "has not
included instruction in the art of, as I believe you
call it, tailing people. She must have known she
was being followed. When she was past Fillmore
she suddenly turned into a vacant lot. When I
had reached it, she had disappeared. I don't know
where she went."

"Probably dodged into some back yard," Prevost said.

"Well, I could think of nothing to do but to
walk back and forth along the street, then to con-
ceal myself in the shadow of a building and wait.
But she didn't reappear and at last I gave up and
came home. I did not confide in anyone. There had
been alarms and excursions enough already. If you
had brought us a woman who might be Rowena,
I would have had a few remarks to make, but the
following night that woman was killed. Since

she was wearing Rowena's raincoat, carrying her
purse and so on, I had to believe she was Rowena.
Though I still thought that on Wednesday night
that woman seemed determined and purposeful
and not at all a poor ghost trying to remember
who she was.

"And," Sophia said, going to a desk that was lit-
tered with small, chunky brown childrens' classics
of sixty years ago, "I'll give you a list of names
of women who had most to do with our rummage
sale. . . . There. Good afternoon, Inspector."

Prevost grinned but he said meekly, "Good afternoon." In the hall he paused and looked toward
the stairway to the third floor. Then he shook his
head. "No, I won't talk to Daphne again. You may
tell her or anyone else all that you know, Chris, if
you like. And I'll go on about my business now."

Which business Chris supposed concerned the
list of names Sophia had given him. He would
have been surprised and vaguely uneasy if he had
known that Prevost drove straight to Russian Hill
Place and passed the next hour talking to Major
Dundas.

Meanwhile, after looking at his watch, Chris
shrugged and climbed the stairs to Daphne's quarters.

Daphne had progressed to the chaise longue,
in a pale pink negligee, the Persian in her lap and

the Siamese on her shoulder. Her hair was artfully arranged; the negligee and the cats became her but she looked her age.

"Well, Daffy, it seems that for once you were right," Chris said as he sat down and began to tell her the results of their findings for the day.

Daphne did not try to give the impression that her fanciful little brain could not grasp his involved story and when he had finished she said only, "I knew that woman wasn't Rowena. I would always have known, though I suppose I would have had to accept her if the rest of you had. I have some family pride, too."

Then she went on more characteristically, "But the wickedness of it! Whoever killed that woman knew that if we believed she was Rowena, *I* would be suspected of having killed her. But everyone knows better now. Whoever directed the conspiracy killed her and I had no reason to engage in any such scheme. It was to my interest, financially, that Rowena should never return."

"Yes, but Prevost will say that it is just possible, not probable, that *you* believed that woman was Rowena, Daffy."

"Who cares what the stupid police may say? And Mark couldn't have had anything to do with the conspiracy, either. He couldn't have married a false Rowena or expected to be appointed trustee of her property if we'd decided she must have one. But with Rowena dead he will gain financially, through me, when the estate is settled."

"A false Rowena could have paid Mark off in cash, if he dreamed up this plot," Chris pointed out. "And will Mark really gain financially through you?"

"I'll help him, within reason, when I have money," Daphne said lightly. "But he takes an over-pessimistic view of things. I scolded him for not confiding in me until today, though I know that his pride was wounded because he couldn't go on giving me everything, as he always had and still wants to do. But Vibert's is an old shop and can't be in any real danger of collapsing. Mark is tired and ill and easily discouraged. In six months he won't need any money to keep it going."

"You'd throw a drowning man a rope, wouldn't you—if you had nothing more important to do at the moment?" Chris stood up. "No, we won't discuss it. I have to meet Anice. We're going to the French quarter for dinner tonight."

XII

Because they found a family restaurant that was not too crowded, Anice and Chris were a long time over their dinner and it was after nine o'clock when they arrived at Russian Hill Place.

Michael opened the door and murmured hastily, "I'm sorry to say that Mr. Lovell 'just dropped in' a few minutes ago," before he took Anice's coat.

He supplied them with drinks; they sat down and the men talked of the occupation of Japan, reconversion and demobilization. Miss King and Mrs. Dundas preferred to discuss the possibility that there would be nylons by Christmas and the chances that Anice might be able to acquire a dozen sheets before she and Chris were married.

But at last Bob put down his glass and said, "Why don't we say what's on our minds? I'm not thin-skinned. Sophia told me what she'd learned from you and Prevost, Chris. She thought I should know how things stand. If you and Anice came here for any special reason, just consider that I'm not present."

"I've nothing to say that I object to saying before you, Bob. I understand that Michael wanted to ask Anice one or two questions."

"I intended to ask Anice what Daphne's attitude toward divorce is," Michael said. "Perhaps you know, Chris, but I'd rather hear Anice on the subject."

Anice looked uneasily toward Chris. "I think I do know, but—"

"Then tell us, dear. I don't mind."

"Daphne approves of divorce as an institution. She thinks we should be 'civilized' about it. Which means she'd expect Mark to be 'civilized' if she wanted to divorce him. But if the shoe was on the other foot, she'd be furious and fight him if she could."

"Yes," Bob said, "Daffy wouldn't like the world to know her husband found her anything but irresistible. And if she would consent to be obliging, she'd want a whopping big alimony."

"Yes, she'd think she was entitled to alimony," Anice agreed. "Well, that's better than taking in washing but we don't know that Mark wants a divorce. I was only guessing when I told Chris I thought he might have met some girl while he was in the Army."

"You guessed right. Mark didn't tell me the gal's name and I don't know that he would make the mistake of marrying her—"

"'Mistake?'" Michael said.

"Sure. Mark went for this girl because she was so different from Daffy. An old-fashioned home girl who pampers a man and defers to him. That would appeal to poor old Mark, but I also gathered the girl's the sort who read a book once and then rested on her laurels. Maybe Mark doesn't realize that yet, but you know that sort of woman would soon bore him."

"Yes, Bob, but it's not 'a new circumstance for a man of first-rate abilities to be captivated by very inferior powers,'" Chris said. "However . . . Tell me, Michael, in all your experience, have you ever been concerned in another such—"

He stopped as the doorbell rang. Valerie opened the door so quickly that they all had ample opportunity to see Mark regarding Joel with open dislike and resentment while Mr. Gloster tried to maintain his usual attitude of elegant nonchalance without lighting a Murad or an Old Gold.

They hastily rearranged their faces but took seats as far apart as possible and did not thereafter speak directly to each other. Joel explained that he had wanted to walk to clear the cobwebs from his brain and, finding himself in this neighborhood and remembering Mrs. Dundas's very cordial invitation to drop in at any time, had ventured to impose upon her kindness and . . .

Mark disposed of the brandy and soda that Michael handed him in a fashion that suggested his throat was merely a funnel, and broke in rudely, "I wanted to call on you. Joel insisted on tagging along. He thinks that I am in a dangerous frame of mind tonight. I am. Having failed to borrow money from anyone, I have achieved a desperate sort of gaiety. Thank you, Major, I will have another."

"Have you appealed to Sophia?" Bob asked.

"Sophia has no money. I thought you'd know that, Bob. I know because my broker is Sophia's broker. I, like Sophia, couldn't leave well enough alone. I wanted," Mark said bitterly, "to leave my poor, helpless little wife well provided for in case I was killed in action. You can't blame the stony-hearted bankers for not thinking highly of my business ability when they look over the record."

"But I'm surprised at Sophia," Bob said. "I considered her very hard-headed besides being 'a wonderful manager.'"

Chris saw Anice frown involuntarily. "You don't consider Aunt Sophia a good manager?" he said.

"Chris, I hate to keep criticizing, but I think Miss Sophia is just efficient. She manages to run that old barn of a house without good servants, better than most women would. But she spends so much money to do it. It'd never occur to her not to have some kind of food just because it costs too much, or not to ask people to dinner because that costs money, too. She takes for granted you always have fine linen and dishes and flowers, even when you have to buy them. She buys expensive old books just because she thinks she needs them for references for her writing. None of you people have any idea what economy or managing really is," Anice finished without rancor.

"She's quite right, you don't," Michael said.

"Do you?" Joel inquired skeptically.

"I do, Mr. Gloster. I know what it is to have one nickel, which once would buy a bowl of soup, or coffee and doughnuts. Soup is more filling but coffee is more stimulating.

Which to spend your nickel for was quite a pretty problem."

Michael paused and added blandly, "Since you are not thin-skinned, Mr. Lovell, and you seem to be running over with brotherly love, has Mr. Vibert tried to borrow money from you?"

Bob reddened. "Yes, he did, though he's man and brother enough not to say so. I can lend him some money; I'm not broke. But no junior officer who tries to keep up with the Joneses lives on his pay, especially when people suppose he has a very good private income. That's a secret shared by several dozen people. If it wasn't, I'd tell you to mind your own damned business."

"*Lo credo!* What were you about to ask me, Chris, when our last two unexpected guests arrived?"

"I think I meant to ask if any of the cases you have helped solve have resembled this one?"

"No, except as all murder cases are alike in a few important and a few superficial characteristics. In the last but one, two people were involved in a little matter of negligent homicide. One of the parties wished to talk; the other decidedly did not. Deliberate murder was the result of that difference of opinion."

"You mean that Rose Tanner and someone else was linked in a scheme that was at least mildly criminal; that Rose wanted to talk and someone was determined that she shouldn't? If we suppose that she knew who killed Hunt, everything would have been very simple if she had been able to talk before being killed."

"Yes, Chris; it's very simple when one of two partners in crime is willing to turn state's evidence," Michael said. "And when the going gets tough, the accessory before or after the crime almost always does want to sing. A clever detective sometimes manages to play the accessory off against the murderer if he suspects the identity of both but hasn't evidence enough to arrest either. The difficulty is to manage to keep the accessory in the land of the living until he will talk. Too often the accessory, innocent or otherwise, is a murderer's second or third victim."

Mr. Vibert had finished his second drink and was feeling it. He said, "Do you know who hatched up this scheme to pass the Tanner woman off as Rowena?"

"No," Michael said, as bluntly, "I do not."

At this point Valerie rose and began to empty ash trays. Her guests were too well-bred to take the hint immediately. They talked for a while of current movies and the street- and cable-car service in their beloved city—with acerbity. But before Mrs. Dundas began openly to yawn, they rose and said good night.

Bob offered to take Joel and Mark home but Mark said curtly that he preferred to walk. Bob and Joel drove away and Chris tucked Anice into Daphne's car which he had again borrowed without permission.

"I wonder," Anice said, as they turned into Union Street, tailing a squat, gray E car down the hill, "what Michael would have asked me if the others hadn't turned up? Well, perhaps he did find out what he wanted to know, though . . . Chris, I'm hungry."

"After our enormous dinner? Tut-tut! At this rate you'll be a little dumpling in ten years."

"I'm afraid of that, Anice sighed. "Valerie has such a gorgeous figure. But she's fairly tall. It's runts like me that can't stand an extra five pounds. Though Daphne's short and she's stayed thin. Brandy never seems to give her an appetite but it has me. Could you eat scrambled eggs?"

"I'd rather have bread and cheese. Don't you know that old phrase: 'bread and cheese and kisses?'"

Anice laughed and fitted her head into his shoulder. "Well, cheese isn't rationed now and kisses never were. . . ."

In his own room at eleven o'clock, Chris settled himself to read. He had partaken generously enough of brandy and kisses to be pleasantly stimulated and not at all sleepy. He tried to interest himself in the familiar pages of *Persuasion*.

But though he had always insisted and proved in print that there was deep, if suppressed, passion to be found in Jane Austen if one looked below the surface, tonight Miss Austen's beautifully mannered dialogue merely annoyed him. He threw his book down and lay staring at the ceiling.

He thought: I'd like to talk to someone but there is no one in this house to whom I could speak freely. I'd like to talk to my father. I'd like to tell him about the war and talk to him about Rowena and go out to the kitchen and make coffee that would float a brick and watch him eat cold beans with raw onions. I'd like . . .

Chris shook his head and muttered, "Good God, in another minute I'll be quoting poetry about 'vanished hands and voices that are still.'" He put out his light, flopped over on his stomach and said determinedly, "I'm going to sleep!"

Eventually he did sleep and tonight he did not dream. When he awoke, as suddenly as he had the night before, he woke knowing that he had heard a shot fired near at hand.

He was on his feet in an instant; reached his door and shook it futilely when he found it locked.

Then he heard Bob Lovell's voice, loud and urgent. "Let go, damn it! Goddamnit, let me go! I tell you it's no use! This is the pay-off and if you try to stop me, it will only mean . . ."

The pounding of heavy feet on the stairs and men's voices shouting, drowned Bob out. Chris picked up a chair and swung it against his door until a panel shattered. Through the jagged gap he saw Bob. He had his hands on Joel's shoulders, not so much struggling with him as supporting him.

"Take it easy, Joel. There's nothing you can do now. The Marines have landed and—"

From the third floor, slightly muted by distance and a closed door, came the sound of a second shot.

XIII

Chris sat in St. George's study, slumped down in the old desk chair, reading a letter that was deeply creased and rather soiled from having been carried in a billfold for some months. Chris had put on the glasses that, before 1942, he had worn frequently.

There was black lace on the paper before his eyes but the writing he had to read was not the usual frenzied hen-tracks of a doctor. Harold Baird had preserved the legible, characterless handwriting of his schoolboy days. He had written:

I am writing this because I know that when Joel hears the story I will tell him tonight, he should have some proof to back up his statements or people might not believe him.

When I knew I was going to die before long and decided I'd die quickly, I couldn't decide right away who to talk to. I finally decided that Joel is discreet and can keep a secret where some of the others might not. And I like some of them too much to face them with this story.

I'm a good enough doctor to know my mother won't live long so I'll tell Joel that and let him decide how soon he'll tell the others what I'm going to tell him about Rowena.

Because I know Mother would die without telling the truth and that means I have to talk while I can or no one will ever know what became of Rowena.

I know that I always let Mother push and prod me along. At one time she thought it would be fine for me to marry Rowena and I liked her all right. But then I met Jean—my wife—and I *had* to marry her. After that I never gave Rowena a thought and Mother certainly never mentioned her then.

So, though I'd still see Rowena, I wasn't prepared for what happened. I wouldn't have supposed Rowena could have acted like she did. She'd always seemed so placid and well-bred.

But she sat across from me at my desk that night, insisting I didn't really love Jean and that even if she didn't have as much money as Jean, she'd "make it up to me." I tried to be tactful but finally told her I loved Jean and would, even if she was poor. Rowena acted like she didn't believe me and threatened to kill herself if I wouldn't do what she wanted.

I didn't believe her and let her see I didn't. She said if she did kill herself, everyone would know why as soon as they read her diary. I tried to treat her like a hysterical patient. That didn't work. She opened her purse and brought out a Colt .45.

I still don't know if she pointed it at me or herself. I tried to take it away from her and somehow it went off and there was Rowena lying dead across my desk.

Then Mother appeared. I didn't have to do much explaining to her. My idea was to wipe my prints off the gun, call the police and tell them it was suicide. Which it had been!

But Mother said: "Even if you wipe off your fingerprints and put Rowena's on the gun in the right place so the police will believe it was suicide, this will ruin you. Professionally and with Jean. She's idealistic and she won't marry you if she believes Rowena killed herself because of you. We must get her body away from here!"

No one had heard the shot. My office was at the side of our house and there was the width of two gardens between it and the next house. Later I knew our neighbors hadn't been home that night. When the gun went off, it was right against Rowena and that muffled the sound.

Then the phone rang. It was a patient who thought she was dying when she had gas pains. Mother whispered: "Tell her you'll be with her in fifteen minutes." Because, that way, if the police asked if I'd used my car, I could say I had and prove why I went out in it.

The garage was near the house and couldn't be seen from the street. We got Rowena into the back of the car and covered her. But we hurried so that we forgot her purse that had fallen to the floor; the raincoat she'd taken off and put on a chair when she came in; and the umbrella she'd laid on the same chair.

I called on my patient and Mother sat in the car. I shouldn't have done that but no one we knew passed by. They wouldn't have been surprised to see Mother waiting for me if they had. She often went on night calls with me and waited outside like that.

Then we drove out past Lake Merced and buried Rowena after a fashion, in the sand. It was a dark night, rainy; and we had just a small flashlight. There were trees and we turned off the road in a place where no one was apt to notice a car on a night like that. I'm afraid that's the best description I can give of the place where she is. Probably the sand's shifted by now because she's never been found. I thought she would be and if I'd known no one would find her, I might not have . . . But I suppose Mother would have persuaded me, regardless.

Mother was furious when she realized we were saddled with some of Rowena's things. She wanted to burn them but you can't burn an ivory umbrella handle. And it would have looked odd to build up a hot furnace fire or even one in the fireplace so late at night.

And I had something to do. Mother had already said: "If that is St. George's gun, it may be missed. I know it's kept in the dining room sideboard but if you put it back, I believe the police could tell that it's been fired recently. But your father's gun is just like St. George's and hasn't been fired for years."

We had Rowena's purse with her keys. And then I remembered what she'd said about keeping a diary. Mother agreed I'd better get the diary if I could. So I got into the Talcott house; put Father's gun in the sideboard; took the silver out and put it on the dining room table and opened a window in the kitchen.

Mother said that was stupid, but I wasn't sure someone might not wonder why Rowena's diary couldn't be found. I thought I'd better make it look like someone had tried to rob the house that night so I left things upside-down in Rowena's room and her jewelry all over the bureau. I found the diary under her lingerie, took it home and burned the pages a few at a time.

But I wouldn't destroy Rowena's coat and so on, even when months went by and her body wasn't found. Mother said I was a weak fool but I guess I felt that some day I might tell the truth and that no one would believe my story without some tangible proof.

We knew when St. George hired a private detective but we didn't suppose he'd succeed where the police failed. It got to be July, and Jean and I were to be married the last of the month—and one night Henry Hunt called on us.

I never was sure how much he knew, but I wasn't hard to bluff. And he did know about the two guns and the diary and said the police would like to know about them. I lost my head and said it hadn't been murder. Hunt said he didn't think it had been or he wouldn't have asked me to explain. Mother tried to stop me, but I told Hunt the truth.

Hunt said I'd had a tough break and he'd been having some tough breaks himself and needed ten thousand dollars. If we could raise that, in cash, he'd forget what he knew. As simple as that.

Mother had held onto her old-fashioned jewelry and, since she never wore it, no one would miss it. She said she wouldn't risk trying to sell it, but perhaps Hunt could? He said, very calmly, that he knew how to dispose of it. He took it away with him and we never heard of or saw him again. Mother didn't trust him, but I had a hunch he'd keep his bargain and he did.

I don't say I didn't go on and enjoy life—till Jean died. I'd tell myself it hadn't been my fault, and it doesn't matter where one's body lies, and that the truth would make Rowena's folks more unhappy than not knowing she might not come home some day. Just wishful thinking.

After Jean died, Mother kept me in line by saying she was a tired old woman—she was and ill, besides—and that I'd never betray her. I wouldn't if I was going to outlive her. But Mother would keep alive to look after me, by sheer will power if she knew I was going to die, and she would never speak, so I must.

XIV

Chris laid the letter down without comment. He took up a neatly typewritten document that Joel had prepared early that evening because as he had said, "I'm the sort who instinctively puts all communications in writing. And I am a physical coward and I was frightened. One can't speak from the grave so I wrote this while I could. . . ."

It began without preamble:

I was greatly shocked at what Harold Baird told me the night he died. But it was like Hal to leave it to someone else to do a disagreeable task. I did not even guess that he meant to kill himself that night.

He gave me his written confession in a sealed envelope and asked me not to "use" it until morning. Of course I asked: "Why?" He said: "I promise you I will be here in the morning." And he was, dead in his bed. That wasn't cricket of Hal. He also insisted that I take Rowena's purse, raincoat, and Sophia's umbrella with me. I hid them in my room that night.

I read his confession before breakfast the next morning and was not surprised when a neighbor brought us the news that Hal was dead. Sophia at once went over to the Baird home to be there when Mrs. Baird arrived. That was no time to "break the news" to Sophia.

I did intend to speak to her immediately after the funeral, and then that didn't seem to be the best time either. I gave myself a few days to think. I had been very fond of Rowena and am fond of Sophia. I delayed performing a painful task and then—I will be frank—it occurred to me that Hal's mother would be well off and might pay well for his confession and my assurance that I would forget it forever.

My own income is infinitesimal and when the estate is settled I will be without employment unless I can make work for myself collecting and publishing St. George's letters. But Sophia and Chris do not think well of the project and Daphne is indifferent to it. I am temperamentally unfitted for any other sort of work. I do not care to face competition in a workaday world and already, since the war is over, jobs are not so plentiful.

But I soon learned that Hal had only a life interest in his wife's considerable property. Mrs. Baird inherited only his personal property which amounted to very little. The home was mortgaged almost to the extent of its value. So I decided not to approach Mrs. Baird after all.

By then I was in an embarrassing position. Sophia was going to ask why, when Hal died in December, I had kept his secret until middle January. Sophia is tactless and I am sensitive to criticism.

I can't say what I would have done if I had never met Rose Tanner. For years I have had a secret taste for low company, a result of having lived with the superior Talcotts for so long. I often relax by spending occasional evenings in bars, drinking and talking to anyone who will talk to me if I pay for the drinks.

Most of these persons were women but I seldom went home with one of them. I am naturally fastidious. I met Rose in a bar on Bush Street. In time she admitted she hadn't been born Rose Tanner and that she had been an actress. I don't know where; probably in summer stock in the East.

Around 1938 or '39 she was in a serious automobile accident. She said that she had been ill for some time, put on weight, lost ambition and had drifted ever since. She was not attractive but she was shrewd and intelligent and I enjoyed talking to her. Eventually I told her who I was.

She remembered the Talcott case. She laughed and remarked: "I might pass for Rowena, seven years older, a lot fatter and with a scar on her head."

So the first seed was sown. I amused myself by considering if it would be possible to pass Rose off as Rowena. I realized that

I had useful stage-properties in my possession: the raincoat, purse and Sophia's umbrella. I thought: a dress would be even more convincing proof that the woman wearing it must be Rowena.

I have always been observant regarding women's clothes. Rowena valued my opinion and taste. She had showed me the frock she wore the night she disappeared and said that Mrs. Baird had one like it. Afterwards I was always aware of that dress whenever Mrs. Baird wore it.

It was sheer luck that Mrs. Baird brought a bundle of old clothing to Sophia in January and that it lay in the hall for some time. Merely as a matter of foresight, I looked for the dress in question, found it and hid it. How was I to know that Michael Dundas could say that dress had belonged to Mrs. Baird and not to Rowena?

Meanwhile I had gone on seeing Rose and without saying anything that would compromise me, I suppose that, insensibly, I had been preparing her for what might come. I told her the terms of St. George's will and I recall that we talked of a number of famous cases involving imposters. But of course nothing could be done so long as Mrs. Baird, who knew Rowena was dead, was still living.

In February, three things happened. Mrs. Baird did die, and I ran into a chap who remembered that St. George had employed Henry Hunt to search for Rowena. He remarked that Hunt was back in the city. That was convenient. Hunt would have to be dealt with and I had wondered how that could be done unobtrusively and safely when he lived in Los Angeles.

And then Chris was reported missing. I am very fond of the dear fellow. I was grieved to think that he was dead. But it seemed to me quite unnecessary that Daphne should inherit Chris's share of Rowena's share of the estate.

I crossed the Rubicon and spoke frankly to Rose. She was not shocked. In fact, she flattered herself that she had led me on and encouraged me to plan. That, of course, was pure vanity on her part.

But she had given the matter some thought. She said that her handwriting would have to be reasonably like Rowena's. She said: "I have a talent for copying handwritings. That's one reason I've changed my name several times. Give me some of her letters and time to practice and I'll pull it off."

She added that I needn't fear that she had a criminal record; that her fingerprints were not on file. She said also that she had moved around a great deal and did not believe she could be traced back more than six months.

It was our plan that she should turn up, pretending to be Rowena but suffering from partial loss of memory still. She would remember leaving the house to play cards with the Lymans and then—blackness, confused memories of pain and illness, recollections of being in unfamiliar localities . . . I do not need to furnish a blueprint, I am sure. "Rowena" would have clung to me and we would have married with, I am sure, since I do know my Talcotts, the blessing of the entire family.

I began to coach Rose in a thousand details and fortunately she was a "quick study." Also, by April I was amazed to see how much like Rowena's handwriting Rose's appeared.

She also began to "establish" her new character. She moved to a respectable rooming house, found work in a laundry and stuck to it. It was quite possible that she would be traced back to the Vine Hotel and she did not intend to deny she had lived there. There was a woman there with whom Rose had been a little too friendly but Rose insisted that she had put on an act for Miss La Grayce that would take care of her and that she was not the sort who would volunteer information to the police.

I insisted that we must have some jasmine scent and it wasn't until March that Rose found some. I did not intend to ask anyone to believe that I smelled jasmine in Rowena's old room unless that odor actually was present.

So we did not rush matters and I consider that I have been the victim of circumstances. I am not to blame because I was obviously the ideal person for Hal Baird to confide in, and it was sheer accident that I met Rose. I think my plan was not lacking in brilliance. It was my helpers who wrecked the scheme.

Because Hunt had to be dealt with, I thought he could be brought to heel when I showed him Hal's letter which made clear the fact that Hunt had blackmailed the Bairds and suppressed evidence. But I do not like the crude approach and I knew that Hunt was slippery, devious, a tough customer. And I knew that he had a weakness for women.

Rose agreed that it might be unwise to approach Hunt undiplomatically and said that the woman angle was promising, but that she would never get anywhere with Hunt, a connoisseur of women. And that is how Anice came into this.

XV

When Chris was reported missing she was furiously angry. She had gambled on marrying him to the extent of living with us when she disliked most of us, and conducting herself circumspectly when she didn't wish to. And Chris was probably dead so she had wasted her time. She could not deceive me as to her true feelings.

So she was ripe for my suggestion that she deal with Hunt for us. Also, she could be useful because she was an "outsider" and occupying Rowena's room. We wished to accustom the family to the idea that Rowena was alive by staging various incidents that would give them no choice but to believe that ghosts walk or that Rowena was alive.

We intended that Rowena should be "found" by the police. They would be more apt to accept the testimony of Anice, the "outsider," regarding those odd happenings,

than that of those of us who had known
Rowena.

Also, I suspected the others would be reluctant to talk and I would have to follow
their example. But it would be natural for
Anice to "tell all," appearing to be badly
frightened.

She was to be given twenty-five thousand
as soon as possible, if she handled her part
in the business successfully. She remarked
that we could not very well double-cross her;
and, while she would have to wait for her
money, it was something to look forward to
until another "rich sucker" came along; and
that it would be a pleasure to "do" Daphne
out of "a wad of dough."

Anice simply went to Hunt's offices when
he had opened them and asked Hunt for a
job. He did not give her one, but things took
their natural course. How could I guess that
she would find the little bounder so attractive that she became intimate with him? She
calmly admitted it. She said: "Didn't you
want me to take care of Harry? I don't mind
at all. He has a marvelous technique and he's
my kind of person."

So she met Hunt frequently, at night in
his offices. On two occasions she was seen

by the janitor, an unsavory individual named Sheely. He stared at her and leered. At the time she didn't care too much, but later on she worried a great deal about Sheely.

Because she didn't understand Hunt after all. She didn't know he had a wife and large family to whom he was deeply devoted. She didn't guess that he had a sentimental streak and that there were some taboos that he would not violate.

Of course, by April we knew that Chris was alive. But it seemed probable that he would lose a leg if he recovered otherwise. Before May, we could not be quite certain that he would live and it was July before we knew that the doctors had saved his leg.

That was why Anice went on "playing ball" with us even after we knew Chris was alive. She was not so happy about the scheme after that but I "kept her in line" by threatening to expose her; and, regarding Chris, she did not want to "count her chickens before they were hatched," and had no intention of marrying a one-legged man.

So, in June she "put her cards on the table." Hunt not only refused to cooperate; he struck her and threw her out "on her ear." Therefore, we decided that for a time, at least, the scheme must be abandoned. When Anice knew, in July, that Chris would return un-mutilated, she was only too anxious to abandon the plan, so that Chris would inherit one-half and not one-quarter of St. George's estate.

Rose and I drew the line at murder, you see. And how could I foresee that when Chris came home he would get in touch with Hunt and that Hunt would decide to tell him everything and warn Anice that he meant to do so? Could I have guessed that Anice, now determined to marry Chris and the Talcott money, would kill Hunt so that he could not tell Chris the truth about her . . .

Chris suddenly put Joel's manuscript down on the old desk though he was only two-thirds through it. He remarked, dully and impersonally, "As a writer, Joel is longwinded and too much given to enclosing common expressions in quotation marks. And in spite of his protestations of friendship, he disliked and resented the Talcott family, didn't he?"

Neither Michael nor Bob answered him. Bob picked up a whisky decanter and poured himself another stiff drink, murmuring, "'Mother, dear Mother! ere I die, Give me three grains of corn.'"

He added, "Here it comes," at very nearly the same moment as Chris said, "Michael, why didn't you warn me?"

Michael, who had been standing by the window, unconsciously straightened his straight back, came over to the desk and yanked one of the old, leather-covered chairs close to it. He sat down and unbuttoned his coat but in the end he only said, "*Che sará, sará*. No doubt what shall be, will be, but—"

"Chris, there are a few things that no man can tell another point-blank. A friend does not dare to give you his candid opinion of the woman you intend to marry because he values your friendship—"

"And neither does a foster brother," Bob said. He came over to Chris and put his free hand on the younger man's shoulder. He went on, awkwardly, "I loved your father, Chris. He took my own dad's place and you all became my family. I'm seven years older than you are. I'm an average man. I don't understand women instinctively. But a guy can learn, you know, and I have learned."

"Mr. Lovell couldn't bring himself to tell you that when he tried to console Anice she made a play for him," Michael said. "Or that he was certain that she was thoroughly familiar with the terms of your father's will. And if he had told you, you wouldn't have believed him, Chris. You didn't believe anything Daphne said about Anice. I gave you every chance to use the brains you were born with. You are a scholar; you have often eagerly pounced on a careless utterance, phrase or even a word used carelessly and made something of them—"

"What facts did you ever give me?"

"All that I myself had, Christopher. It occurred to me the day after Harry was killed that it was possible there had been a scheme afoot to produce an imposter to take Rowena's place. And I asked you almost from the beginning *why* Harry had decided to talk. Harry had kept his trap closed for going on seven years. Why should he talk merely because Rowena was alive and beginning to regain her memory?

"She'd save him the trouble when she became more rational. If Harry wanted to escape the consequences of having let someone buy him off six years ago, he would either have cleared out hastily or have dealt with Rowena before she could talk. He did neither but was killed before he could talk."

"You might," Chris said, "have argued that someone didn't want Hunt to tell me that Rowena was alive?"

Michael drew a deep breath and pressed his hand against his ribs. *"Por Dios,* think! You were told Harry was clever and shrewd. Would he have risked blackmailing anyone, neglected to report his findings to your father and the police, if Rowena had been alive and apt to regain her memory and give him away when she did?"

Chris flushed. "You're right. Go on."

"When I began to wonder if your ghost was neither a ghost nor Rowena but an imposter, it was evident that Harry's cooperation would be necessary to such a scheme. We knew the day after he was killed that he'd come into money when he needed it badly and just after he'd worked three months on the Talcott case and that, therefore, he must have known more about Rowena than he had told.

"Very well: who told Harry about the plan to put someone in Rowena's place? The person who dreamed up the plot, you might answer. But I knew, and you were told and it was common knowledge, that Harry had a weakness for women. One who didn't know Harry as well as I did might naturally think that he could best be approached by an attractive woman.

"I would never have employed even so attractive a girl as Anice to handle Harry but I knew that though he had a weakness for women he was not weak where they were concerned. I told you so, Wednesday morning. I also told you that Harry did not object to hitting a woman when he thought it necessary.

"I asked myself what woman could have been used to attempt to handle Harry. Since the 'ghost' must have resembled Rowena greatly she wouldn't be Harry's type. Daphne was obviously the one person who could have no part in a plot to foist a false Rowena on you, so Daphne was out. But I knew as soon as I met her that Anice *was* Harry's type.

"And then, I couldn't help being impressed by the fact that in February you were reported missing and that, according to Anice, the manifestations began then. That could be coincidence but it might not be. Also, from February to July Harry was in the city without his family. He and Anice were both on the loose during the same period of time."

"You told me what sort Hunt was," Chris admitted. "You told me the fact that I was reported missing in February was important though you didn't tell me why. You deliberately misled me on that point."

"Yes. But I did tell you that Harry had a quick temper and that he'd never let a mistress influence him or interfere with his family life. You knew that Anice was supposed to have fallen on the stairs and bruised her cheek that night in June when the last of the manifestations, according to her, occurred. You said yourself that nothing happened after that and presumed that was because Harry had refused to cooperate. Why didn't you add Anice's bruised cheek to that? She had to account for it and did so with that remarkable story of seeing Rowena elocuting in the living room and being so frightened by the spectacle that she fell on the stairs."

"That 'remarkable' story made my blood run cold."

"I suppose it did, Chris, but you had only Anice's word that it was true and it was very 'stagey' as Nick would say. And, as Joel tells us, it was pure invention. Anice had spilled the works to Harry and he hit her and tossed her out. And warned her to tell her pals to give up their plans.

"When Anice learned that you were coming home soon, with two legs, she was anxious to move; to appear to have been ill-used by your family. The story that she later told you of her fright not only accounted for that bruise but explained to you why she had been forced to move. I tried to approach Anice with an open mind but immediately, at the Copper Kettle, she ordered brandy and water. So did Daphne—"

"Daffy was copying Anice," Bob said, "because Anice could hold her liquor and Daffy got the notion perhaps it was *what* you drank that was important, not what kind of head you have for booze. And brandy and water isn't an unusual concoction—"

"But it did happen to be Harry's," Michael said, "and for every person who orders brandy with plain water there are twenty who take it with soda. Then Anice used the term 'sandhouse' and that is railroad slang for rumor, gossip, surmise. Harry, his wife told us, had once been a railroad cop. I've often heard him use that expression. Valerie says he did when he talked to her. Harry had two pet phrases: 'it's better than taking in washing' and 'Mother told me there would be days like this.' Anice used both of them to me when we were dancing Wednesday night—"

"She has used both expressions in my hearing," Chris said. "Not that either phrase is unusual but I said to myself that people pick those things up from their friends or reading. I could have told you Anice didn't use those expressions once, but you didn't ask me—"

"It wasn't too important," Michael said. "Joel goes on to tell us that Anice became impatient. He and Rose Tanner meant to wait at least a month after Rose had moved to Mrs. Sawyer's before they

staged any disturbing incidents to suggest Rowena
was alive. But Anice began, a very few days after
you were reported missing, to suggest that a ghost
was walking in Rowena's old room.

"That wasn't fatal. It was left to her to rear-
range the contents of her bureau as Rowena might
have done. She could not prove Rowena had done
that or the story she was to tell of often feeling someone had been in that room while she was
sleeping. But she became confused or careless. If
I remember correctly, Anice told you, speaking of
finding her bureau drawers had been put in order:
'That first week in February the first odd things
happened.' And then, 'A week later I sat up in bed
. . . and in a minute smelled perfume.'

"That is, she told you that she first smelled
jasmine in the room in February, but it was not
until March that a woman answering Rose Tanner's description purchased jasmine scent from a
Chinese merchant."

"I see," Chris said. "Prevost started to comment
on that this afternoon and stopped and didn't go
on. Isn't that true?"

"Yes. He began to be interested in Anice then
because another fact hit him in the face. Rose
bought two flasks of jasmine but only one was
found in her room. We agreed, when we realized
the manifestations were part of a scheme, that

the perfume, which was smelled by Sophia and
Daphne, too, must have been scattered about the
room. When Nick saw the flaw in Anice's story
to you he thought how easy it would have been
for someone to turn the second bottle of perfume
over to Anice and for her to scatter the perfume
about Rowena's old room. Which is what Anice
did do. Joel says . . . Do you want to read the rest
of his deposition?"

"No!" Chris said. "Joel's attempts to justi-
fy himself give me the nearest thing to butterfly
belly that I've experienced since our LCI headed
into the beach at Salerno. Does Joel tell you anything you hadn't guessed?"

"Very little. He explains how the program proceeded. Anice 'appeared' beside Daphne's bed in
May and frightened her by seeming to be trying
to wake her as Rowena used to do. Rose wrote the
note that was pinned to Daphne's pillow in May—
again by Anice. It was safer for her to do those
small chores though they intended that eventually
someone should see Rose Tanner in the house.

"She was to leave Sophia's umbrella in your
father's study on a night when Joel thought everyone would be at the theater. He didn't have time
to warn Rose when Sophia decided at the last moment to stay home. So Rose tangled with Sophia

in the study but, as we've already said, that turned out to be one of their best manifestations.

"Then in June Anice approached Harry and we've already discussed the results of that little chat. Soon afterward she knew you would return in one piece. Then she was between the devil and the deep. It did not suit her plans for you even to wonder if Rowena might be alive. But she could not be certain that someone, probably Sophia, would not consult you when you got home.

"And Anice had to tell you some story that would explain why she fell on the stairs and why she had left the old homestead. The story she told you made her appear both brave and persecuted and on some points the others must back her up. Whatever she told you, they had to risk Sophia's talking to you and Mark's adding his bit. But they didn't suppose you would take any action; certainly not such prompt action. They thought you would be tired and that you were lacking in decision. I suspect you were when your father was alive," Michael said bluntly. "They certainly didn't expect you would go straight to Hunt, not knowing you'd learned something about Hunt from an Army pal.

"Harry had told Anice to tell the other two to forget their clever scheme but that he would not inform against them unless they forced him to.

Harry didn't know you'd be coming home. When
you did and wanted his help, he decided to give it
to you."

"And you have kept asking, 'Why?'" Chris said.
"I see now why you did, but I don't know the
answer."

"Because he had something to tell you that
affected only you," Michael said. "He was an odd
mixture and, as Joel said, there were some taboos
he wouldn't violate. He always gave a sucker a
break and I'm afraid he considered you a sucker,
Chris."

"So far as Anice was concerned?"

"Yes. And he meant to tell you about Anice. You
were a soldier, home from the wars with a gimpy
leg; and you heard Mrs. Hunt say 'that Harry has
a son in the Navy' and thought nothing was too
good for the boys in the services."

Chris nodded. "And Hunt did ask me about my
Army service over the telephone and he did say
that I was 'entitled' to some peace of mind." He
smiled bleakly. "I don't suppose he thought that
knowing the truth about Anice would add to my
peace of mind, but I fancy he argued that I de-
served better than her."

"I'm sure he did. According to Joel, Anice had
told him about you. Joel called on Rose Monday
afternoon to warn her that you would be home

that night and to be ready to clear out if necessary. He didn't know what Anice would tell you or what Sophia might say to you and what your reactions would be.

"Rose wasn't easily frightened so she stayed on at Mrs. Sawyer's. On Tuesday evening, Harry called on her. Anice had been so sure of herself that she had told Harry everything, even where Rose lived. And Harry told Rose that he intended to spill the works to you, Chris, the next morning.

"You will remember that we agreed that only Harry could have told his murderer where he would be at approximately eight-fifteen. He could not have contacted any of you by telephone between six-fifteen and about eight o'clock. Mark Vibert walked out on you around seven, but Harry had left his offices by then so Mark couldn't have contacted him there. Harry's time was pretty well filled until eight-fifteen when he turned up on our doorstep. He not only talked to Rose Tanner but had a sandwich on Polk Street.

"After you left the house around eight, Harry might have managed to reach Sophia, Joel or Daphne by telephone. He could not have reached Mr. Lovell before eight- fifteen because he was taking Anice home—"

"Look," said Bob, who by now had absorbed far more than three grains of corn, "I know I'm a junior officer and you're a hell of a swell of a major—but stop calling me Mr. Lovell."

Michael grinned briefly. "Very well, Bob took Anice home. That took him at least ten minutes and he'd need twenty to drive back to his own apartment and would have to garage his car before he went up to it., By that time, Harry was talking to Valerie. Then this afternoon I was a fool for luck. I stopped at one of our neighborhood groceries on my way home. The proprietor is only twenty years removed from Sicily and he would never have gone to the police to volunteer information.

"But I can speak his villainous dialect so he told me at once that Harry used his telephone Tuesday night. That was around eight o'clock. Harry dialed a number and got no answer. He started to go; then went back and dialed again. He got his number and talked for some time. You could argue that he dialed two different numbers but it was possible that he only tried the first one again and got it on his second try—because in those few minutes the person he wanted to talk to had reached home. And Anice definitely was not home at a little before eight and just as definitely was at home by a few minutes past eight."

"I can testify to that," Bob said. "And when Anice got out of the car, I thought I heard a telephone ringing in her place though I had no reason to give it a second thought."

Michael said, "Well, if it was Anice that Harry talked to from Luigi's store, she had about thirty-five minutes to get from her apartment to Harry's car. If you know your local geography, you know she could have done that and then had thirty minutes to get home and be there when you arrived, Chris. According to Joel, that is what she did. Harry gave her the same warning he had given Rose. Anice insisted on talking to him. I suppose Harry felt he owed her a personal interview. Since he told Chris he couldn't meet him later that evening he probably expected to see her. He warned her beforehand because he was on his way to—he believed talk to me and tell me the whole story.

"Anice told Joel he did try to avoid a personal interview but she offered to meet him anywhere he chose; in fact, suggested she had better, since her roommate was home. And the poor damned fool told her where his car was parked. She came to it with an old gun of her father's and waited for him."

XVI

"Joel tells us," Michael went on, "that he had listened in on Chris's conversation with Harry Tuesday evening. He wanted to warn Rose that Harry would talk to Chris the next day. When Chris left the house that night, he risked telephoning Rose and they met in a bar on Fillmore.

"Rose hadn't so far to go as Joel so she didn't leave Mrs. Sawyer's until eight-thirty-five. She knew what time he telephoned and when he met her; so, when she learned the next day that Harry was dead, she knew that Joel hadn't killed him. Rose drew the line at murder. She waited all Wednesday for Joel to contact her and when he didn't, she went to the old homestead to talk to him, not knowing that again, only Sophia would be there."

"I should have seen that what Aunt Sophia told us this afternoon helped eliminate Bob," Chris said. "Aunt Sophia's story made it clear that Rose Tanner hadn't come to the house that night to haunt it. So she must have come to see someone and she could not have counted on seeing Bob there privately, if at all."

Michael nodded. "As Nick realized at once. Well, Joel got in touch with Rose on Thursday. She was for immediate confession. Mrs. Sawyer could alibi her and she could alibi Joel for the time of Harry's death. She insisted that you wouldn't prosecute them for attempted fraud—"

"She was right," Chris said, "and I dare say Joel points out that although she had little to lose by confession he preferred to continue being the old family friend and Father's literary executor?"

"Yes," Michael said. "He does point that out in his lamentations. After a long argument, he and Rose parted without coming to any decision. Joel went on and met Anice during her lunch hour. She simply told him the truth—that she had killed Harry and said: 'What can you do about it?'

"In the end, Joel said that Harry had been a crook, anyway, so he wouldn't talk if Anice would be a good little girl from then on. But he added that Rose wouldn't be so lenient or, at least, they would probably have to scrape up some money to persuade her to leave the city at once and promise her more, later on.

"Anice was too practical to care for the idea of paying blackmail to Rose for the rest of her life. You left her around nine on Thursday, Chris. She went to see Rose after that. At that point we have to guess what happened. Joel doesn't know and Anice died without talking—"

"I think," Chris said, "that I'll take a drink, Bob, unless you intended to finish the decanter alone. A stiff one. . . . Thank you. Go on, Michael."

"We can only suppose that Rose told Anice she had decided to talk that night; that she would array herself in Rowena's coat, what she presumed

was her dress and carry her purse to help prove
her story. That was an unnecessarily theatrical
way of doing the job but the whole affair had been
theatrical and I fancy Rose had something to do
with that. And of course the stage-properties
would be some proof that she wasn't lying when
she accused Joel.

"Anice told Joel that she had a duplicate made
before she turned her latchkey back to Sophia
when she left here. So she was able to let herself
into the house to wait for Rose. And she would
naturally prefer that Rose die here where, the police would argue, anyone who lived in this house
could easily have killed her.

"We know that Harry and Rose were killed by
the same gun and that gun was in Anice's possession tonight, proof that she did kill Rose. As to
the janitor, Al Sheely, we have to guess again. Joel
says that Anice worried a great deal about Sheely;
said she knew that he hadn't forgotten her even if
he didn't know her name—yet.

"We must suppose she slipped out before her
roommate was awake yesterday morning, went to
Sheely, persuaded him to go up to Harry's offices
with her and talk there. I'd think, from the evidence of the wine bottles in his kitchen and from
what we know of his habits, that he was probably
slightly fuddled still, so early in the morning. But

she was a pretty woman and she may have offered
him money at once. He went with her. It's still
guesswork to say that he did not object when she
put her arms about him, the better to stab him in
the back. He was very slight and though it must
have taken some doing, even Anice could have gotten him onto the wall bed; then shut it up, hoping
it would be some time before his body was found.

"And, with one more danger to herself disposed
of, Anice had time to get back to her apartment
before her roommate was stirring, to talk to Prevost
and assure him she was going to work as usual.

"But," Michael continued, "Sheely's death was
another arrow pointing to her. We presumed he
was killed because one of you visited Harry late
at night and Sheely saw Harry's visitor. But if the
visitor had been a man, that wasn't so damning.
Joel or Bob or Mark could have said they wished
to consult Harry professionally about the strange
doings at the old homestead and no one could have
proved that that was or wasn't true. Miss Sophia
could have told the same story and no one would
have suggested her relations with Harry were anything but businesslike even if they believed the
business in question ended in murder.

"But no one, in view of Harry's reputation
would ever believe Anice's visits to his office were
strictly a matter of business. I have a low mind,

of course. When I wondered if Harry had slept in his offices before his family came back here, I wondered who Harry slept with. Besides, he made a point of speaking to Valerie about *sleeping* in his offices.

"Today we were swamped with facts," Michael said. "We could guess what had happened to Rowena and that a conspiracy had been planned to take over her inheritance, but we still didn't know who had planned the affair—"

"You spoke the truth when you said earlier to-night that you didn't know?" Chris said.

"Yes. How could we know? But we did suspect that Anice had known Harry and was concerned in the conspiracy and therefore had motive to kill Harry and Rose Tanner—and opportunity in both cases. But she could not have planned the conspiracy in the beginning. She wouldn't have had the necessary knowledge of Rowena. Therefore there must have been three people in the plot and Anice still had an accomplice who could give her away. After he'd talked to Sophia this evening, Nick came to see me and I told him everything I knew or thought about the case. He agreed that Anice must be watched and that Bob was no longer un-der suspicion."

"So Michael called me," Bob said, "and asked me to come to their place and he laid his cards on the table. I had to agree with him about Anice. And I said I'd give the impression, when you two came, that I'm hard up and might want money, badly. That was so Anice would think I was still a suspect."

"And," Chris said bitterly, "you got us there so that you could point out to Anice that partners in crime usually fall out and that it is always the accessory before or after the fact who wants to squeal."

"Yes. We wanted to trap Anice. What makes you think she wouldn't have tried to dispose of Joel eventually, whatever was said at our house tonight? And why," Michael said coolly, "do you take for granted that when Anice had tired of you and the life in an university circle that you'd have wanted, she wouldn't have decided that it was better to be a wealthy widow than a bored wife? She would have been very bored, and I fancy you were afraid of that in your saner moments."

"Yes—yes, I was. I used to wince at some of her expressions like 'going steady' and her grammar, and then I'd tell myself not to be an intellectual snob and . . . What happened here tonight?"

"Nick put Costello on Anice," Michael said. "But he meant to be in at the kill and wanted me with him. I should have refused his invitation but I thought—well, I tossed discretion to the winds and changed my clothes." He indicated his slacks and leather jacket.

"Yes," Chris said, "you thought that when explanations were in order, I'd rather have them from you than Prevost. You were quite right, I would."

Michael flushed, as he always did when anyone recognized the fact that though he was brutally offhand with fools and the merely foolish, he often took on disagreeable duties that no one else cared to assume.

He said quickly, "Nick and I took cover across the street. When we were beginning to be very, very weary, Anice appeared and let herself into the house. Bob can take the story up from there—"

"Well," Bob said, "Prevost hesitated about putting a cop in the house without permission in case nothing happened. But I had my key and there was no reason I shouldn't let myself in and wait. So I hid out in the catchall closet in the lower hall with the door open a crack. I had a long wait, too. Finally I heard the front door open and saw Anice go by me. I'd been warned not to open the door for the police too quickly. By the time I had, I got to the second floor just in time to hear the first shot as I turned on the lights.

"I yelled and started toward Joel's room where I thought the shot had been fired. I think Joel yelled, too. Anice burst out of his room with a gun in her hand. I grabbed at her and missed her and she streaked up the stairs to the third floor.

"Before I could follow, Joel rushed out, simply gibbering. He grabbed me and when you broke your door in to get into the hall, Chris, I was still trying to throw him off. He clung like a leech and Prevost, Michael and another cop had already charged by me up to the third floor when I waved them on."

"Anice had a key to the bedroom doors—one key fits all of them," Michael said. "She had locked Sophia and you in, Chris. But she lost her head when she found she'd put a bullet, not into Joel, but into a mound of pillows he had arranged in his bed while he slept on a couch in his room. He wasn't easy in his mind about Anice tonight and he took no chances, but he was still badly frightened when she shot at the dummy in his bed.

"I suppose she was beyond thought by then. She had no reason to suppose that the police suspected her even slightly and then suddenly, the police were here. We cornered her in one of the vacant rooms on the third floor. Prevost warned her not to shoot; he and Costello had their guns out. She had one in her hand and she turned it on herself. That's all, Chris."

"Yes, that very definitely is all." Chris got up. "I had better get some rest. There will be a good many—arrangements to be made tomorrow."

"Look, wouldn't you like me to—" Bob had moved within kicking distance and Michael kicked him. Bob's eyes watered but he heroically refrained from rubbing his shin.

Chris said courteously, "I hope you'll sleep here tonight, Bob. And I will see you in a few days, Michael."

His facial muscles contracted into what slightly resembled a smile. Bob took a hesitant step toward the door that Chris closed behind him.

"No. Chris doesn't want our brotherly sympathy just now," Michael said. "Do you remember your feelings the first time a woman made a fool of you and an older, more experienced man said: 'Well, I could have told you what she was like, but—?'"

"Do I not?" said Mr. Lovell. "She was a pretty little redhead and St. George said to me . . . Well, we'll skip that. I'll let Chris tough it out by himself. I know you think I'm a well-meaning, clumsy ox and lack the light touch as a comforter."

Michael smiled and did not deny it but he said, "I think you're a hell of a good guy, Bob. So would you mind taking me home in your car? All this has been pretty rugged. . . ."

"It has! I'd forgotten you were afoot since Prevost went off and left us here. My bus is parked two blocks down."

"I suppose," he added when they were in the car, "that Valerie is waiting up for you? But since you told her everything you told me before Chris and Anice turned up at your place tonight, maybe she just went to sleep."

Michael sighed. "No, I have no hope that she will be anything but discouragingly wide-awake."

Valerie was. She was sitting up in bed with a book she was not reading.

Michael came to a full stop in the doorway and inquired tunefully, "'Have I stayed away too long? If I came home tonight, would you still be my darling, or have I stayed away too long?'"

"Since you have come home this morning, my darling, I'll forgive you. I don't need to ask if your plan worked out."

"Don't you?"

"No. You look regretful because of Chris and triumphant because you do like to guess right. I am sorry for Chris and will do my best to console him when given an opportunity. But I've been thinking about us and what you want to do with the rest of your leave. People know you're here and we had four more invitations after you went off tonight. That makes seven to date and that is only the beginning."

Michael sat down and began to take off his shoes. "You win, dear. Where do you want to go?"

"Oh, if you would rather stay here—

"No. Tomorrow morning we'll start out and go where our fancy takes us. If we stay here we'll have to submit to being wined and dined or else. I have not your excellent digestion or your patience with the bores one encounters at ceremonial dinners. Since I have been lucky enough to come back in one piece, I object," Major Dundas said firmly, "to being killed with kindness."

COACHWHIP PUBLICATIONS
CoachwhipBooks.com

VIRGINIA RATH

DEATH AT
DAYTON'S FOLLY

COACHWHIP PUBLICATIONS
CoachwhipBooks.com

VIRGINIA RATH

AN EXCELLENT
NIGHT FOR
MURDER

COACHWHIP PUBLICATIONS
CoachwhipBooks.com

THE DARK
CAVALIER

VIRGINIA RATH

COACHWHIP PUBLICATIONS
CoachwhipBooks.com

MURDER

with a theme song

VIRGINIA RATH

COACHWHIP PUBLICATIONS
CoachwhipBooks.com

POSTED
FOR
MURDER

VIRGINIA RATH

COACHWHIP PUBLICATIONS
CoachwhipBooks.com

EPITAPH FOR LYDIA

VIRGINIA RATH

COACHWHIP PUBLICATIONS
CoachwhipBooks.com

A DIRGE FOR HER

VIRGINIA RATH

COACHWHIP PUBLICATIONS
CoachwhipBooks.com

COACHWHIP PUBLICATIONS
COACHWHIPBOOKS.COM

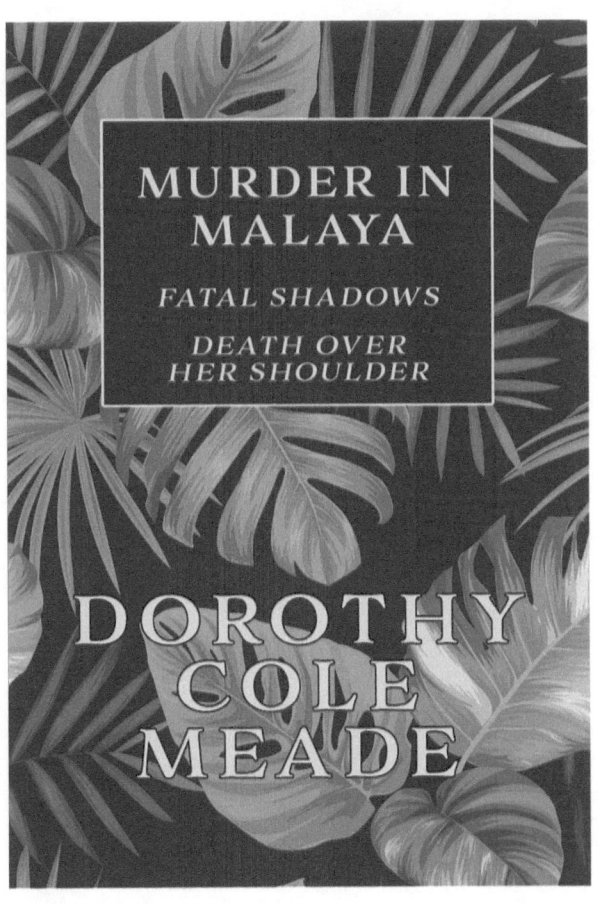

MURDER IN
MALAYA

FATAL SHADOWS

*DEATH OVER
HER SHOULDER*

DOROTHY
COLE
MEADE